A WOMAN SCORNED

JULIE ROBITAILLE

B⧉XTREE

First published in the UK 1991
by BOXTREE LIMITED, 36 Tavistock Street,
London WC2E 7PB

1 3 5 7 9 10 8 6 4 2

ISBN: 1 85283 602 4

Typeset by Litho Link Limited,
Welshpool, Powys

Printed and bound in Great Britain by
Cox & Wyman Ltd., Reading, Berkshire

A catalogue record for this book is available from the
British Library

Prologue

'Good morning, people – let's come to order,' Douglas
Brackman said, entering the room and getting right down
to business in his usual brisk manner. 'We have a lot on the
agenda today.' He sat down, glancing quickly around the
conference table at the McKenzie Brackman staff, then
looked at his watch. 'Leland will be here in a few minutes,
with what I'm certain will be some extremely good news
for everyone, but in the mean time let's take a look at what
we have pending on our calendars. Arnie, how's the
Morrison divorce case going?'

Arnie Becker's grin was shark-like. 'We've got Alan
Morrison by the short hairs,' he said happily. 'My all-time
favourite private eye, Ilene Lester, managed to get some
beautifully clear shots of Mr Morrison *in flagrante delicto*
with not one but *two* amazingly nubile young women,
neither of whom is his wife.' Arnie's eyes sparkled.
'Twins!' he added gleefully.

'Wow,' said Michael Kuzak through a mouthful of
doughnut. 'Twins . . .'

'And in focus,' Arnie nodded.

'All right, enough of that,' Doug Brackman said uncomfortably. 'Stuart. How's the Taggart tax problem coming
along?'

'I have more files in my office than I can even count,'

1

Stuart replied. 'If I can't stall the Government on this one, we're in deep trouble here.'

'When's the audit scheduled?'

'I don't think it's even going to get to that point,' Stuart replied.

'Good,' said Doug 'Now —'

'Douglas,' Ann Kelsey interrupted him, 'come on! What's the good news?'

'You'll see,' Douglas replied smugly. 'It's a surprise.'

'Oh, come on, Douglas, give,' Victor Sifuentes said, with a nod of agreement in Ann's direction. 'That's not fair.'

Doug Brackman allowed himself to smile just a little. 'Trust me,' he said. 'It's worth the wait.'

Abby Perkins groaned softly, and glanced sideways at Jonathan Rollins, who seemed unusually preoccupied this morning. 'What do you think, Jonathan?' she whispered. 'Is it going to be yet another of Doug's special cost-cutting methods? Is that what we're supposed to be pleasantly surprised about?'

Jonathan shrugged unhappily; he looked as though he couldn't care less what Douglas Brackman had up his sleeve this morning.

'Michael,' Doug continued, 'the Chisolm case – where do we stand?'

Michael grimaced. 'This one's a bitch,' he said, 'and it's just getting worse. Derron Holloway has decided to make this his latest *cause célèbre*, and we are not looking very good.'

'Well, what did you expect, Michael?' Jonathan demanded, suddenly coming to life. 'Did you really think the black

2

community would just sit back and watch quietly while a white cop gets off for murdering a black kid who just happened to get in his way?'

Oh, thought Abby, with sudden comprehension, so *this* was why Jonathan looked like a storm-cloud. This racial case had already garnered huge media coverage and divided the community, and now it looked like it might just divide the staff at McKenzie Brackman as well.

'No, I . . .,' Michael began to protest. 'Listen Jonathan, I need to talk to you about this again. . . .'

'Forget it, Michael,' Jonathan said, making an obvious effort to control his anger. 'You already tried it, and I already refused.'

'Refused *what?*' Brackman demanded.

'Refused to be co-counsel on this case,' Jonathan told him. 'I will not be used as a token black in this case.'

Doug Brackman glanced at the two lawyers. 'OK,' he said mildly. 'Let's talk about this later. Personally, however, I might be a very good idea for you to work with Michael on this one, Jonathan.'

'You think it would look really good for McKenzie Brackman to demonstrate how liberal it is to the jury by having a black lawyer defend a guilty white cop!' Jonathan snapped. 'And I won't do it!'

'How do you even know he's guilty?' Michael Kuzak demanded. 'You haven't so much as looked at the evidence.'

'Oh, Christ!' Jonathan sighed. 'Spare me . . .'

Just at that moment, the door to the conference room opened, and all eyes in the room turned expectantly towards it. Lovely blonde Grace Van Owen, looking cool and impeccable, came through the door, followed by Leland McKenzie, who was smiling broadly.

'Ladies and gentlemen,' Leland said, 'I'd like you to meet your newest partner.'

There were exclamations of surprise and delight from all around the table. Grace was familiar to all of them; throughout her career, first as an assistant district attorney, and then, for a brief time, as a judge, she had often been a formidable opponent whose savvy legal strategies and absolute observance of ethics had earned her the respect of her peers.

'Did you know about this?' Stuart whispered to Michael Kuzak.

Michael nodded, 'Leland cleared it with me,' he said. Grace and Michael had been romantically involved several years back, and Leland McKenzie had wanted to make sure that Grace's addition to the firm wouldn't cause any personal problems. Michael and Grace had both assured him it wouldn't: they had moved far beyond that love-affair, and had managed to develop a strong and genuine friendship in its place.

'Grace is replacing Rosalind Shays?' Ann asked delight-edly.

'This is terrific!' Arnie said emphatically. 'Welcome aboard, Grace.'

Leland and Grace seated themselves while more excited congratulations flew around the conference table.

'Talk about a contrast in styles!' Stuart exclaimed.

'Well, yes,' Leland McKenzie said with a smile, 'she is, and it is. But unfortunately', he continued, his expression abruptly turning sober 'I'm going to have to be the bearer

4

of bad news as well as good.' Leland looked around the table. 'I just got off the phone with Jack Sollers. It seems that he's been retained by Rosalind Shays in a lawsuit she's filing against us!

A shocked hush fell over the table for an instant. Then the lawyers began to react, one question piling on top of the next.

'*What* lawsuit?' Abby asked. 'What on earth is she suing us for?'

Stuart whistled softly. 'Rosalind Shays is suing us?'

'Oh, Jesus,' Douglas Brackman groaned. 'Is that woman ever going to stop haunting this firm?'

'Apparently not,' Leland shook his head. 'At least, not unless we pay her the half a million dollars she claims we owe her for wrongful dismissal.'

'*What!*' Arnie yelped. 'That's ridiculous! *What* wrongful dismissal?'

'Half a million?' Abby echoed disbelievingly. 'Is she kidding?'

'That woman practically ruined this firm!' Ann Kelsey snapped. 'How can she possibly be suing us? What are her grounds?'

'She claims it was a case of sex discrimination,' Leland said.

'Sex discrimination?' Michael echoed in disbelief. 'I don't believe it! What grounds could she possibly have? She was never treated unfairly – Christ, you brought her in as a full partner! How can she make any sort of claim based on her gender?'

'I had no idea,' Leland replied. 'But if this thing actually goes to trial we'd better be prepared.' He glanced around at the unhappy faces of the lawyers. 'Let's just hope that it never happens,' he added.

'Amen!' Michael exclaimed.

'Well,' Victor said half-jokingly, turning to Grace, 'welcome to McKenzie Brackman.'

Chapter One

'I've seen Jack Sollers at work,' Michael Kuzak said soberly, 'and I've got to tell you that the idea of going up against the combination of Rosalind and Sollers is enough to make any sane lawyer nervous.'

The partners were in conference in Leland McKenzie's office late the next afternoon. Rosalind Shays and Jack Sollers were due to arrive any minute to see if there was an agreement they could all come to, rather than see the sex discrimination lawsuit go to court.

'We absolutely cannot let this thing go to trial,' Ann said nervously. 'We just have to make it . . . go away.'

'I completely agree – but not for half a million dollars,' said Doug.

'Half a million,' Stuart repeated gloomily. 'Why doesn't she just ask the firm to declare bankruptcy?'

Leland Mckenzie watched as his staff's morale seemed to crumble before his eyes, and he suddenly found himself on the defensive. 'I don't know why all of you are acting as if we've already lost,' he said sharply. 'Believe me, I've thought about this from every angle, and there's no way she can win this suit.'

'That's not really the point,' Michael said. 'The point is that Rosalind is acting like the classic woman scorned, and I have a feeling she'd like nothing better than to humiliate this firm in public. And let's face it, this firm has had more than enough trouble in the recent past, and we absolutely *cannot* afford this kind of negative publicity.'

'Got that right,' Arnie Becker chimed in.

Douglas shot Arnie a look of annoyance. 'And you ought to know,' he said pointedly.

'And exactly what's that supposed to mean?' Arnie responded defensively.

Doug's eyes narrowed. 'You know what it means,' he said. 'I'm not the one who tried to sneak out of here like a thief in the night with my clients' files. I'm not the one who made a global reputation sleeping with his clients!'

'At least none of my clients got *paid* for sex!' Arnie's snide reference was to Doug's steady girlfriend for the past six months, Marilyn Hopkins, who was a professional sexual surrogate.

'Oh, come on, guys,' Michael interjected, trying to cool things down, 'let's not take it to the personal level – we don't have to sink that low. Anyway, let's face it. Collectively' – he glanced at the people around him – 'there's plenty of dirty laundry that could be aired about the firm. This could get extremely ugly, and we've got to present a united front.'

Just then, Roxanne Melman knocked lightly on the door, then stuck her head into the room. 'They're here,' she announced, her mobile face reflecting the tension in the office all too clearly.

'Have them wait for just a moment, Roxanne,' Leland said. He faced the partners again. 'For now,' he said, 'Douglas and I will handle this alone. Maybe facing just the two of us will calm things down a bit. I really do believe I

8

can get Roz to agree to a compromise.'

As the lawyers filed out, passing a very composed-look-ing Rosalind Shays, and her attorney, Jack Sollers, Ann shot a sharp glance in Roz's direction. Then she leaned over and spoke softly in Stuart's ear. 'That bitch never compromised on anything in her life. And, even though Leland thinks he can settle this things right now, I don't.'

Markowitz shrugged philosophically. 'You never know,' he said.

'I know,' Ann said grimly. 'Believe me, I know.'

'Come on, Ann,' Stuart said with a smile, attempting to cheer his wife up, 'don't be so negative. After all, she doesn't have a leg to stand on in a sex discrimination suit.'

'I'm not so sure about that,' Ann said softly, but Stuart had already moved out of earshot.

*

'Roxanne! Oh, I'm so glad I caught you.' Corrinne Hammond Becker, Arnie's wife of four months, stopped breathlessly in front of Roxanne's desk. 'How are you doing?'

'I'm fine, Corrinne,' Roxanne replied, barely glancing up from her word processor. 'Arnie's in his office, you can go right in.'

'Well, I really came by to talk to you, too.'

'You did?' Roxanne looked up, surprised.

Corrinne nodded, smiling. 'Are you really, *really* busy right now?'

Roxanne smiled briefly. 'Yes, of course I'm busy. Your husband has a pretty hectic schedule.'

9

'Well, don't I know that!' Corrinne smiled. 'We are both *so* overloaded! Planning for this ski trip, getting Arnie's study at home redecorated, hauling Chloe around for rehearsals in the Hallowe'en play – gosh! it's just so much to keep track of!'

'I'm sure it is,' Roxanne agreed pleasantly, although to her Corrinne's hectic schedule sounded pretty easy to manage.

Corrinne cocked her head to one side, her eyes sparkling and her shiny chestnut hair catching the light. 'That's why I was wondering if I could possibly persuade you to give me some help.'

'With what?' Roxanne asked.

'Well, Arnie simply *has* to give me the names he wants on our Christmas-card list. I mean, here it is October, and we've only just scheduled the photography session for the cards, and I really don't have the faintest idea which of his clients should be on our combined list. And you know Arnie – pinning him down to that kind of task is just about impossible.'

Roxanne nodded. 'I know. But what is it that you would like me to do? If you want to borrow the Rolodex and take it home . . . well, I mean, maybe overnight for *one* night; but, Corrinne, I really need it here in the office.'

'Of course you do,' Corrinne agreed. 'I know that! That's why I was hoping I could persuade you to go through it for me!'

'What?' Roxanne said, startled.

Corrinne didn't seem to notice Roxanne's dismayed expression. 'I'm sure it wouldn't take up all that much of your time, Roxanne, and that way the Rolodex wouldn't

10

have to be out of the office at all!' She flashed her most charming smile. 'Could you do that, do you think? Just go through it and make a list of the people I need to send them to?'

'Gee, Corinne,' Roxanne said, 'I'm really swamped right now . . .'

'Oh, I'll merge the lists!' Corrinne assured her. 'You wouldn't have to do that . . .'

Roxanne sighed. 'I just don't know where I'd find the time to —'

'Oh, *please*, Roxanne,' Corrinne begged. 'You're so efficient, and I'm just not familiar with Arnie's clients . . .'

Just at that moment, Arnie stuck his head out of the door, still staring at a sheath of papers he held in his hands. 'Rox,' he said without looking up, 'I need these pages filed right now for the Musiel divorce, and —'

'And what?' Corrinne said teasingly. 'Don't you need to take your adoring wife to lunch?'

Arnie looked up with a smile of surprise and delight. 'Hello, darling!' he said, hugging her. 'Of course I want to take my adoring and adored wife to lunch! Rox,' he continued in a business-like tone, 'this needs to be done yesterday!'

'Oh, Arnie,' Corrinne said, brushing an imaginary thread off his collar, 'don't torture Roxanne. I just asked her to do a big favour for me – you know, the Christmas card list.'

'That's good,' Arnie said, nodding. 'That won't take long. Rox, you don't mind, do you?'

'Of course she doesn't, darling!' Corrinne said happily. 'And aren't you just the luckiest man – a wife at home and a wife at the office? Right, Roxanne?'

11

'Right, Corrinne,' Roxanne said softly. 'He's a lucky man.'

She watched with growing resentment as Arnie pulled on his jacket and strolled out of the office with Corrinne on his arm. Roxanne realised she was getting very tired of all this. She loved working at McKenzie Brackman, she liked the feeling of being kept busy by important work, of being an indispensable part of the support system in the law office. But she most certainly did *not* like being given orders by her boss's wife, a woman who could do with a little more to fill up her own time.

It wasn't that Corrinne was a bad person; on the contrary, Roxanne – despite her own feelings for Arnie Becker – thought that marrying Corrinne was quite possibly the smartest thing Arnie had ever done. At least it had put an end to his seemingly incorrigible catting around. But the plain fact was that Roxanne Melman was an excellent legal assistant, not a personal maid. And Corrinne, whether she was doing in on purpose or not, was treating her like domestic hired help.

Now, there, she thought, was a basic difference between the two of them. Roxanne had enough money from her divorce from David to choose not to work, but it would never have occurred to her not to do so. Working was too much an integral part of her identity and her happiness. Corrinne, on the other hand, seemed to have made the transition quite easily, jumping from her first marriage to a rich man to her second to Arnie; and she didn't seem to be troubled in the least by her lack of career or interest outside her own home and family.

Roxanne sighed again and began to go through the

12

Rolodex. She might as well get the task out of the way, she thought.

'Hey, Rox, what's wrong?' Abby Perkins asked. 'You look as though you just lost your last friend. It's not this Rosalind Shays thing, is it?'

Roxanne looked up at Abby and shook her head. 'No,' she said. 'Although having that looming over our heads doesn't exactly make the office atmosphere a barrel of laughs, does it?'

Abby smiled ruefully. 'No,' she agreed, 'it certainly doesn't. So what is it – man trouble?'

'You *could* say that,' Roxanne said cautiously. After all, it *was* man trouble. There was this trouble with Arnie at the office. There was trouble at home with Murray, her eccentric father, who had recently been diagnosed as having Alzheimer's disease. And there had been a disappointing series of dates with men whom her friend had fixed her up with.

'Boy, don't I know it,' Abby agreed. 'Men are impossible.'

Roxanne nodded in agreement. 'Yes,' she said, 'they are.' Then she added ruefully: 'And so hard to find!' They both laughed.

'Tell you what,' Abby said impulsively. 'Why don't we go out to lunch and talk about it? Maybe getting it off your chest will help. Who knows?' she added with a shrug. 'Maybe getting it off *my* chest will help, too. What do you say?'

'Good idea,' Roxanne said gratefully. Abby was a discreet woman, and in the past had proved herself to be a good friend as well. And Roxanne was certain that if she

13

chose to tell Abby what was really bothering her it
wouldn't go any further.

'How about later this week?' Abby suggested. 'I've got
to be in court this afternoon.'

'That's fine,' Roxanne agreed, already feeling relieved.
As Abby walked away, she turned her attention back to the
Christmas card list, feeling just as resentful as she had
before.

*

Leland McKenzie and Douglas Brackman sat composedly
at the conference table, merely nodding politely as
Rosalind Shays and her lawyer, Jack Sollers, entered the
room. Rosalind, a woman who rarely let her emotions
show, looked as cool and calm as she always did. Jack
Sollers was a physical match for her. A good-looking man
in his early fifties, he was fit and well groomed, dressed
impeccably in a suit which seemed to cry out Savile Row
rather than Rodeo Drive.

There were no preliminary pleasantries exchanged; there
was no need for them. Everyone in that room knew precisely why they were there: to come to a monetary agreement
with which they could all live. There was no point in beating about the bush.

As soon as Rosalind and Jack Sollers had seated themselves across the table, Leland began to talk business.
'Now, Rosalind,' he said directly, 'this is the offer. One
hundred and twenty-five thousand, and no admission of
liability.'

Sollers smiled thinly. 'This suit isn't a joke, Leland,' he

14

said.

'I know that,' Leland replied, keeping his temper in check. 'No one treats half a million dollars as a joke. But let's be rational about all this, shall we?' He glanced from Rosalind's calm face to Jack Sollers, including both of them in his offer. 'Come on, Jack, Rosalind, we all know what's going on here. There was no bad faith; there was no sex discrimination. You've got no case.'

But Douglas Brackman noted uneasily that neither Rosalind nor her lawyer seemed disposed to jump into the conversation, either to agree or to disagree. And Doug knew that that was a bad sign: they had something up their collective sleeve, and they were just giving Leland enough rope to see if he would hang himself – and the firm – before they revealed their trump card. Douglas could feel his stomach knot up with anxiety.

But Leland didn't seem to be fazed. He merely looked calmly across the table at them and continued. 'And both of you know damned well that the only reason I'm even digni-fying this with *any* kind of financial settlement is so that we can avoid the embarrassment of a public spectacle. Which', he added in a warning tone of voice, 'none of us needs.'

There was a tense silence in the conference room. Then Jack Sollers spoke. 'Five hundred thousand,' he said matter-of-factly.

'You have got to be kidding!' Brackman yelled, startled out of his resolve to stay calm. No one came to the bargain-ing table really expecting to have their initial demand met.

'Of course I'm not kidding,' Jack Sollers said flatly. 'Five hundred thousand, and that is rock bottom.'

'You're out of your mind, Roz!' Leland snapped.

15

Rosalind stared him straight in the eye, but said nothing.

'Kindly refrain from speaking to my client in that manner,' Sollers warned him.

'This is some kind of game you two are playing!' Leland said, barely able to control his fury.

Jack Sollers shook his head. 'No,' he said, 'it's not a game at all.'

'Well, whatever you think you're doing, you haven't got a prayer,' Leland said grimly. 'You are not getting that kind of money out of this firm!'

Sollers leaned forward, his elbows on the table. 'Leland,' he said, 'we've known each other for a long time – and, believe me, you don't want this one to go forward.'

There was a barely disguised threat beneath his words, and Leland took umbrage. 'I don't know what you think you're getting at . . .' he began.

'If this goes to court,' Jack Sollers said, 'this suit will put you and this entire firm on trial smack in the public eye, Leland. And I think everyone at this table knows that this firm can't stand up to that kind of scrutiny. Don't we?'

'I don't have the faintest idea what you're talking about,' Leland blustered, trying to ignore the disruptions and problems that had cropped up among the staff over the past year or two.

'Well, then, let me try to make it clear for you.' Jack Sollers leaned forward for emphasis. 'By the time I get finished here, McKenzie Brackman will be the laughing-stock of Los Angeles. Other law firms will be shaking their heads at the mess that's been exposed here, and the public will be getting a good hearty laugh at the expense of every-one on the staff. Except you, Leland,' he said, his tone softening slightly.

'And just what is *that* supposed to mean?' Leland enquired defensively.

'Leland,' Jack Sollers said gravely, 'they won't be laughing at you. You will simply be pitied.'

Leland reacted as though he's been stung, then tried immediately to cover his response. He stared Jack Sollers straight in the eye. 'I don't like threats,' he said coldly, 'and I'm not giving her half a million dollars, Jack. No way. Not now; not ever.'

Sollers relaxed in his chair and smiled. 'I have to admit', he said, his smile broadening, 'I was actually hoping you'd say that. I'm looking forward to this one.'

The man really was a barracuda, Doug reflected miserably. He actually seemed to enjoy making other people squirm.

Jack Sollers glanced over at Rosalind, who sat as still and silent as a statue. 'Shall we go, Roz?' he asked.

As the two of them rose, Rosalind stared Leland in the eye. 'Leland,' she said in a soft pointed voice, 'you've just made your last mistake. When this thing is over, you'll wish to God that you'd handed over that five hundred thousand, because you won't have a firm left. But I suppose you'll just have to learn the hard way.'

She turned and walked out of the room, and Jack Sollers followed.

In the deafening silence that followed, Doug shook his head. 'What have they got, Leland?'

'I don't know,' Leland said. 'But we'd better find out before this goes to court. I don't want any nasty last-minute surprises.'

17

Chapter Two

'What a day!' Ann Kelsey exclaimed wearily, kicking off her pumps and curling up on the soft leather couch in their study.

'Boy, you're not kidding,' Stuart Markowitz agreed from across the room, where he was fixing drinks for them.

'Here,' he said, handing her a Scotch and water, 'maybe this will take the edge off.'

Stuart settled himself opposite her in a large comfortable armchair. They clicked their glasses together, then paused, an unexpected silence falling between them.

'Oh God,' Ann said unhappily, 'I can't even think of anything good to toast to!'

Stuart sighed. 'Come on, honey, you just can't let this thing with Rosalind upset you this way. We've got a great team of lawyers, and personally I really don't think this will go far enough to create any kind of serious negative publicity.'

Ann shook her head. 'Maybe you're right,' she said. 'God knows, I hope you are. But let's face it, Stuart, you and I both worked with Rosalind long enough to know what she's like.' She gazed unhappily down into her drink, as if the solution could somehow be found there.

'She's a fighter all right,' Stuart agreed. 'And a good one.'

'It's more than just being a fighter,' Ann said. 'She doesn't take on challenges unless she thinks the odds are on her side, and she'll do anything to win. *Anything*,' she repeated emphatically. 'Clean tactics, dirty tactics, out-and-out sabotage!'

'Let's try to calm down and be rational about this,' Stuart said, thinking someone had to be the voice of reason here; his wife seemed to be going a little bit overboard. 'There *are* a lot of things that have gone on in the office over the past two years or so that no one wants to rehash. But I think she's just banking on that – on us not wanting to go over that stuff again – not on some secret that she wants to spring in an open court.'

'Oh, Stuart,' Ann said softly. 'No. That's not it at all.'

Stuart was startled to see a tear run down Ann's cheek. 'Honey, what is it? What's wrong?'

'Nothing. I'll be all right.' Ann wiped the tear away and tried to compose herself. She took a sip of her Scotch, then set the tumbler on the glass coffee-table. Then she took a deep breath and tried to pull herself together. After all, she thought, there was no sense in delaying what she had to say. 'I have to tell you something,' she said somberly.

Stuart looked at his wife with genuine concern. 'Ann, what on earth . . . ?'

Ann held a hand up to stop him in mid-question. 'I think *I'm* the secret she's got waiting to spring in open court,' she said softly.

'*What?*' Stuart looked at her with disbelief. 'What are you talking about?'

'Stuart,' Ann said, struggling to get the words out, 'do you remember the day Rosalind lost the senior partner-

19

ship?'

'Of course.' How could anyone forget the trauma that had preceded that event, trauma which had threatened to split their office into warring factions?

'Well, right after that happened, I ran into her in the ladies' room; and, Stuart, I swear it was the first time – the *only* time – I have ever seen a chink in that incredible armour of hers. I mean, she was actually showing some genuine emotion. She seemed really sad and really upset by what had happened. Almost . . . I don't know . . . *confused*!' Ann looked pleadingly at Stuart.

'But she's the one who caused what happened, sweetie,' Stuart reminded her. 'If she'd been as honest and above board with all of us as she was aggressive with the clients, she probably could have had anything she wanted at the firm. *Including* the senior partnership. But she wasn't. From the very first day, she was a backstabbing bitch, a sneak and a liar – and it finally caught up with her.'

'I know that,' Ann said miserably. 'Believe me, I know it. I hated her from the moment she walked into the firm! But that day, when I saw her there, just for that moment, I actually felt sorry for her.' She laughed a small bitter laugh. 'And, if there was ever a time when I should have reminded myself how much I really despised her, that was it.'

'Tell me what you said,' Stuart coaxed her. 'It's probably not as bad as you think.'

Ann looked at him and sighed. 'Yes, Stuart,' she said. 'It's just as bad as I think. I told her that if she'd been a man she wouldn't have lost the senior partnership.'

Stuart's eyes widened in disbelief. 'Oh by God,' he said slowly, as the full implication of the words hit him. It was like a physical blow. 'Oh my God! Ann, how could you have said that?'

'You know, Stuart,' Ann said, looking pleadingly at him, 'it's that old attitude: if a man does it, he's considered aggressive; if a woman does it, she's considered a bitch.'

'But Rosalind *is* a bitch!' Stuart exclaimed angrily. 'It has nothing to do with gender!'

'I know, I know,' Ann said miserably.

'Jesus, Ann, how could you? That's her whole case; that's why we're going to get dragged into court!'

Ann just sat silently, staring down. Stuart got up and began to pace. 'OK,' he said, as much to himself as to his wife. 'OK, let's think this thing through. Major damage-control is called for here.'

'But how can we do damage-control when we know what she heard?' Ann demanded. 'I mean, I can't just march into court and contradict her.'

'Why not?' Stuart countered.

Ann looked at him in disbelief. 'What are you saying, Stuart?' she asked.

'I'm saying', Stuart told her straightforwardly, 'that you *might* not remember what you said.'

'Oh Christ!' she exclaimed as the full implication of his words hit her. 'I'm not going to sit here and listen to this! You're talking about perjury!' She stood up angrily. 'I'm going upstairs to check on Matthew.' And with that she strode furiously out of the study.

Stuart fixed himself another drink and stared moodily into the fireplace. This was a mess; there was no way around that. And he'd have to handle Ann with kid gloves – she was too distressed by being in the middle of this thing.

21

Although, Stuart thought, for once it would have been better if his wife could have checked her impulse to be comforting . . . and honest!

'Stuart!' Ann was standing in the arched doorway to the study, looking even more unhappy than she had when she left the room a few minutes earlier.

'What is it?' Stuart asked, alarmed. 'Is something wrong with Matthew?'

'No, no – he's fine. But Rosalita is quitting. Where the hell are we going to find another housekeeper to take care of Matthew while we're at work?'

It was obviously the final straw in a day full of heavy contenders for the title. Stuart moved across the room and put his arm around Ann while tears began to flow in earnest.

*

'Abby! How come you're still here?' Jonathan Rollins, leather attaché case in hand, paused at the door to Abby Perkins's office. 'Burning the midnight oil, or what?'

Abby looked up and smiled wearily. 'Come on in for a minute,' she said. 'I'm just wrapping up the files for the mini-mall case. We settled out of court this afternoon. Talk about last-minute bargaining! And I just want to clear this off my desk so I can start fresh tomorrow.'

Jonathan glanced at his watch. 'I think we both work too hard,' he said half-jokingly.

'It seems to come with the territory,' Abby agreed. 'What are we – type-A personalities?'

Jonathan shrugged. 'I suppose so, if that's the latest label they want to put on normal ambition.'

Abby laughed. 'Oh, come on, Jonathan!' she exclaimed. 'Our kind of ambition isn't exactly considered normal.'

'I suppose not,' Jonathan said, sprawling across the couch in Abby's office. 'But I guess we're both banking on the big pay-off, huh?'

Abby sighed and relaxed in her chair. 'I suppose so,' she said. 'I mean, if I don't make partner this time around, I don't know what I'm going to do.' She paused. 'And I don't know about you, but I'm a little concerned over this trend that Leland seems to be starting – bringing in people to the firm without consulting anyone else.'

'You don't mean Grace, do you?' Jonathan asked, startled.

'Oh, no – not at all,' Abby replied. 'Grace is great, and way out of my league anyway. No, actually I was thinking of C. J. Lamb.'

Cara Jean Lamb was a fireball of a young lawyer who had so impressed Leland McKenzie with her bright aggressive tactics that he had offered her an associate position which included CJ keeping a part of the base fee of any case she brought into the firm.

Jonathan nodded. 'I like her,' he said, 'and she certainly is . . . well, *noticeable*. In court and out of it. But I know what you mean – we seem to be getting a few too many cooks in the kitchen.'

'Exactly,' Abby said. 'I like her, too, but I like the idea of making partner more. I mean, look how many times I've been passed over. And I know damned well that everyone here looks at me as if I'm a wimp. I just don't need any more competition.'

'No one looks at you as if you were a wimp,' Jonathan protested.

'Maybe not,' Abby shrugged, 'but they certainly don't seem to see me as an aggressive fast-tracker, either.'

'So what will you do?'

'I don't know,' Abby said slowly. 'I can't exactly go running out of here without a safety-net. God knows, I need the paycheck. Raising Eric by myself isn't exactly cheap. Or easy,' she added sadly.

'Aren't you seeing anybody these days?' Jonathan asked curiously.

Abby shook her head. 'No. You know – a blind-date here, a fix-up there. Nobody, not really. How's Diana?'

Jonathan smiled. 'Fine. Now, *that's* a part of my life that seems to be running smoothly.'

'She's happy at the Public Defender's office?'

Jonathan nodded. 'Yes. It's more her style than this place is. I guess she's a little more public-spirited than I am.'

'Then, how does she feel about you getting mixed up in the Brian Chisolm case?' Abby asked, curious.

Jonathan frowned. 'I'm not mixed up in it,' he said. 'And I intend to keep it that way.'

'Good luck,' Abby said, sensing that this was too touchy a subject to press. 'But I have to tell you I think you're going to be getting a lot of pressure on this one.'

Jonathan frowned. 'I know,' he said. 'Believe me, I know.'

*

Grace Van Owen looked carefully at Victor Sifuentes, as if she was judging his ability to be tough enough.

'Victor?' she said.

Victor looked up from the legal pad on which he was jotting some pertinent notes, his sculpted face calm, his dark eyes steady. 'What?'

Grace smiled and shrugged. 'Oh, I don't know.' He was tough enough, she decided. And, God, he was gorgeous.

'You worried, Gracie?' Victor asked with a small smile playing on his lips.

'Have you ever seen Jack Sollers at work?' Grace countered. 'He is one impressive piece of legal machinery, Victor. I don't think this is going to be any cakewalk for us.'

'Neither do I,' Victor agreed. 'But what can we do? It's a job that someone's got to do, and we're the logical choices to defend the firm.'

'Victor, tell me something,' Grace said impulsively. 'Do you think it *was* sex discrimination? You were here, and I wasn't.'

Victor paused for a moment, then shook his head. 'You know,' he said reflectively, 'I've gone over it and over it in my head, and I swear, Grace, I can't think of one single thing that points in that direction.' He shrugged with an easy smile. 'I suppose that could just be convenient chauvinist memory-loss, but I don't think so . . . '

Grace smiled back at him. 'Neither do I,' she said. 'I've never seen any evidence of that kind of prejudice in you.' Uh-oh, she thought, time to back off the personal stuff. 'Well,' she said briskly, 'let's go. Time for the staff meeting.'

Actually they were the first ones into the conference room, followed closely by Abby, Jonathan and Arnie, who

25

all seemed to be unusually preoccupied with their own thoughts. Stuart and Ann came in looking even more distracted. What was going on here? Grace wondered. A cloud of doom seemed to hang over the room. As Douglas and Leland strode in, Michael Kuzak appeared as well, and the meeting began.

'OK,' Doug Brackman said, looking around the table, 'as you all know, this is the day. Shays versus McKenzie Brackman goes to court this morning.'

Ann spoke up first. 'I got subpoena'd last night,' she said.

'So did I,' said Abby.

'What?' Leland said, obviously upset by the news. 'Why?'

'You two?' Doug echoed in disbelief. 'Why?'

'What on earth could she want with you two as witnesses?' Arnie Becker asked.

'Well, Rosalind and Abby were pretty friendly,' Michael pointed out. 'Maybe she just wants somebody from the firm who can't completely blacken her reputation in public.'

'Good point,' Leland said grimly. He looked seriously at Abby. 'What are you going to say if you're called as a character witness?' he asked her.

Abby shrugged uneasily. 'I suppose I'll say that it doesn't matter how I felt personally; I was certainly aware of the kind of negative effect she was having on the firm as a whole.'

'Good,' Doug said, nodding in satisfaction. 'That should take care of it.' Then he turned his attention to Ann. 'But you, Ann – you two were like cat and dog from the minute she got here. Why would she subpoena you?'

Ann glanced at Stuart, who nodded reassuringly. 'I think . . .,' she began in a shaky voice. She cleared her throat and began again. 'I think it probably has something to do with a remark I made to her after she lost the senior partnership.'

As Ann finished her sentence, it felt was as though all the people round the table were holding a collective breath.

'Go on, Ann, please,' Doug said, fighting to keep his voice calm.

'Ann, what did you say?' Leland demanded far more brusquely.

Ann looked down at the table, unable to meet her partners' eyes. 'Something like . . . um . . . well . . . that what happened to her wouldn't have happened if she'd been a man.'

After an initial numbing silence, the lawyers all seemed to start shouting at once.

'Oh my God!' said Doug Brackman, looking horrified.

'Ann!' Leland snapped. 'You actually said that to her? Were you out of your mind?'

'Oh Jesus,' Arnie muttered. 'Great. I wonder what we're going to find out next.'

Michael Kuzak simply sat there, stunned, unable even to respond.

But it was Victor whose fury was the most urgent. 'I'm hearing this *now*?' he shouted. 'Now, on the day that we go to trial? I can't believe this, Ann – not only that you could be so stupid as to say something like that –'

'Hey, wait a minute, Victor,' Stuart began to interject.

'Shut up, Stuart!' Victor yelled. Then he seemed to make an effort to calm down. 'Ann,' he said, glaring at her, 'giving that woman exactly the ammunition she needed for a case – that's bad enough! But how the hell could you keep this a secret until now?'

'I'm sorry,' Ann said, her voice nearly a whisper. 'I just didn't know how to tell any of you . . . '

'Well,' Arnie said firmly, 'there's only one way you can handle this, Ann. You simply cannot admit that you ever said that when you're on the stand.'

Ann looked startled, then angry. Her voice was recovered as she snapped at Arnie. 'What are you telling me, Arnie? Am I supposed to lie?' God, she thought, it was bad enough that Stuart had mildly suggested the same thing; at least he'd known to back off. But the rest of the partners . . .

'Yes,' said Arnie. 'Have a convenient memory-loss – it happens all the time.'

'Of course,' said Doug. 'He's right.'

'I can't do that. . . .'

'For God' sake, Ann,' Leland said to her, his voice shaking with anger, 'they are absolutely right. If you say that, you'll make her entire case!'

'And just what do you suggest, Leland?' Ann said. 'You're with the rest of the guys here – you think I should commit perjury?'

Leland fixed her with a serious intense look and chose his words carefully. 'Everyone at this table knows you, Ann. We're all perfectly aware how honest and conscientious you are,' he assured her. 'What I am strongly suggesting is that you remember that the conversation in question took place over six months ago. You couldn't possibly be expected to remember it.'

'I don't . . . I just don't know if I can do that,' Ann said.

28

'You can do it all right,' Leland replied grimly. 'I'd like to remind you that the future of this firm is at risk here. How *much* risk, we didn't really know until right now. This is not the moment to demonstrate once again your much vaunted integrity. Do you understand?'

Ann looked Leland straight in the eye. 'I understand,' she replied angrily.

'Good,' said Doug with a sigh of relief. 'Let's move on to something a little less horrifying, shall we?'

As Arnie began to give the status of a tricky annulment case he was working on, Grace leaned over towards Victor, who sat looking like a thundercloud. 'We have our work cut out for us, kiddo,' she said.

Victor's eyes met hers. 'Tell me about it,' he said.

Chapter Three

It was just as unnerving as the attorneys from McKenzie Brackman had expected it to be. There they sat, all of them, behind the defence table where Grace and Victor were seated. Arnie reflected that they looked just like ducks lined up to be shot – an obvious and unflattering contrast to the plaintiff's table where a composed sober-looking Rosalind Shays sat, while Jack Sollers, using his most intense dramatic voice and posture, addressed the jury with his opening statement.

'This is not a pretty case,' he said sombrely, fixing one, then another jury member with a piercing look. 'The last thing that people like you want is to learn that there are lawyers – often highly paid, respected lawyers – who are simply unable to do their job. Because that', he said emphatically, 'means that any time any one of *you* could unknowingly hire a lawyer who would be inadequate to defend you.'

He strode up and down in front of the jury, pacing, seemingly lost in thought. Suddenly he looked up again. 'And that's really what this trial is about,' he informed them. 'Incompetence.'

'Oh Jesus,' muttered Arnie, shifting uncomfortably in his seat.

'This firm' – Jack Sollers motioned towards the line of

lawyers with a contemptuous wave of his hand – 'this allegedly respected law firm was in such deep trouble last January that they were desperate for someone – someone serious, someone competent, someone even *brilliant* – to help bail them out of their troubles. Because, believe me, members of the jury, they needed the best they could find in order to put their messy home in order.' Then he pointed emphatically towards Rosalind Shays. 'And, ladies and gentleman, this is who they brought in to save their law firm. My client, Rosalind Shays, a woman with an uncompromised reputation for the highest standards and capabilities as a lawyer. A lawyer whose brilliance has been proved again and again.'

Sollers strode to the table and took a sip of water. 'Now, let me set your minds at rest about one thing. When Rosalind Shays joined McKenzie Brackman last January, she was under no illusions about the firm being in trouble. She knew exactly what she was being brought in to do. She knew that the firm was a ship which was foundering, taking on water much faster than it could bail it out. She knew that she was going to have the unwelcome task of repairing that leak. And make no mistake about it – she was up to the task. But '– he paused for a moment of piercing eye-contact – 'there was *no* way that she could have known the level of ineptitude and personal destructiveness that pervaded this incompetent group of so-called lawyers.'

'Object,' Victor said firmly. 'These are licensed lawyers; the phrase "so-called" is misleading.'

Judge Travelini nodded. 'Sustained,' she said quietly. 'Members of the jury are instructed to ignore the phrase. And, Mr Sollers, you will please refrain from verbal flights

31

of fancy.'

'I'm sorry, your honour,' Jack Sollers said humbly. 'I just got carried away.'

'Right,' Grace whispered to Victor. 'He just got carried away. Carried as far as he could get before he hit a speed-bump!'

'This is sounding *awful*,' Victor whispered back. Grace nodded grimly in agreement.

'The head litigator' – Jack Sollers pointed towards Michael Kuzak, who simply glared back at him – 'was so invested in a murder trial – for which, by the way, he wasn't even getting paid –'

'*Object!*' Victor said more emphatically. 'We *all* do *pro bono* work, your Honour; it's hardly fair to cite defending people who can't afford our kind of firm as *criticism*.'

'You didn't let me finish,' Jack Sollers said.

Judge Travelini nodded. 'I'm going to allow it, Mr Sifuentes. But, Mr Sollers, please don't linger on this line; move along.'

'What I began to say', Jack Sollers said with a little smile, 'was that because of Mr Kuzak's very charitable actions in a murder case he had no time left for the criminal cases he was getting paid for. And when he couldn't handle what he was being *paid* to handle, the firm to chose to send Stuart Markowitz, a tax attorney with almost no trial experience, into litigation.'

Stuart flushed in anger as the members of the jury stared at him. 'Jesus,' he whispered to Ann, 'he makes it sound as if I'm a book-keeper!'

'Shh.' Ann patted his hand comfortingly. 'I've got a feeling this is nothing compared to what's coming.'

32

'While this was going on,' Sollers continued smoothly, 'the firm's matrimonial lawyer – he nodded contemptuously in Arnie Becker's direction – 'was busy, *very* busy – throwing himself into the making of home videos for do-it-yourself divorces. And when he wasn't being sued for malpractice he was engaged in copying and stealing the firm's files while he planned and carried out a midnight defection to another firm. The only thing which brought him back was the threat of a suit by the firm against him – and the *honour*' – Sollers's voice dripped with sarcasm – 'of becoming a partner!'

Sollers paused again for effect, while the jury stared at Arnie Becker as though he was an alien creature. Arnie attempted to look innocent.

'Then', Sollers said, 'we have Leland McKenzie, the senior partner in the firm, who was old and tired enough to admit he needed help – the kind of help my client could provide. That in itself is fine; but what *isn't* fine is that he reneged on his word as soon as Rosalind Shays had pulled the firm back from the brink of disaster –'

'Object!' Victor shouted. 'Move to strike – there was no brink of disaster!'

'Sustained,' Judge Travelini agreed.

'And the administrative partner, Douglas Brackman,' Jack Sollers continued without missing a beat, 'seemed to have been undergoing some sort of personal identity crisis. There wasn't much time left to do a lawyer's job after he was through trying toupees, then braces, and while he romped through a series of well-known affairs with women, including his own father's mistress and a professional sexual surrogate!'

33

Brackman closed his eyes, appalled at hearing himself described in such a fashion. It wasn't that Sollers's statements weren't true; it was the sleazy spin he put on them, and the implied contempt. Douglas had never felt so humiliated.

'Now, ladies and gentlemen,' Sollers said with a smile, 'ordinarily I'd tell you just to take a look at this mixed bag of kooks and whackos, and to laugh at their various antics. But,' he said, holding up a warning finger and suddenly looking very grave, 'what happened in the firm, what these people did to my client, wasn't one bit funny. Facing almost certain bankruptcy, McKenzie Brackman put their collective heads together and came up with a solution. My client, Rosalind Shays, was that solution. They brought her into the firm for the sole purpose of rescuing them from disaster – excuse me, your Honour – from severe financial and client-related problems. And they brought her in as a senior partner. That's how much they needed to have her credibility to show to the world.'

'He's really good,' Abby whispered to Ann.

Ann nodded. 'He's so good he's scary,' she agreed. 'This is going to be a nightmare, Abby.'

'The evidence will show', Sollers continued, 'that Rosalind Shays not only brought them the credibility they needed, but she also brought them clients – and she brought them *money*. In short, she brought McKenzie Brackman the kind of profit and prestige they had never before had. And then' – he leaned forward at the jury-box to emphasise his words – 'only then, after she had accomplished all of this for them, this little boys' club decided they didn't really want a woman at the helm for them. And they got rid of

34

her. Just like that,' he said, snapping his fingers. 'After she had served her purpose, they dumped her.'

Sollers took another sip of water, then faced the jury once again. 'You know,' he said in a conversational tone of voice, 'as a rule I don't even think about taking cases where the defendant is another attorney – it's too messy. Call it professional courtesy, call it anything you like, but most of the time I'm simply not comfortable with the idea of it. And I certainly don't like to be in the position of attacking other lawyers – it's too much like turning on one of your own.'

'Haven't sharks always been known to do that?' Abby murmured.

Arnie smiled thinly in response.

'But when Rosalind Shays asked me to represent her in this case, when I saw what these people had done to her – the unbelievable level of deceit, and the quite blatant sexual discrimination that had occurred – I had to rethink my position.' His eyes narrowed, and his voice dropped a notch. When he spoke again, he sounded tougher, more emphatic. 'Ladies and gentlemen, after I spent a little time thinking about this case, I took it. Oh, yes,' he said, glancing angrily over at the McKenzie Brackman staff, 'I took it all right. Because as a fellow-member of the Bar I was, quite frankly, *embarrassed* by this behaviour. *Ashamed* of what they did. People like this degrade the entire profession. And we're going after them.'

He learned forward, his hands resting on the front of the jury-box. 'You and me, we're going after them. Appealing to the overwhelming evidence, appealing to the truth, appealing to your fundamental sense of what is fair, what is

35

right – and what is *wrong* – you and I, ladies and gentle-men, together, we're going to teach this unscrupulous bunch of thieving sharks a lesson they will *never* forget.' He glared over at the defence table once more, then back at the jury members. 'Thank you,' he said quietly, then turned and walked to the plaintiff's table, where Rosalind Shays, dressed all in black, gave him a look of gratitude and sadness.

'That was a remarkable performance,' Arnie whispered to Doug Brackman. 'Maybe Sollers missed his calling when became a lawyer instead of an actor.'

'For Christ's sake, Arnie,' Doug Brackman snapped impatiently, 'all good trial lawyers are actors. Take a look at Rosalind Shays if you want to see a bit of stellar-quality performance; she's actually behaving as if she had a normal emotion coursing through the icy water in her veins!' Then he sank moodily back into his own thoughts about the accu-sations Jack Sollers had levelled at him personally. And what he was going to do about them.

*

'Roxanne, I'm sorry to keep bugging you. . . .'

Roxanne looked up from her typing to see Corrinne smil-ing and looking just a little embarrassed. 'What is it?' she asked coolly.

'Well, I wanted to thank you for getting the Christmas list together so quickly; it will really be a big help. We are just so crunched for time.'

'Oh, well,' Roxanne shrugged, relaxing a little, 'that's OK, Corrinne. It really wasn't any big deal.'

36

'Oh, good,' Corrinne sighed. 'I was hoping you'd say that, because I do have just one more tiny little favour to ask you.'

'What's that?' Roxanne said, reverting to a cooler tone.

'Well, Travel Time botched the plans for the ski trip. I can't believe how disorganized they are. I mean, how do you run a business that way and expect to get anywhere? Anyway, not only didn't they get us on to the Friday-night flight that I specifically requested, but they didn't even reserve Chloe a spot in the Beginner Show Bunnies. And she just has her heart set on it. Besides, how are Arnie and I going to get in any serious skiing if we have to look after Chloe?'

Roxanne wondered briefly if Corrinne was going to ask her to come along as Chloe's babysitter. Wouldn't that be a joke!

'So do you think you could get things straightened out for us?' Corrinne asked.

Roxanne shook her head negatively. 'That has nothing to do with me, Corrinne,' she told her. 'You need to talk to Liz Cohn she's the one who handles all of the firm's scheduling at the agency.'

Corrinne shuddered. 'Ugh! Liz Cohn is the travel agent from hell,' she said. 'I think she hates me because I married Arnie . . .'

Roxanne bit her lip to keep from telling Corrinne that Liz Cohn was two years away from retirement, obese, and looking forward to the time when she and her husband could hop in their camper and travel across the country, visiting their grandchildren.

'Oh, no,' Roxanne said soothingly, 'I'm sure she'll

straighten things out for you, Corrinne.'

'Oh, Roxanne, *please*? I just can't deal with people like that – and you're so efficient!'

Efficient – exactly what she *wasn't* going to be if Corrinne kept taking up her time bugging her with these silly requests for help. Roxanne sighed. Sometimes, she thought, it was easier to switch than fight. 'OK,' she said.

Corrinne beamed. 'Oh, that is so sweet of you!' she exclaimed, tearing a page from her Filofax. 'Here's a list of what needs to be done. You are such an angel!'

'Corrinne, is that really you?'

Roxanne looked up to see Gwen Taylor, the stunning secretary who had recently gone to work for Stuart Markowitz full-time, smiling at Corrinne. 'It's me, Corrinne. Gwennie Taylor!'

'Oh my God!' Corrinne exclaimed. 'I can't believe it!' The two women hugged, and Corrinne turned to Roxanne. 'This kid used to be our mascot in school. Her sister Laura and I took her to buy her first bra!' She turned back to Gwen. 'What on earth brings you here?' she asked. 'Are you retaining my husband in some fabulously pricey divorce settlement?'

Roxanne saw Gwen's big eyes widen in what seemed to be shock. 'Arnie Becker is your husband?' she asked faintly.

'Yes. We've been married for almost five months now. But what are you . . .?'

'I'm a secretary,' Gwen said hastily. 'I work for Stuart Markowitz.'

'Oh, how fabulous!' Corrinne laughed. 'We'll all have to get together, you and me and Arnie, and go out for a drink.'

38

'I . . . um . . . I'd love that,' Gwen said, slipping away. 'I've really got a lot to do, Corrinne – this is a hectic day but I'm sure I'll be seeing you around!' And she was gone.

'What an amazing coincidence,' Corrinne mused. 'Well, I'd better be moving along, too. Thanks again Rox. I really appreciate this. 'Bye now!' And with a wave she was gone, leaving Roxanne to surmise that what she had always suspected – that Arnie and Gwen had slept together right before he married Corrinne – must be true.

*

Court resumed session after a tense gloomy lunch in which the McKenzie Brackman staff dissected Jack Soller's opening statement so many times, and drew so many possible conclusions about his strategy, that it began to not even make sense to them. There was a pervasive feeling of unease, and not even Leland, with his avuncular reassurances, could make the attorneys feel that a great deal of damage hadn't already been done.

They filed back into Judge Travelini's courtroom, looking, according to Arnie, like a pack of beaten Indians.

'Now, Victor,' Leland said, tapping the young lawyer on the shoulder, 'don't forget: be clean, be quick, be strong. Make your points and get out. It's the only way we're going to be able to counteract what Sollers had already tried to lay down in the jury's mind.'

Victor nodded. 'I know, Leland,' he said patiently.

Then he turned to Grace, who was jotting notes on a lined yellow pad. 'I *should* know,' Victor whispered. 'He's only told me the same thing about twelve times since noon!'

'Are you nervous?' Grace asked sympathetically.

Victor thought for a moment, then shook his head. 'No,' he said, 'not really. But I do think it's going to be an uphill battle.'

Grace nodded, and then both arose as the bailiff announced the judge's arrival. Marilyn Travelini sat down, then nodded to Victor. 'Mr Sifuentes,' she said.

Victor walked to the front of the courtroom calmly with his customary easy self-confidence. Grace watched him intently, focusing on every move, every word. Victor nodded to the judge, then turned to face the jury. His voice was as cool and deliberate as his demeanour. He had to demonstrate to them that Jack Sollers's approach was not his approach, and to calm them down from the emotional pitch to which Sollers's opening diatribe had raised them.

'Ladies and gentlemen,' Victor began in a low authoritative voice, 'now is the moment when you put behind you what my learned opponent' – and he threw a small mocking smile at the plaintiff's table – 'so theatrically told you. Because' – and here he stared at each juror, making sure the eye-contact was established – 'the evidence which I will submit to you will show beyond a doubt that Rosalind Shays is a phoney, bringing a phoney case before you. Ms Shays is *not* the injured party here. She is a dishonest and highly manipulative person who will betray – who *has betrayed* – anybody who gets in the way of her self-promotion.' He threw a dark glance at Rosalind, whose composure didn't seem in the least bit ruffled by his words.

'Rosalind Shays was not voted out of her temporary position of senior partner because she is a woman. There is no case of sexual discrimination to be found here, no matter what Mr Sollers would like you to believe. Rosalind Shays was voted out because she is a liar and a sneak, and she cannot be trusted – least of all by those who, as her law partners, should most be able to trust her.'

Victor's face darkened. 'I'm sorry to be so blunt, but that is the truth. Rosalind Shays wants you to believe that she's the classic woman scorned, but that couldn't be farther from the truth. She is a liar and a cheat; she's the person with the knife ready to plunge into anyone's back for the sake of her own advancement. And *that* is why she is no longer a part of McKenzie Brackman. There is no other reason.'

He paused to make cold hard contact with Sollers and Rosalind. Then he turned back to the jury. 'They think they're coming after *us*?' Victor permitted himself a small sardonic smile. 'Wrong, ladies and gentlemen. We're going after *her*.'

Chapter Four

Jack Sollers didn't appear to have been the least bit impressed by Victor's brief but strong opening statement. Staring at the opposing counsel, Grace Van Owen thought she could detect an effort on his part not to look too gleeful. Grace had to admit to herself that she had been grudgingly impressed by his handling of the situation. He had a right to seem confident. It was good to project confidence; in the jury's mind, it generally meant you had complete faith in your client. But it could be a delicate line to tread between confidence and smugness, an attitude which could – and often did – backfire on lawyers. Grace felt herself hoping devoutly that Jack Sollers would let his mask slip long enough to let the jury see what he really thought.

'All right, Mr Sollers,' Judge Travelini said with a nod in his direction. 'Let's begin.'

'Yes, your Honour,' Sollers replied respectfully. 'The plaintiff calls as its first witness Mr Stuart Markowitz.'

There was a general, almost tangible jolt of surprise which could be felt all along the row of defendants. This was completely unexpected.

'What the hell is he doing?' Victor murmured to Grace as he rose to his feet. 'Objection, your Honour. This witness is not on their list.'

Sollers flashed a brief thin smile at Victor which the jury

42

couldn't see; but this time Grace could see that there really *was* the unmistakable look of smugness he'd been so successfully avoiding. Grace felt an icy finger of worry.

'He's on *your* list, Counsellor,' Sollers reminded Victor.

'I know he's on our list, Mr Sollers,' Victor replied impatiently, 'and he's prepared to testify. But for *us*, not for *you*.'

'He can testify for whoever he wants,' Sollers said with an easy shrug. 'I'm simply requesting that he testify *now*.'

'And I'm objecting to that,' Victor said through clenched teeth.

'Counsel,' Judge Travelini interjected, 'we're wasting time here. This is a court of law, and I expect the business conducted herein to be done so expeditiously. Do I make myself clear?'

'Yes, your Honour,' Victor said, 'but if Mr Sollers intended to call this witness as part of his case he should have included him on the list I was given.' He was clearly alarmed at this unexpected turn of events.

'Stuart,' Ann whispered worriedly, clutching his arm, 'what are they trying to do?'

'Calm down, Ann; it'll be all right,' Stuart replied, although he was feeling far from calm himself. He had a terrible feeling that this little surprise testimony was going to make him look like a fool. Given Soller's description of him during his opening statement, what else *could* he think?

Judge Travelini looked sternly at Victor. 'What is the big deal, Mr Sifuentes?' she asked. 'You were planning to call him anyway. It's not as if you've never heard his name before.'

43

'But he was scheduled to be our fourth or fifth witness, your Honour, and that is considerably down the road. I haven't had a chance to prepare his testimony with him and I – '

'That's the point!' Jack Sollers broke in. He winked at the jury, who seemed to be quite interested in the legal bickering that was going on in front of them. 'I don't want the rehearsed version. I think we're all more interested in the truth.'

'Objection!' Victor shouted. 'How dare counsel impugn the testimony of –?'

'That will be enough, Mr Sollers,' Judge Travelini interjected. Then she looked in Victor's direction. 'Mr Sifuentes, I'm overruling your objection. The witness will take the stand.'

'Then I move for a continuance to allow discovery –'

'No,' the judge, said, frowning.

'Your Honour!' Victor said, dismayed.

'This is a waste of time, gentlemen, and I believe it made it amply clear just a few minutes ago that I do not tolerate wasting time in the courtroom. Call the witness, and let's get on with it.'

Victor and Grace exchanged glances. They quite obviously had to back down.

'Mr Stuart Markowitz,' the clerk said.

Clearly ill at ease, Stuart rose and walked to the witness-stand, where he raised his right-arm, gave his name and was sworn in.

'Now, Mr Markowitz,' Jack Sollers said smoothly, 'you are a tax attorney, are you not?'

'That's correct,' Stuart said stiffly.

44

'And would you please tell the court in your own words just why the plaintiff, Rosalind Shays, was brought into your firm as a partner?'

'Who else's words would he use?' Ann snarled under her breath.

'Well, uh . . .' Stuart paused and tried to collect his thoughts. 'The firm was becoming less profitable than it had been in the past, and we all felt that we could use somebody new who could help us expand our client-base.'

Sollers nodded, stroking his chin thoughtfully. 'And would you say that Ms Shays accomplished that for the firm?'

'Yes,' Stuart said without elaboration. If Sollers was expecting him to roll over and just give him what he wanted, Stuart told himself, Sollers had another thing coming. Sollers was going to have to prise it out of him.

'In fact', Sollers continued, 'the truth is that during her short tenure at McKenzie Brackman my client increased the firm's revenues, did she not?'

'Yes,' Stuart acknowledged.

'By . . . let me see . . . by thirty-two per cent. That's correct, isn't it, Mr Markowitz?'

Sollers was obviously going after Stuart's testimony in a way that left no room for convenient memory-loss or vagueness: a tax lawyer would most definitely have those kinds of numbers at his fingertips.

Stuart nodded curtly. 'That would be right, yes.'

'And would it also be right to say that at the time Rosalind Shays joined the firm McKenzie Brackman was in considerable disarray, to the point that it nearly wasn't functioning?'

45

'The firm was functioning just fine,' Stuart snapped. 'There was no disarray!'

'Is that so?' Jack Sollers nodded thoughtfully. 'Just fine?'

'Yes,' Stuart said.

'Well, I'd be interested to know – and I'm certain the members of the jury would, too – just how a tax attorney such as yourself, an attorney with no litigation experience whatsoever in nearly nineteen years of practice, was suddenly thrust into the position of appearing in court.'

Stuart looked offended. 'I wasn't thrust into anything. I was totally prepared to litigate,' he added, trying to keep his feelings of anger and embarrassment at bay. Jesus, he thought, this guy really went for the jugular. Or the balls.

'Really?' Sollers cocked a greying eyebrow in disbelief. 'And just what was it that prepared you so well for litigation, Mr Markowitz? Did you watch a lot of Perry Mason reruns?'

'Objection!' Victor yelled, leaping to his feet. The members of the jury were chuckling.

'Sustained,' Judge Travelini said. 'Mr Sollers, you are out of line, and you know it. Please stick to an acceptable line of questioning or you may well find yourself in contempt.'

'I apologise, your Honour,' Jack Sollers said with patently false humility. Then he turned his attention back to the stand. 'I've looked at your trial record, Mr Markowitz,' he said. 'Your first case concerned a woman suing someone over a bad dating service, and your next one, I believe . . . oh, yes, *that* was the one involving an elderly rabbi whose hand had slipped during a bris.' He smiled at the jury.

'That's Jewish ceremony in which a boy is circumcised,' he explained.

The jury could barely contain themselves. 'That bastard is getting them in the palm of his hands,' Victor whispered to Grace.

'I told you he was going to be hell to go up against,' Grace replied softly.

'Yes,' Stuart admitted. 'Those were my first two cases. But I did a good job in both,' he added firmly.

'No doubt,' Sollers said dismissively. 'But let's move on. Why don't you tell the members of the jury how you would assess your performance in the next trial – the major personal injury trial where you represented a man who had been held as a political prisoner and had been tortured by electrocution?'

'I was ready,' Stuart said resentfully. 'I was completely prepared.'

'Oh Jesus,' Ann murmured. Abby reached over to pat her hand in sympathy. That case had been terrible, emotionally and psychologically. And Stuart, she knew, had yet to come to terms with the outcome of it.

'I doubt that your former client thinks that,' Jack Sollers shot at Stuart.

'Objection!' Victor yelled.

'Withdrawn,' Jack Sollers said placatingly. Then he turned to Stuart again, fixing him with a controlled dramatic stare. 'And who in the firm believed that you were ready to handle that case?' he asked.

'Well, for one,' Stuart replied in a clipped tone of voice, 'Rosalind Shays! She was a senior partner, and she okayed it.'

47

'Based on your head litigator's ill-founded recommenda-
tion!' Sollers snapped.

'Objection,' Victor said. 'This is irrelevant and –'

'It isn't at all irrelevant!' Sollers said to the judge. 'It
goes to show what a shambles McKenzie Brackman was in.
This man had no business in court! He's an accountant with
a law degree!'

'Objection!' yelled Ann Kelsey, springing to her feet.

'You can't make an objection, Ms Kelsey,' Judge
Travelini said, not without sympathy. 'You aren't the attorney of record here.'

'Sit down, Ann!' Arnie Becker yanked her back down
into her seat, where Ann sat fuming.

'And would you tell us what the outcome of this torture
trial was, Mr Markowitz?' Sollers pressed on. 'This trial at
which the defendant actually took the stand and *admitted*
that he'd helped wire your client's genitals and had sent
electric currents through his body. He admitted his guilt,
and what *happened*?'

There was a dead silent pause. 'We lost,' Stuart said
finally. He looked down, finding it difficult to contain his
emotion.

'That's right, Mr Markowitz. You lost. You're such an
outstanding lawyer that you managed to lose a case which
any first-year associate partner should have been able to
win.'

'Objection,' Victor said wearily.

'Mr Sollers!' Judge Travelini admonished him. 'I warned
you . . .'

'I'm sorry, your Honour, but I happen to think that this is
a perfect example of how McKenzie Brackman *wasn't*

functioning when my client stepped in and literally saved the firm.'

'Are you through with this witness?' Judge Travelini asked mildly.

'Yes, your Honour.'

Judge Travelini fixed a calm knowing look on Sollers. 'Then, I think it's time for us to break for the day,' she said.

There seemed to be a collective palpable sigh of relief among the McKenzie Brackman lawyers. They watched as Rosalind Shays, followed by Sollers, swept out of the courtroom without so much as a glance in their direction.

Leland spoke first. 'I want to see everyone in the conference room at five,' he said sharply. 'No excuses. We have some serious rethinking to do.' Then he marched out of court, his back ramrod-straight.

'That was a fiasco,' Abby said.

'We took a pounding,' Arnie Becker agreed. 'Does anybody here happen to know a good hit-man? It might be cheaper than this.'

'Don't even joke about that!' Doug snapped, then turned on his heel and walked out.

'Well, in that case,' Arnie continued, 'does anybody around here have a sense of humour?'

The gloomy faces around him seemed an eloquent response.

'I know,' Arnie admitted with a sigh. 'We're in big trouble.'

*

When he returned to the office, Arnie was surprised to find

Roxanne distant and curt with him. Instead of greeting him with concern, instead of asking him how the day in court had gone, she surveyed him with cool appraising eyes.

'Arnie,' she said, handling him a stack of messages, 'I need to talk to you.'

'Oh, Rox, does it have to be now?' Arnie said wearily. 'You have no idea how busy —'

'Yes,' she snapped. 'I do have an idea how busy you are, and yes, it has to be now.'

'OK,' he said, resigned, 'come into my office.' Maybe it was just pre-menstrual tension, he thought. 'But would you mind getting me a Perrier first?'

'Get it yourself,' Roxanne said.

'Oh Jesus,' Arnie muttered. 'What have I done now?' He walked across the office into the small kitchen area where the communal office refrigerator was housed, and fished a chilled bottle of Perrier out of it. A Scotch and soda would, he thought, be preferable. Then he trudged back to his office and motioned Roxanne to come in.

Roxanne closed the door behind her and stood there, her arms crossed against her chest. It did not bode well, thought Arnie; it was a very defensive posture. He had the distinct feeling that this was going to prove to be more than a simple case of PMT.

'OK, Roxanne,' he said, 'what's going on?'

'Arnie,' she said, 'this is very difficult for me to say to you. I know how much you love Corrinne, and how much she loves you . . .'

Oh God, Arnie thought, please don't let this be about Gwen. Please don't let Roxanne know about that . . .

'. . . and I understand that maybe she thinks that as your

50

secretary I'm sort of . . . well, sort of part of the package that she got when you two got married.'

So it wasn't Gwen, Arnie thought, relieved. But what was Roxanne talking about? 'What package?' he asked, genuinely bewildered. 'I don't know what you're talking about, Rox.'

Roxanne sighed. 'Honestly, Arnie,' she said, 'sometimes you are just so oblivious.'

'To what?' Arnie repeated.

'To the fact that Corinne treats me as if I was hired help.'

'Oh, come on, Roxanne,' Arnie said, shaking his head in disbelief. 'Is all this about helping her put together the Christmas card list?'

'Yes, Arnie,' Roxanne replied patiently. 'It *is* about putting together the Christmas card list – which, in reality, meant me taking time to cull through that overextended Rolodex of yours and create the list myself. It's about having to spend time changing your travel plans because Corinne isn't happy with Liz Cohn, or doesn't want to deal with her, or something. It's about arranging a babysitter for Chloe, and making *sure* that your dinner reservations at L'Hermitage on a Saturday night – just you and Corinne, not a business dinner – are confirmed. It's about being asked to pick up your ski jackets from the cleaners, for God's sake!' She stared angrily at him.

Arnie sank down into the luxurious leather couch beneath his office window, a window which displayed a spectacular panoramic view of Los Angeles. When you could see it, that was. He realised suddenly that he was exhausted. 'Rox,' he said gently, 'sit down. Come on.' He patted the couch beside him, but Roxanne shook her head and remained standing.

Oh Jesus, he thought, she really was upset. But what was he supposed to do? 'Listen,' he said, 'this is just a little too much for me to deal with right now. This trial is turning into a circus; I feel like I don't have a minute for anything except work – I just can't handle any more problems.'

Roxanne looked steadily at him. 'I'm sorry, Arnie,' she said, 'but there's really no way around this. I'm afraid you're going to *have* to deal with it, like it or not. I'm not trying to create trouble – I want this all to work out – but I have to be treated with the respect that I deserve, and I just don't feel like I am.'

Arnie looked up sharply, stung by a new thought. 'Rox,' he said, 'you wouldn't consider . . . I mean, you're not thinking about leaving, *are* you?' He felt a sudden surge of panic at the idea of not having Roxanne there for him, the way she had been for years. 'I mean, I couldn't handle that, I really couldn't!'

'In that case,' Roxanne replied, 'just please have a talk with Corrinne and set things straight, all right?'

'All right,' Arnie said, giving in, although the idea was about as appealing as playing with a snake. Corrinne was loving and sweet-natured, but she managed somehow to always get her way. 'I'll try.'

'OK,' Roxanne said, not giving an inch. Then she turned to leave.

'Oh, by the way,' Arnie called after her as she opened the door, 'is the Halperin deposition ready?'

Roxanne glanced back at him. 'No,' she said, 'I'm afraid I'm behind on all of that. The Christmas list took more time than I thought it would.' And, with that parting salvo fired, she walked out.

'Oh Jesus,' Arnie muttered to himself, 'what next?' Then he remembered what was next: a certain-to-be-gloomy, verging-on hysterical post-mortem of the horrible day in court.

Chapter Five

'How did it go today, darling?' Corrinne asked as Arnie came into the spacious foyer of their luxurious Malibu home. 'Was it awful? Oh, Arnie, I can tell by your face that it was!' Corrinne hugged him sympathetically, then gave him a lingering kiss on the lips. 'Come into the study and I'll fix us drinks, and you can tell me all about it.'

Arnie nodded and tried to smile, but the smile was at best a strained one. 'OK,' he said gratefully. Thank God he had a wife who was as sweet and understanding as Corrinne.

'Hi, Arnie!' Chloe sang out, skipping down the stairs. 'Guess what happened in school today?'

'Not now, sweetheart,' Corrinne began.

'No, it's OK,' Arnie said, picking Chloe up and swinging her in the air. She was all blonde curls, huge eyes and smiles. He had never really thought about having children himself, but he had discovered that he absolutely adored being stepfather to Chloe, who was like a constant ray of sunshine. 'What happened in school?' he asked, setting her down again.

'Miranda brought her snake to show and tell,' Chloe said, her eyes getting even wider. 'And it was really big, and I picked it up and everything, and now I'm not afraid of them any more!'

'Well, that's terrific,' Arnie said with a smile.

'So . . . can I have one?' Chloe asked.

'One what?'

'Snake,' Corrinne said, rolling her eyes. 'I've already told her that I don't think it's such a good idea.'

'Oh, please!' Chloe said earnestly. 'I'll take care of it, I promise!'

'Honey,' Arnie said, squatting down so he could look her in the face, 'do you know what snakes eat?'

Chloe nodded. 'Bugs – that's what Miranda said.'

'Well,' Arnie said, 'maybe. But I think that when they get bigger they need to eat other animals – like mice and things.'

Chloe wrinkled up her nose in disgust. 'Ugh.'

'Well, that's probably why Mommy isn't really so enthusiastic about you getting a snake. I mean, would *you* want to feed a mouse to the snake?'

'No!' Chloe shook her head vehemently.

'And I wouldn't want to, and I know your mom wouldn't want to . . . so who would feed the poor snake?'

'Rafaella?' Chloe said hopefully.

Arnie stifled a smile at the thought of their live-in housekeeper willingly getting anywhere near a reptile: Rafaella, who kept all sorts of amulets and charms in her room to ward off evil spirits. 'No, honey,' he said, 'I don't think so. You see, having a pet is a responsibility, and that means you have to be the one that will take care of it.'

'Mice and all?' Chloe asked doubtfully.

'Uh-huh.'

Arnie watched Chloe's mobile face as she considered then rejected the idea. Suddenly she lit up again. 'Well,

55

then, what about a pony?' she asked.

Arnie and Corrinne exchanged glances over the little girl's head.

'Let's talk about that another time, honey,' Corrinne said firmly. 'Now, why don't you go and clean up for dinner and watch some television while Arnie and I have a little private time?'

'OK,' Chloe said obligingly, and skipped off.

'God, she's good-natured,' Arnie said.

'Like her mom,' Corrinne said with a smile. 'Come on, sailor, you look all done in.'

Arnie followed his wife into their large comfortable family room and threw himself down on the couch. 'It was awful, Corrinne,' he said, shaking his head. 'Not just the courtroom itself, but afterwards in the conference room at the office. God, you should have heard it – everyone freaking out, everyone trying to put the blame on someone else.' He sighed, remembering the near-chaos that accompanied the conference late that afternoon.

'Here,' Corrinne said, handing him a tall gin and tonic, and sitting down next to him. 'Tell me all about it.'

Arnie winced as he recalled the frayed tempers and flying accusations. 'That bastard Sollers pulled a fast one – he put Stuart on the stand and reamed him about his trial record. So we get into the conference room and Doug immediately starts screaming at Stuart, telling him he shouldn't have been so passive, and naturally Ann jumps right in and starts yelling at Doug not to upset Stuart, who is looking like he's having a complete anxiety attack . . .'

'Ouch,' Corrinne said with a shudder. 'How awful, especially with his heart and all.'

'His heart *and* Leland's heart,' Arnie agreed gloomily, remembering back just a few months when both those men had been in hospital with heart trouble. 'So then Ann starts telling Stuart he should take his medication, he's not looking too good; and I decided it was time for someone to play referee, so I jumped in and tried to say that we should just settle the damned case and make it go away.' He paused and took a long swallow of his drink. 'But no one wanted to pay any attention to that, and then Doug turns on Abby and starts screaming at her that she'd better come through on the stand . . .'

'Whew,' Corrinne whistled softly. 'I'll bet she loved that.'

'Hah! You should have seen her. I swear I thought she was going to leap for Doug's throat, and who could blame her? And Grace, who was also trying to be the voice of reason, kept getting shouted over, and Victor looked as though he was about to explode.'

'So what was the net result?' Corrinne asked, snuggling up to Arnie.

Arnie shook his head ruefully. 'There wasn't one,' he said. 'I guess whatever happens in court tomorrow will be the net result. I swear, Corrinne, if the firm gets through this in one piece, I'll become a religious man.'

'That'll be the day,' Corrinne smiled. She stroked his cheek gently. 'I'm glad this week is over for you. We do still have the reservations for L'Hermitage tomorrow night, right?'

'Oh . . . uh-huh,' Arnie said, his mind suddenly and unpleasantly jogged back to the conversation he'd had with Roxanne earlier.

57

'Good,' Corrinne continued. 'You know, Chloe's going to be with her dad for the weekend. Maybe we should just get a cottage at the Beverly Hills Hotel, order champagne, and have ourselves a properly decadent weekend. What do you think?'

'Ah . . . .' How the hell was he going to bring this up? he wondered.

Corrinne suddenly sighed. 'You know, Arnie, I guess this probably isn't the best of all possible times to bring up another problem, but I've been meaning to talk to you about something that's really been bothering me about your office.' Corrinne bit her lip. 'I don't know how else to say it, but I just can't believe how possessive she is of you.'

'What?' Arnie exclaimed, startled out of his musings. She couldn't mean Gwen, could she? 'Who?'

'Well, Roxanne, of course!' Corrinne looked up at him, clearly puzzled. 'Who else do you think I'd be talking about?'

'Oh, Roxanne, of course.' Arnie sighed with relief. Then, just as quickly, he realised he was about to be attacked on the other flank. Maybe he could head it off at the pass. 'Rox just gets moody, Corrinne; she gets really bad PMT.'

'Well, that may work just fine in France as a murder defence,' Corrinne said, her fine brow wrinkling, 'but it won't wash with me.'

'Listen,' Arnie said, 'she's feeling overloaded right now, with Murray and all . . .'

'No, that's not it.' Corrinne shook her head decisively. 'I know what she's been going through, but I really think she resents the hell out of me.'

'Why should she resent you?' Arnie said.

There was a pause, and then Corrinne sighed. 'Because you're in love with me. Because you married me. Because she's cut out of that entire part of your life now; she doesn't have to take care of you any more, or massage your ego, or juggle your girlfriends . . .'

'She hated doing that,' Arnie protested. It was true; Roxanne *had* hated it.

Corrinne shrugged. 'Maybe. But it was better than nothing. She was really close to you.'

'She's still really close to me,' Arnie said softly. He owed Roxanne that much.

Corrinne nodded. 'OK, and maybe that's part of the problem, too. I mean, maybe that's part of *my* problem. I guess I just don't like you having an office wife – much as I might joke about it.'

'I'm married to you,' Arnie reminded her. 'Not to Roxanne.'

'I know that! But I feel like I have to compete with her for your attention,' Corrinne said, pouting prettily. 'Think about it, Arnie. How would you feel if I spent all day, every day, in an office with a man who worshipped me?'

'I'd hate it,' Arnie admitted.

'Would you be a little . . . *jealous*?'

'Yes,' Arnie replied uncomfortably. He knew he was just digging himself in deeper and deeper, getting further away by the sentence from the place in the conversation where he could actually bring up the problems Roxanne had asked him to talk about with Corrinne.

'Maybe it's time for you to start thinking about letting Roxanne go,' Corrinne suggested.

Arnie was startled out of his discomfort. 'No!' he said

59

sharply. 'I'm not firing Roxanne,' he said. 'I wouldn't do that.'

Corrinne shook her head and sighed. 'She really needs to get over this fixation she has with you, Arnie. She needs to get on with her own life. And maybe you need to stop depending on her so much, too. Just think about it, OK?'

Arnie had the sudden overwhelming feeling that the walls were closing in on him. His secretary, who also happened to be his best friend, wanted him to tell his wife to back off. And his wife wanted him to fire his secretary.

'OK?' Corrinne asked, more pointedly.

Arnie looked into her big blue eyes and, for the first time in their relationship, denied her something she wanted. 'No,' he said softly. 'I'm not firing Roxanne, and that's all there is to it.'

But that wasn't all there was to it, and Arnie knew it as surely as he knew that he had to go into court tomorrow, as surely as he knew that the knots in his stomach were getting tighter. Neither woman was just going to drop her grievance. And just how he'd get himself out of this mess was anybody's guess.

*

Douglas Brackman and Leland McKenzie were still in the office at seven-thirty, trying to figure out an angle to keep the damage at a minimum. But neither man seemed to have the energy to keep on rehashing what had gone on in court earlier, and there were certainly no easy or obvious solutions presenting themselves.

'I don't know, Doug,' Leland said, shaking his head sombrely, 'maybe we actually *should* consider settling out

60

of court, just to stop the publicity. I never dreamed it would get this nasty this fast.'

Doug sighed, a heavy heartfelt sound. 'Neither did I,' he admitted. 'And I have an awful feeling we haven't seen anything compared to what's coming. But, Leland,' he added with a frown of concern, 'I also don't know if we can really even *afford* to settle this thing. The firm is just getting back on its financial feet!'

'I know,' Leland said, his voice as heavy as Doug's. 'God, I rue the day I ever brought the viper into this nest!'

'Hindsight always has perfect vision,' Doug reminded him. 'So don't beat yourself up about it. How could you possibly have known what she was going to do, what she even capable of doing?'

Leland sighed again and shook his head. 'I don't know, Doug,' he said. 'Maybe I should have checked her out more thoroughly, talked with more of the people from the other firms she worked for . . .'

'Water under the bridge,' Doug said, trying to get Leland off the self-blame track.

'Well, you're just full of clichés tonight, aren't you?' Leland asked moodily.

'Don't snap at *me*, Leland; we're about to go under, and we need all the camaraderie we can muster. Which', he reflected, thinking back on the Tower of Babel that had been their conference room a few hours earlier, 'our co-workers seem to be distinctly lacking at this point in time.'

Suddenly the phone rang, a shrill unexpected sound in the empty offices, and Doug and Leland exchanged surprised shrugs.

'Leland McKenzie,' Leland said into the receiver. He

listened for a moment, then handed the phone to Doug. 'It's for you. It's Marilyn,' he said. 'She sounds a little upset.'

*

Twenty-five minutes later, Doug was knocking frantically on Marilyn Hopkins's front door. He hadn't been able to get much substantive information out of her on the phone, just that there had been some kind of terrible accident and that she needed help immediately. He had to come over, Marilyn had insisted, in a voice that was shaking with hysteria. He had to come over and help her. Right now!

With barely a word to Leland, Doug had fled from the office and, breaking all speed limits along the way, he had raced to her apartment, terrified that someone had hurt her. After all, her profession was sexual surrogate, and even though the screening process was tight it couldn't be perfect. In that profession, how could there be any guarantees that some sicko – real *sicko*, not just someone with impotence problems, like Doug had had when he had retained her services – wouldn't slip through the cracks? Someone with a fetish for knives or whips or . . . Oh God, he thought, pounding furiously on her door, please let her be all right!

Suddenly the door was cracked open half an inch, and Marilyn, her eyes wide with fear or shock, looked out at him. 'Oh, Doug! Thank God it's you,' she exclaimed, opening the door just wide enough to pull him hastily inside.

She didn't *look* hurt, Doug saw with relief. Her hair was a little messy, and she was wearing an old towelling bathrobe and bunny slippers, but she didn't appear to have been knocked around or physically abused in any way. He clutched her by the arms and stared down at her pale face. 'Are you OK?' he demanded.

She nodded, but he could see that she was shaking like a leaf. He hugged her close for a second, then said: 'It's OK, Marilyn; it's going to be all right. I'm here now. Just try to calm down, take some deep breaths and tell me what happened.'

But she just sagged against him, speechless, so Doug tried again. 'Are you sure you're not hurt?' he asked. 'Talk to me.'

Marilyn shook her head. 'No,' she said faintly. 'I'm not hurt; I'm fine.'

'Then, what is it, darling?' he asked.

She pulled away from him, took a deep breath and stared up at him. 'Come here,' she said, leading him towards the bedroom where she saw her patients. Doug had the sudden sinking feeling that he didn't really want to see what was in that bedroom, but he was here, and there didn't seem to be a choice.

'Look,' Marilyn whispered, pushing open the door and gesturing towards the room.

Doug's eyes roamed over the tastefully decorated room, all the soft subdued colours specially chosen to put nervous clients at ease. At first, he didn't see anything amiss, other than the bed covers, which had been pulled down and seemed to have been hastily thrown aside. But then his eyes moved from the top of the bed to the floor beside it.

'Oh Jesus,' he whispered as his mind digested what his eyes were seeing.

63

Lying on the floor beside the bed, face down, was a huge mountain of a man. From what Doug could see, he appeared to be completely naked, except for a black cowboy hat, a pair of cowboy boots, spurs and a holster. He must have weighed a good four hundred pounds, Doug thought irrelevantly, unable to tear his eyes away from the mound of white flesh. More to the point, he was quite obviously dead.

'What happened?' Doug asked finally when he was able to speak.

'It must've been a heart attack,' Marilyn said, her voice still quivering. 'One minute he was fine, and the next he just started to clutch at his arm and gasp for breath, and then . . . .' She broke off, chewing her bottom lip. 'But I swear to God, Doug, when he came for his first consultation with me, and I saw how much he weighed, I *made* him get a stress test. And I read the report, and I *swear* he was supposed to be in good health.' Marilyn looked as though she was about to burst into tears.

'Are you are he's dead?' Doug asked, hoping against hope that perhaps this was just some temporary aberration. Like a coma.

'Well, he's been in that same position for an hour!' Marilyn snapped, her voice tinged with incipient hysteria. 'And this certainly wasn't supposed to be a part of his therapy!'

'OK,' Doug said, trying to make his voice sound soothing, 'let's both just calm down and try to be rational.'

'But I don't know what to do!' Marilyn wailed.

'First,' Doug said, 'we have to notify somebody – I mean, we can't just let him lie there like that. Does he have

64

a . . . *wife*?' He winced at the idea of breaking this kind of news to a spouse.

'No,' Marilyn shook her head. 'He's divorced. *Was* divorced, I mean.' Then she started shaking again. 'I just don't know what to do, Doug. Nothing like this has ever happened to me before.'

'It's going to be OK,' Doug promised her, although he wasn't at all certain it *was* going to be OK. He forced himself to think of options. Did you call the police in a case like this? The paramedics? The National Rodeo Association? 'You're a legitimate sex therapist; no one's going to make a fuss about this.'

'No, it's not going to be OK at all,' Marilyn said, shaking her head. 'And unless we do some really fast thinking there is most definitely going to be a fuss.' She looked up at him pleadingly. 'Oh, Doug,' she said, 'the man lying there is Jerome Miller.'

Doug felt himself blanch. 'The State Senator?' he managed to choke out.

Marilyn nodded. 'Yes.'

'Oh, no,' Doug whispered.

'And I really can't afford this kind of publicity,' Marilyn said nervously.

'Oh, my God . . .'

'And, besides, I'm not even sure he had a permit for the gun . . .'

Doug began backing out of the doorway as he started to feel the beginning of a panic attack coming on. 'I've got to get out of here, Marilyn,' he said. 'I can't be found here!'

'Doug, you've got to help me!' Marilyn cried, clutching his arm. 'You can't just leave me!'

The publicity was going to be bad for *her*? Doug thought, his mind jumping erratically around. This was all he needed to add fuel to the courtroom fire that was raging around McKenzie Brackman. Wouldn't Jack Sollers just love to get his hands on this! Doug headed rapidly towards the front door.

'Where are you going?' Marilyn demanded.

'I can't stay, Marilyn!' Doug's voice was as shaky as hers. 'After I leave, wait for a couple of minutes and then . . . just call the police!'

As he reached for the doorknob to let himself out, the doorbell rang abruptly, and Doug nearly jumped out of his skin. 'Oh, my God!' he hissed. 'Why didn't you tell me you had already called them? I've got to get out, I've got to . . . Where's the back door?'

'It's OK, Doug, relax,' Marilyn said softly, putting a soothing hand on his arm. 'It's not the police – it's just my eight o'clock appointment. I'll get rid of him.'

Doug found himself cowering in the background as Marilyn, running a hand hastily over her hair, opened the front door. 'Oh, Howard,' she said, 'I'm sorry, I've got the flu. I know I should have called, but I must've fallen asleep.'

Doug heard the man murmur something.

'No, I'm sorry, you're just going to have to go home, Howard,' Marilyn said more firmly. 'It won't work. Trust me, the mission is scrubbed for today.'

The mission was scrubbed? What on earth did *that* mean? Despite his mounting nervous tension, Doug couldn't resist peeping through the curtains which covered the front windows as the man returned to his car. He was wearing a silver space helmet.

'Oh Jesus,' Doug said softly. 'Oh sweet Jesus.' He put his head in his hands and tried to stop the splitting migraine that he just knew was coming on. 'What have I got myself into?'

Meanwhile Marilyn had returned to the door of the bedroom, and was hovering there, seemingly unable to walk into the room all the way.

'Doug,' she said thoughtfully, 'would it be better if I just took the gun and hid it?'

He started at her as if she was crazy.

'Oh,' she said, misreading his expression. 'You're right. I guess that would be considered concealing evidence, wouldn't it?'

Doug sagged against the wall. 'Do you happen to have an aspirin?' Doug asked.

Chapter Six

When court resumed in the morning, only Arnie Becker, Doug Brackman and Leland were sitting behind the defence table. Everyone else except Stuart had prior commitments – meetings or cases due in court.

During their vitriolic and, Victor felt, mostly pointless rehashing of the fiasco the day before, the attorneys for McKenzie Brackman had been able to agree on only one thing: not to cross-examine Stuart. Everyone at the conference table agreed that the sooner Stuart was out of the mind and eye of the jury members the better. With that in mind, Stuart stayed at the office this morning, chafing at his humiliation on the stand the previous day, and more than willing to remain out of sight, nursing his wounds in private.

Victor had also managed to corner Jack Sollers the previous afternoon and he had demanded to know who Sollers planned to call for his next witness. Victor didn't intend to let his opponent get away with any more surprises like the one he'd managed to pull off the day before. But Sollers now appeared to be following the predictable course for the moment: he told Victor he intended to call Rosalind Shays to the stand.

After Rosalind was sworn in, Jack Sollers approached the witness-box and smiled reassuringly at his client, who tried to smile bravely back. In a dark charcoal suit and a lighter-grey blouse, her cheeks untouched by blusher, her lips pale and set, Rosalind looked every inch the injured party.

'Look at her,' Doug hissed to Leland and Douglas.

'She's doing the grieving widow routine.'

'Except that she's really more like Lady Macbeth,' Doug said pointedly.

Leland nodded unhappily in agreement. Better than anyone, he thought, he knew exactly the kind of act Rosalind could put on – and how well she could play any part that suited her purpose. And he wasn't looking forward to this performance.

'Now, Ms Shays,' Sollers said in a low soothing voice, 'let's start at the very beginning. After Leland McKenzie made the offer to you to join the firm as a full partner, tell the jury, how did you feel about the prospect of joining McKenzie Brackman?'

'I was flattered and excited about the position, and about the possibilities and challenges it appeared to offer,' Rosalind replied. Then she looked up at Sollers, then glanced briefly towards the jury-box. 'But I was also some-what nervous about going there – at least, at first.'

'And why was that?'

Rosalind smiled a small self-deprecating smile, which quickly disappeared. 'They had the reputation of being such a close-knit firm,' she said, 'and I was' – she shrugged – 'well, I was obviously an outsider. I really didn't know how I'd be received.'

'But you did accept the offer,' Sollers said.

'Yes,' Rosalind confirmed.

'With the doubts you had about the firm —'

'Objection!' Victor pounced on the last question before it was out of Sollers's mouth. 'The witness didn't say she had any doubts about the firm!'

'Sustained,' Judge Travelini agreed.

'I'll rephrase,' Jack Sollers said easily. 'Tell me, Ms Shays, what exactly made you decide to accept?'

'I suppose it was . . . well, *ego*,' Rosalind admitted quietly. 'They as much as admitted they were looking for a saviour, and that intrigued me. It presented a very . . . well, *romantic* kind of challenge.'

'And in your own opinion, Ms Shays, do you believe you lived up to that challenge?'

Rosalind looked straight at Sollers, eyes wide, all sincerity. 'I know it's going to sound self-serving,' she said, 'but I *did* think I lived up to it. I still think I did. More than lived up to it, in fact. I brought in new clients, and I generated over three million dollars in revenues. I also' – she glanced quickly towards Leland, a reproachful look 'kept existing clients who *weren't* happy with the firm from walking out the door.'

Victor and Grace sat silently at the defence table. Both of them knew they couldn't challenge or object at this point, no matter what kind of damage Rosalind was causing – because, unhappily, everything she had said so far was the truth. And things would only get uglier if Jack Sollers decided to bring in witnesses to verify what Rosalind was saying.

'And how did the firm react to your performance?' Sollers asked.

'They appeared to be very happy about it,' Rosalind told

70

him. 'So happy, in fact, that they made me senior partner.'

'Uh-huh,' Sollers nodded solemnly. 'And then one day it all changed, didn't it?'

Rosalind paused, sighed and nodded. 'Yes,' she said quietly. 'It did.'

'Can you tell the court exactly what happened?' he asked gently.

Rosalind seemed to struggle for composure.

'Talk about great performances,' Victor jotted on the pad in front of him. Grace looked at the words and nodded gloomily.

'One day I was told very abruptly and unexpectedly that I didn't . . . *fit in*,' Rosalind said, her face reflecting the pain she had felt. 'Leland . . . Leland McKenzie came to me and said. . . .' She seemed to struggle to find the words. 'He said it just wasn't working out. And he asked me to resign quietly.'

'And then what happened?'

'When I told him that in all conscience I simply couldn't do that, he said . . . She paused again for dramatic effect. 'He said that he would break me. And that's what he did.'

Victor glanced over at the jury, whose faces uniformly seemed to reflect a belief in Rosalind's words and a great deal of sympathy.

'Please tell the court exactly what transpired after that,' Sollers urged Rosalind.

'A partners' meeting was quickly arranged, and at it I was told in no uncertain terms that it would be best for me just to leave the firm without making a fuss about how I was being treated. It was perfectly obvious to me that the entire thing had been orchestrated behind my back.'

71

'Objection,' Victor said firmly. 'Conclusory.'

'Overruled,' Judge Travelini said just as firmly.

Victor glowered, but remained silent.

'Please keep going, ma'am,' Sollers said.

'Then . . . I left,' Rosalind said simply.

'And did you leave the way they wanted you to leave – quietly and without a fuss?'

Rosalind nodded. 'Yes,' she said. 'I did. At that point, I suppose, I felt that it would be the best thing for everybody concerned if it was done that way. And I think I was still stunned by what had happened. I was still putting the firm's interests before my own. And I thought I could live with it.' She glanced over at the jury-box, an expression of vulnerability on her face. 'But I found I couldn't. I just couldn't.'

'And so you initiated this lawsuit,' Sollers prompted her.

'Yes,' Rosalind said more firmly. She lifted her chin in a gesture of defiance. 'I did. They had brought me into the firm because they were falling apart. Then, after I saved them, after they didn't need me any more, they got rid of me. It was shabby —'

'Objection,' Victor said.

'Overruled.'

'Please continue,' Sollers told Rosalind.

'When I reflected on it in the clear light of day, I saw what had happened. Rather than share with me the profits I had brought in,' Rosalind said, 'they threw me out. And that just isn't right.'

Sollers paused to let her words sink in. 'But, Ms Shays,' he said gently, 'with all due respect, you seem to have landed on your feet.'

'Damn him,' Victor said softly. 'He had to get that in

first, didn't he?'

Grace nodded and sighed. There went another chance to damage Rosalind in the eyes of the jury. 'I warned you about him,' she said.

'I suppose you could say that,' Rosalind agreed. 'But the truth is that I will always wear the blemish of this so-called failure. To the legal community in this city, I'll always be the woman who couldn't cut it as senior partner. And, because of that, I'll very likely never get a second chance to prove that that's wrong!'

Sollers nodded thoughtfully. 'And, tell me, is being senior partner so important to you?'

Rosalind nodded. 'Yes,' she said in a near-whisper. 'It is.'

'Why?' Sollers pressed.

Rosalind paused again. She appeared to be struggling to find the right words, although Victor was certain she had come to the stand with every bit of this presentation well prepared and rehearsed.

'Being senior partner is . . . *was* my dream,' Rosalind began. 'All my professional life I wanted . . .' She seemed to be fighting back tears. 'Well, ever since my husband died nine years ago . . .'

'I told you,' Doug muttered, 'it's the grieving widow!'

'He probably died just to get away from her,' Arnie whispered to Doug.

'Ever since then,' Roz continued, 'the only thing I've had in my life is my career. And that dream – the dream that one day I would be accorded the respect and implicit admiration from my fellow-attorneys that goes along with that. I've worked very hard to get to the place where I

73

would even be considered for that position. And that's why I was so . . . so very proud when it came true at McKenzie Brackman.'

'Break out the Kleenex,' Arnie muttered. 'And a nice chorus of violins.'

Doug buried his head in his hands and groaned quietly.,

'I don't think I've ever felt that I had made a greater contribution to any firm than I had at McKenzie Brackman,' Rosalind continued. 'And when they made me senior partner it was a complete confirmation of all that I'd accomplished there. I knew that I had *earned* the title, the position of senior partner. As difficult as it had been, that just made it all the more gratifying.'

'Please go on,' Soller urged her gently.

'And that's why it made it so . . . so . . . 'Rosalind seemed to suck in her breath in an attempt to stem a flood of emotion and tears from coming to the surface. 'That's why it was do devastating for me, professionally and personally, when they . . . took it away from me.' Here her voice began to quiver. 'They just took it away.' She brushed her hand across her eyes, then looked at Judge Travelini. 'I'm sorry, your Honour,' she said.

There was a hush in the courtroom. Finally Jack Sollers broke the thick silence. 'I have nothing further, your Honour,' he said in a subdued voice.

Rosalind sniffled, trying to gather herself together.

'I think we'll break until tomorrow,' Judge Travelini announced, her expression and voice revealing no reaction to the emotionally loaded testimony she had just heard.

As Rosalind stepped out of the witness-box, Jack Sollers took her hand and squeezed it in a gesture of compassion.

No one on the jury missed the gesture.

From the defence table, Victor and Grace watched in gloomy silence as Sollers escorted Rosalind back to the plaintiff's table just long enough to gather up his papers and attaché case and make a quiet exit from the courtroom.

'Look at them,' Grace murmured to Victor, motioning subtly towards the jury-box.

'I know,' Victor sighed. 'If this went to decision right now, they'd find for her and award her the goddam moon!'

Grace nodded grimly. 'Well,' she said, 'I guess we'll just have to pull a few rabbits out of our own hat, won't we?'

Victor smiled briefly. 'They'd better be some impressive rabbits,' he agreed. 'Big mean rabbits with excellent teeth.'

'Grace, Victor, I want to see you in my office this afternoon at three,' Leland said briskly.

'More raking over the coals?' Victor asked Grace softly.

She shrugged. 'We'll see.'

*

'And then there was this guy named Alex.' To her surprise, Roxanne found that she was actually able to laugh about it now, over salad and iced tea with Abby Perkins. For the past hour they'd been swapping date horror-stories, commiserating with each other about how difficult it was to meet someone who was even marginally acceptable enough to go to the movies with. They hadn't even tackled the subject of serious relationships, agreeing early on in the conversation that the world seemed to be just one huge void where that was concerned.

'And what did Alex do?' Abby asked, already starting to

grin at what she was sure would be yet another calamity story.

'Well,' Roxanne said thoughtfully, 'I'm not exactly certain I could tell you what he *did*. For a living, that is. He drove a battered fifteen-year-old wreck, and there was literally no place to sit in it – it was crammed to overflowing with leaflets, exhibits, maps, and fast-food wrappers from up and down the coast. I couldn't believe that my cousin Amy would do this to me – I mean, she said he was a "dedicated environmentalist". Ha! The guy was more like a rolling bag-person. Either that, or his dedicated environmental work meant picking up garbage and saving it in his car!'

'So what did you do?' Abby smiled sympathetically.

'I've finally learned to stick up for myself,' Roxanne said. 'At least, a little! I took one look at the car and turned around and headed back to the house. He came scurrying after me, wanting to know if something was wrong. Can you believe it? What a creep! I told him that I just didn't see how I could possibly enjoy an evening with someone who was so obviously dedicated to one thing, and one thing only. Especially when the one thing seemed to be garbage!'

'Well,' Abby said with a grin, 'at least the one thing only wasn't sex.'

'Oh, *sex*,' Roxanne groaned. 'Does anybody even *have* sex any more? I mean, between fear of communicable diseases and fear of commitment, what's left?'

Abby shrugged. 'Don't go by me,' she said, her face suddenly sombre. 'The last time *I* had sex the guy had a really big surprise up his sleeve.'

'What?' Roxanne asked, her eyes widening.

76

Abby smiled cynically. 'The usual surprise, I guess – for a naïve idiot like me. He turned out to be married.' She grimaced with distaste at the memory of the investigating officer who'd been so sympathetic when she'd shot a man in self-defence. So sympathetic that his attempts to comfort and reassure Abby had become a flaming affair. Before she learned the truth.

'How awful,' Roxanne said. 'Did you . . .? I mean, had you got emotionally involved?'

'Very,' Abby said bitterly. The memory was still painful. 'Luckily I was so outraged when I found how that any kind of positive emotion I had felt for him just flew out the window. And was replaced by hate.' She shook her head. 'You never think it can happen to you,' she said, a little bemused. 'At least, I thought I was smarter than that.'

Roxanne shrugged. 'No one's smarter than that if the guy is a good liar,' she said. 'Don't beat yourself up about it.'

'No, I'm not. I've finally got past that stage,' Abby told her.

'What stage have you reached?' Roxanne asked, curious.

'Now I just don't trust anyone.' Abby shook her head. 'Pitiful, huh?'

'Well,' Roxanne said, 'do you think either one of us could possibly come up with one positive thing to say about mankind – I guess I mean *men*, don't I?'

Abby laughed. 'Give me a few days to think about it,' she said.

'All I want is to go out with someone who's normal!' Roxanne told her.

'You know,' Abby said thoughtfully, 'I met this man in the elevator the other day. An accountant. He works up on the eighteenth floor in that huge firm, Bannister and Kaplan, something or other – I can't remember the whole name. Anyway he was definitely looking.'

'An accountant?' Roxanne said dubiously, picturing a nerd with leaking ballpoint pens in his pocket. Or her own ex-husband, who'd been a salesman, not an accountant, but who definitely qualified for the title of nerd.

Abby shrugged. 'The guy was kind of cute and, like I said, he's definitely interested. I turned down coffee with him because I had to master some briefs for court, but if I bump into him again why don't I see if he's got a friend? Maybe we can double, then it won't be so awkward.'

Roxanne shrugged. 'I don't know,' she said.

'Oh, come on,' Abby urged her. 'Why not? There'll be two of us – and, besides, that firm is overloaded with males. Now, that's a rarity, Rox. There's got to be at least one other single guy who's presentable!'

'You think?'

'Sure!'

'How do you know he's single?' Roxanne asked her.

Abby grinned. 'No ring, and he was carrying a carton of leftover takeaway with him on his way home. That reads single to me.'

'I don't know,' Roxanne said again.

'Come on, Roxanne, we've both got to get cracking on this. I mean, I don't want to stay single for the rest of my life, and you don't, either.'

'Divorced,' Roxanne reminded her.

Abby waved it off. 'Same difference. I think we have to look at this process as . . . well, as *work* ! It's like that old saying, you know, that finding a job is full-time work.

78

Well, I've got news for you: finding a man is even *fuller-*time work!'

'It's true,' Roxanne agreed gloomily.

'Then, you'll do it?' Abby pressed her.

Roxanne finally nodded. 'OK, why not? See what you can do.'

'Good,' Abby said, attacking her salad with renewed relish. 'Now, tell me what else has been going on. How are things at home?'

Roxanne sighed. 'It's just awful,' she confessed. 'Taking care of my dad was no picnic to begin with – I mean, you know how weird he is anyway. But now *this*, this Alzheimer's diagnosis. . . . God, Abby, it's so frightening. I came home the other night, and he was trying to dial Pepi's to order a pizza, but he couldn't get the numbers right and he just kept repeating them over and over, and wondering why he couldn't make the phone work for him.' Roxanne found she suddenly had to struggle to keep back a flood of tears. 'And Murray is terrified, too. I just don't know how I'm going to handle it.'

Abby put a sympathetic hand on Roxanne's wrist. 'Just try to take it one day at a time, Roxanne. Maybe they'll find out that one of those cures they're working on can be used.'

Roxanne shook her head. 'Maybe,' she said in a low voice. 'But somehow I have the awful feeling that it's going to be too late for Murray.'

'Anything I can do,' Abby said sincerely, 'just let me know.'

Roxanne nodded and tried to smile. 'I know, Abby,' she sighed. 'And I appreciate it, believe me. But listen,' she said, trying for a lighter note in the gloomy conversation. 'I didn't come to lunch just to spill out all of my personal problems on you. Let's talk about something else. How's Eric?'

Abby's face lit up at the mention of her young son's name. 'Great!' she said enthusiastically. 'His baseball team made it into the regional finals. He's so excited!'

'I'll bet!' Roxanne exclaimed. 'How great for him.'

Abby nodded. 'And he's doing really well in school, too,' she said. 'They're putting him into the magnet programme for gifted kids next year when he goes to junior high.' She smiled. 'Maths and science,' she mused, 'he sure didn't get those gifts from me!'

'You're lucky,' Roxanne told her. 'I'd love to have a child.'

Abby grinned again. 'Well,' she said, 'let's get cracking on the accountants – you never know what the side-benefits might be!'

Roxanne laughed. 'OK,' she said, 'I guess you've sold me!'

'Now,' Abby said, 'there's something else I've been meaning to talk to you about.'

'What's that?' Roxanne asked.

'How are you standing up under the pressure from the new Mrs Becker?'

Roxanne's eyes widened. 'Oh, no!' she exclaimed. 'Am I that much of an open book?'

'No, no . . . that's not it at all,' Abby hastily reassured her. 'Don't worry, this isn't office gossip or anything.'

'Thank God!' Roxanne breathed a sigh of relief. That was all she needed to complicate an already complex situation.

'It's just something I've noticed,' Abby told her. 'She always seems to be around, and she always seems to be asking you to do something for her.'

'I know,' Roxanne sighed. 'And the truth is it's not going all that well. I'm pretty angry about it, and I finally broke down and talked to Arnie about it the other day.'

Abby snorted derisively. 'And what did Mr Non-commitment, Mr Avoidance say?'

Roxanne shrugged. 'He sort of agreed to do something about it,' she said. Then she looked at Abby, who wore a doubtful expression, and nodded in agreement. 'I know,' Roxanne said. 'This has yet to be seen.'

Chapter Seven

Victor poked his head into Grace's office and pointed to his watch. 'Come on, Counsellor,' he said, 'it's time for the daily raking over the coals.'

Grace smiled at him. 'You're in an awfully good mood for someone who knows he's about to be raked,' she commented, standing up and pulling on the jacket to her white linen suit.

'Seeing you always put me in a good mood,' Victor said lightly.

Grace looked at him in surprise, and felt her heart skip a tiny beat. Then, quickly, she looked away. There had always been an unspoken attraction between then. Once, several years ago, that attraction had manifested itself in a goodnight kiss which had turned from a friendly peck on the lips into an unexpected and passionate exchange. Good friends that they were – and dutifully taking account of the fact that Grace was still seeing Michael Kuzak, although the relationship was in its rocky latter stage – they had discussed the kiss. Both of them had agreed it didn't mean anything, not really. They were both adults, these things happened, and that was that. Neither of them mentioned it again.

But, quite obviously, that *wasn't* that. The physical attraction remained, kept purposefully in the background, and neither acted on nor addressed again. Keeping a distance had been relatively easy as long as they didn't see each other every day. And there had been another wrinkle in the mean time: Grace was certain that Victor had been genuinely in love with a pretty video director named Allison. It had been Grace to whom Victor turned when Allison was raped; and it had been Grace who represented Allison in the trial afterwards. Allison was a spirited, bright and extremely likeable young woman, and Grace had genuinely hoped that things would work out for her and Victor. But after the ordeal of the trial Allison had simply been unable to continue the life she'd been leading – the memories of everything leading up to the attack had become too painful for her. They had to be cut out of her life; and part of the cutting-out involved breaking up with Victor. So now there was no Allison, there was no one in Grace's life, and she and Victor were in close contact every day.

'Is something wrong, Gracie?' Victor asked, a look of curious concern on his sculpted face.

'Oh . . . no!' Grace replied, startled out of her reverie. She hoped she wasn't blushing. 'No, really, everything's fine. I was just . . . um . . . thinking about something else. I've just got so many things on my mind these days. . . .' She busied herself collecting and stacking papers, as if putting her desk in order was the first priority here. Finally she looked up at Victor, a studiedly bright smile on her face. 'Well,' she said cheerfully, 'let's go.'

'Stiff upper lip and all that?' Victor asked.

'You bet,' Grace replied as they left her office and headed down the hall.

Leland and Doug Brackman were waiting for them in Leland's office. They both looked exceptionally sombre as Grace and Victor entered, but there was nothing unusual about that – these days, everyone at the firm seemed to be walking around with personal and professional black clouds hovering above them.

'Leland. Doug.' Victor nodded to them. 'What's up?' he asked, coming right to the point.

'What have you got planned for Rosalind's cross-examination?' Leland responded in kind.

Victor grimaced. 'What a performance! She's a better actress than I bargained for,' he said. 'I think the best thing would be for me to get in and get out as quickly as I possibly can – stop her from wreaking any more havoc up there in front of the jury, and try to get someone up there quickly who will dilute the effect she's had.'

'And?' Leland demanded. 'What then?'

Victor had consciously to stop himself from getting ruffled at what seemed to be a somewhat hostile challenge coming from Leland. After all, he told himself, Leland was undoubtedly the most worried of any of them – it was his name on the door, and that name was getting tarnished. 'And,' he said deliberately, keeping his voice and face calm, 'while she *is* up there, basically try to get her to admit that she wasn't liked here and wasn't trusted.'

'That's not enough,' Leland barked. 'That won't work. I want you to —'

But Victor cut him off with a raised hand, already certain he knew the direction Leland was heading in. 'I know what you're thinking, Leland, but this isn't the time to attack her. It would be a big mistake right now. First, we have to do

84

the prep work, we have to begin to undermine her credibility in a subtle way.'

'We don't have the time to be subtle!' Leland snapped.

'Then, we have to create it,' Victor said firmly. 'Don't forget, the jury really likes her right now, and if we go for the jugular they're just going to —'

It was Leland's turn to cut Victor off. 'I know what you think,' Victor,' he said. 'And I disagree. That's one of the basic problems we're having. And the other problem is that you haven't been aggressive enough.'

'*What?*' Victor stared at him in disbelief. 'What are you talking about?'

Leland stared him with a steely expression. 'First,' he said curtly, 'you let Jack Sollers beat up on Stuart on the stand, and make him look like an inept fool —'

'That is ridiculous!' Victor exploded, but Leland kept right on talking.

'– when you should have been protecting him —'

'Leland,' Grace interjected, 'that's hardly fair. We didn't even know Sollers was going to call Stuart!'

Leland ignored her. 'His opening was purely malicious, and you should have objected to *that*, first! Then you should have objected further to the adjournment this morning after Rosalind's direct —'

'How could I object' Victor demanded. 'Judge Travelini said she had personal matters tying her up this afternoon!'

'You know damned well that the jury is going to have eighteen hours to dwell on how we mistreated poor sensitive Rosalind . . .'

'Of course I know it! But what the hell was I supposed to do – tell the judge she couldn't take any personal time . . .?'

'The problem is that you're intimidated by Jack Sollers,' Leland barrelled on.

Victor felt his temper rising. '*You're* the one who's intimidated here!' he snapped. 'You aren't thinking straight about this, Leland. Now calm down and try to look at this thing rationally.'

Leland shook his head. 'I'm sorry, Victor, but there has to be a change made here, and —'

'What changes? What exactly are you getting at?' Victor asked.

'Starting now,' Leland announced, 'you're second chair, Victor.' He turned his eyes on Grace. 'Grace, you're taking over.'

'Leland!' Grace protested.

'*What?*' Victor asked, reeling in shock.

'You heard me,' Leland said firmly. 'You both heard me.'

There was a moment of dead silence, and then Grace spoke. 'Leland,' she said reasonably, 'I think this is a mistake. I happen to agree with Victor's strategy. Attacking Rosalind at this point could play right into her discrimination claim.'

McKenzie fixed his gaze on Grace. 'Not if the attack comes from another woman,' he said.

Grace was stunned into silence. She hated hearing it, but underneath she suspected that Leland might, in this particular instance, be right. A jury was certainly less likely to read sexual discrimination into the case if the lawyer on the attack was also a woman.

Doug cleared his throat and finally entered into the discussion. 'We hashed this out before you come to this

86

meeting,' he said, 'and our feeling is that the only way we can win this trial is to destroy Rosalind Shays. And if Grace is the one who destroys her, let's face it, the whole thing will look a lot cleaner.'

Victor's face was dark with anger, but he tried to restrain himself from flying off the handle and saying anything he might regret later. 'This is the wrong way to do it,' he insisted. 'You're both panicking.'

'Victor, no one is suggesting that you aren't a good lawyer . . .,' Doug began.

'That's right, Doug,' Victor said flatly. 'You aren't suggesting it – you're hanging a banner out which proclaims it!'

'We are doing what we feel we have to do to win this case,' Leland said stubbornly.

'And I'm telling you that this is dead wrong. Your strategy couldn't be more off-base.'

'Leland,' Grace said, 'listen to me. This is a very risky way to approach this trial. Rosalind is good, too damned good. And this angle of attack leaves us no other options.' She looked seriously from Leland to Doug. 'If we go after her and we *don't* get her, we will look worse than we ever dreamed possible. And we will definitely lose this case.'

Leland stared back at Grace, his eyes determined behind his steel-rimmed spectacles, his mouth grim and set. 'Then, you know exactly what you have to do, Grace,' he said. 'You have to get her. You damned well have to get her.'

*

Leland looked up in annoyance as someone knocked on his

87

office door forty-five minutes later. 'Come in,' he said impatiently. God, he couldn't wait to get out of here today, he thought. This had better not be yet another office crisis he had to settle; that little scene with Grace and Victor had been downright uncomfortable. He hated to pull a switch on Victor that way, but he was convinced it was the right decision to make.

'Do you have a minute, Leland?' Jonathan Rollins asked, stepping into the office. 'I need to talk to you about something. In private.'

Leland motioned him to come in and shut the door behind him. 'Sit down, Jonathan,' he said, trying to curb his irritation. After all, it wasn't Jonathan's fault that the Rosalind Shays case was going go badly. 'What is it?' he asked.

'Michael just informed me that I'm going to be the second chair on the Chisolm case,' Jonathan said, 'and I think I've made my opinion on that case amply clear to everybody. I just can't do it.'

'And why not?' Leland said wearily. 'Are you going to tell me again how you don't believe that Chisolm is innocent?'

The Brian Chisolm case was yet another thorn in McKenzie Brackman's side. Jonathan clearly believed that the white officer, Chisolm, had killed a black teenager who got in his way simply because he was black, and should stand trial for murder. Michael Kuzak believed the officer was being railroaded because of pressure from the black community. And it hadn't helped a bit when – after the District Attorney's office offered Chisolm a plea-bargain down to involuntary manslaughter, a plea-bargain Michael urged Chisolm to take – the offer had been abruptly withdrawn. The public's attention had been tightly focused on the racial aspect of the case by the entrance into the already circus-like media atmosphere of black activist Derron Holloway, who was very convincing when he announced dire consequences if the racist officer got away with the killing. The limelight had caused the DA's office to think twice about tarnishing their image by letting Chisolm plead down, and that's when the offer was withdrawn. Kuzak had been furious, and rightly so.

'It doesn't matter one way or another what I think about this case, Leland,' Jonathan said, shaking his head. 'What matters is that Michael is so afraid that Brian Chisolm isn't going to get a fair trial, so afraid that he might actually be convicted, that he's telling me I have to assist him in the case because he needs me as *window dressing*!'

'So?' Leland asked brusquely. 'What's the problem?'

Jonathan stared at him in disbelief. 'The *problem*, Leland, is that I'm being asked to function as a pawn here, just because the media has turned this into a circus, and it's suddenly become a race thing!'

Leland sighed. 'Jonathan,' he said, trying to remain patient, 'I just got out of a meeting at which I told Grace Van Owen that I want her to take over lead counsel in the Rosalind Shays mess because she's a woman. What's the difference?'

Jonathan absorbed the news, then snorted and shook his head in disgust. 'Maybe there's no difference at all,' he said, 'but does that make either one of these things right?'

'Right is relative,' Leland said.

'Oh Christ!' Jonathan exclaimed. 'Come on, Leland, I

can't believe you actually said that. I'm telling you I won't do it!'

'Yes, you will,' Leland replied. He could feel himself starting to get angry and upset. 'And I don't want to hear any more about it.'

'But this firm has never forced lawyers to take cases,' Jonathan protested. 'Get someone else . . .'

Leland stood up and began to pack briefs and documents into his briefcase, a signal that he wanted to bring this meeting to a close. 'No,' he said, 'I'm not getting anyone else.' He looked up sharply at Jonathan. 'You know what we're up against right now, Jonathan. We're struggling to keep our heads above water. Everyone in the firm is tied up, and we just can't keep all of them happy all of the time.'

'And I also know that the only reason I'm getting stuck with *this* case is because I'm black,' Jonathan flared again.

'That's right!' Leland snapped in agreement. 'Just like Grace on the Shays case. Just like I did the age discrimination case last year because I'm the oldest lawyer here – complete with a hearing aid —'

'But –'

' – and just like Ann Kelsey took the lead in that obstetrics case we had last year because she was quite obviously pregnant at the time.' He sighed and tried once more. 'Look,' he said, 'this is a business. We have to use whatever gives us the advantage in any given case. And in this case, Jonathan, it happens to be your skin colour. It's a fact of life.'

Jonathan tried another tack. 'Leland,' he said, attempting to match the senior partner's more equable tone, 'Brian

Chisolm may very well be innocent. I know that, and I'm not trying to tell you anything else. But I have to look at this from another angle as well.' He paused.

'What other angle?' Leland asked, curious.

'I . . . well, I know I don't usually talk about this kind of thing, but I've always felt that I'd like to try my hand at something different somewhere down the line. I'd really like to think that some day, with my background, I could be a strong effective voice for the black community.' He looked Leland straight in the eye. 'And you know and I know that if I go up against Derron Holloway now that will never happen.'

'Well . . .,' Leland said.

'No,' Jonathan shook his head. 'There's no *well* or *maybe* about it, and you know it. If I have to be in court for this case, I'll always be known as the guy who took on the righteous Derron Holloway. And the guy who didn't fight for his own community.'

Leland massaged his brow thoughtfully and sighed. Then he looked up at the young lawyer across for him. 'I'm not unsympathetic to that, Jonathan,' he said. 'Believe me, I'm not. But, no matter what your future aspirations are, we have to operate in the present tense. Derron Holloway is not our client. The black community is not our client. Like it or not, Brian Chisolm is our client, and right now he needs all the protection we can give him. And that protection includes you.'

Jonathan seemed to sag into his chair. 'Leland,' he said, 'please reconsider your decision. I'm asking you as a favour.'

Leland shook his head. 'I'm sorry, Jonathan,' he said.

91

'You're going to have to do it. Give Michael whatever he needs.'

'What he needs is a black shadow,' Jonathan said bitterly. 'And it looks like that's exactly what he's going to get.'

Leland watched Jonathan walk out of his office with a sinking feeling. He knew that Michael's decision to put Jonathan on this case was the correct decision. But he also understood the kind of pressure and conflict it was bringing into the sharp young attorney's life. Still, he told himself, ambiguity was a part of life, and often a large part of a lawyer's practice. You had to learn to deal with it, just as you had to learn to deal with your own feelings of ambivalence. For heaven's sake, he thought, annoyed again, you learned that in law school right along with everything else. It wouldn't be news to Jonathan; nor, Leland knew, would it be the last time Jonathan had to face this kind of problem.

Jonathan, Leland was certain, could handle this latest challenge if he chose to; but would he choose to or not? Leland had just gambled on the belief that Jonathan was both too smart and too pragmatic to allow this particular case to become his watershed – to sway his feelings about staying at McKenzie Brackman. But Leland, also smart and also pragmatic, didn't fool himself about the other very real choice Jonathan could make. With McKenzie Brackman already in such trouble, Jonathan *could* decide to walk away from this case and the firm, and that decision could look both morally correct and fiscally sensible.

What a day, he thought. If things didn't begin to get a little easier, maybe *he* was the one who ought just to walk away. Leland sighed. Retirement had never particularly appealed to him – he was too wrapped up in his work to think that having all day, every day, to play golf or watch sunsets or take cruises, or whatever else it was that retirees did, would be satisfying for him – but right at this moment the idea of walking away from this burgeoning mess and leaving it to the younger, more energetic partners to solve *did* have a certain appeal.

Still, he knew, snapping his briefcase shut, there was really no question of getting out right now. He had personally caused the Rosalind Shays fiasco which now threatened to ruin McKenzie Brackman, and he couldn't desert the ship – whether it was floating or sinking. Not until this trial was over, at least.

Chapter Eight

Grace Van Owen stood in front of the witness-box, dressed in a severe black suit and tailored white blouse. She looked perfectly poised and very calm, and it was clear that she was all business. Earlier this morning, when Victor had cornered her in the crowded hallway of the court building and told her to 'nail the bitch to the wall', Grace's last bit of reluctance to take over had slipped easily away.

'You bet I will,' she had promised Victor. 'And it's as much for me as it is for you. This woman has caused too many problems in too many lives already.' It was a thinly veiled reference to what had occurred yesterday in Leland's office.

Victor flashed her his dazzling smile, but Grace could see by the shadows around his eyes that he's spent a rough night coming to terms with Leland's decision. Still, he had gone with her into the judge's chambers and told Judge Travelini that they had decided to switch chairs in the defence. Judge Travelini looked thoughtful; but she didn't, thank heavens, ask any questions. She merely nodded and made a note of it. And nothing had been said one way or another to the jury. Grace had merely introduced herself to them, then proceeded to call Rosalind Shays to the stand for her cross-examination.

Grace stared at her opponent as if taking her measure.

Rosalind was dressed, like Grace, in black; Grace had the thought that in her look and her presentation Rosalind wanted to convey a sense of grief and loss to the members of the jury. But Grace was equally determined to undo every bit of jury sympathy and goodwill that Jack Sollers had accomplished for his client. Two could play at this game, Grace thought, and she could be just as tough as Sollers. And, perhaps even more important, just as tough as Rosalind herself.

'Good morning, Ms Shays,' she began briskly. 'I just have a few questions about yesterday's testimony. I take it you've had enough time to recover from your emotional reaction, haven't you?'

Rosalind nodded calmly. 'Yes,' she said, 'I have.'

'Good,' Grace said, her face a cool mask. 'First, I'd like to clear up one thing for the jury. In your testimony yesterday you repeated a phrase several times – you kept talking about being "forced out" of McKenzie Brackman. Those were your words, weren't they?'

'Yes,' Rosalind said.

Grace looked quizzical. 'Does that mean that you were fired?'

'It was made quite clear to me that I —'

Grace didn't give her a chance to finish the statement. 'Were you fired, ma'am?' she repeated firmly. 'That's all I asked.'

Rosalind paused. 'Not technically,' she acknowledged. 'No.'

Grace leaned slightly forward, her tone still cool, but her demeanour building in intensity. 'Technically,' she said, 'you resigned – is that correct?'

'Yes, but —'

'And you did so without anyone at McKenzie Brackman either directly or indirectly asking for your resignation – isn't that correct?'

Rosalind looked pained. 'I knew I wasn't wanted,' she said.

Grace smiled thinly. 'Yes . . . well . . . quitting because you felt *unwanted*' – she paused to let the sarcastic inflection sink in – ' is quite a different matter from being fired, isn't it?'

'Well, yes, but —'

'Thank you,' Grace cut in before Rosalind could add anything that would qualify her answer. 'Now, referring again to your testimony yesterday, you also suggested that your departure from the firm cost you your share of the profits. But the truth is that you took clients with you when you left, didn't you?'

'A few, yes,' Rosalind said composedly. 'I did.'

'A few,' Grace repeated flatly. She glanced briefly towards the jury-box and saw that they were paying close attention, their interest piqued. Then she looked steadily at Rosalind. 'In fact, Ms Shays, isn't it true that you took not only every client you brought in – the ethics of which no one would dispute – but you also took several pre-existing clients who had been with McKenzie Brackman years before you arrived?'

Rosalind stared back challengingly, but remained composed. 'I didn't force anybody to come with me,' she said with a slight smile. 'There was certainly no coercion involved.'

'And I wasn't implying there was,' Grace said smoothly,

knowing that even now Rosalind was mentally kicking herself for even suggesting such a thing to the jury. 'The point I was trying to make was that you led this jury to believe that you, almost singlehandedly, built this firm up, only to be discarded when you were no longer needed. When in *fact*' – Grace paused again, and looked first at the jury, then back to Rosalind – 'you left this firm much weaker than you found it. When in *fact* you weren't discarded or fired at all. When in *fact* you left McKenzie Brackman voluntarily.' Then she nailed it home. 'True or false, Ms Shays?'

'That may be true, but —'

'And it is also true,' Grace barrelled on, over Rosalind's attempt to digress, 'is it not, that you now make more money than any partner at McKenzie Brackman?'

There was a silent pause. 'Yes,' Rosalind said tersely.

Now was the moment to nail it, Grace thought. 'And do you think that anyone on this jury' – she gestured towards the jury-box – 'could possibly have got that impression, given your performance yesterday?'

'Objection!' Jack Sollers shouted, jumping to his feet. 'The word *performance* suggests —'

'Sustained,' Judge Travelini said. She glanced at Grace. 'Move on, Counsel, you've made your point.'

Grace nodded. She walked over to the defence table and picked up a sheath of papers, then walked back to the witness-stand. 'How many law firms had you gone through before you took the partnership at McKenzie Brackman?' she asked, changing tack.

The question didn't, however, seem to faze Rosalind. 'I had been with seven law firms previously,' she replied.

Grace arched an eyebrow. 'Really?' she said. 'Seven. It seems like you have a tough time getting along with *anybody*, doesn't it?'

'Objection!' Sollers snapped.

'Were *they* all sex discriminators?' Grace managed to get the question in before Sollers shouted out his next objection. It was working, she thought, with the surge of emotional energy she always felt when a cross-examination was going this well; she was most definitely managing to plant the seeds of doubt in the jury's mind, doubts about Rosalind's character, doubts about the truth of what she had claimed on the stand yesterday.

'Sustained,' Judge Travelini said, with a warning look at Grace.

Grace faced Rosalind again, hoping to detect a small crack in the armour. 'Isn't it true, Ms Shays,' she continued, 'that you have alienated almost everybody you ever worked with?'

Rosalind seemed to be far from cracking under the pressure. With a steely glint in her eye, she replied: 'No. That is not true.'

Grace looked thoughtfully down at the papers she held. Then she looked up at Rosalind again. 'Those seven firms total up to four hundred and fifty-two lawyers,' she said. 'Four hundred and fifty-two lawyers with whom you have worked,' she emphasised. 'How many of those colleagues are friends of yours today?'

'Objection!' Sollers was on his feet again. 'What is the relevance of this line of questioning?' he demanded.

Grace looked first at Sollers, then at the judge. 'Her propensity to sever relationships is *directly* at issue, your

Honour!'

'Move to strike!' Sollers yelled in outrage. 'Your Honour!'

Grace moved her glance from the judge to Rosalind and leaned in towards the witness. 'Her inability to get along with the people she works with is *precisely* what's at issue here!' she reiterated, speaking directly to Rosalind.

'I get along with people I work with!' Rosalind said, cracking slightly.

'Mr Sollers,' Judge Travelini said, 'I'm going to allow this. The objection is overruled.'

'Name a friend, Rosalind,' Grace said, making it an all-out challenge. She waved the papers she held in her hand. 'Here they are – all four hundred and fifty-two of your former colleagues. Pick one. Pick out one person here who's a friend.'

'Your Honour,' Sollers protested, 'please! This is badgering!'

'Go ahead!' Grace repeated emphatically, before Judge Travelini had a chance to reply one way or another. 'Choose one. I'll be happy to subpoena whoever it is!'

'Your Honour!'

'That's enough, Ms Van Owen,' Judge Travelini told Grace.

'Sorry, your Honour.' But that apology was simply form: Grace wasn't sorry at all. She felt she had definitely scored points with the jury with that last exchange.

From his seat at the defence table, Victor restrained a smile of triumph. As angry and resentful as he was at being taken off lead counsel, he didn't begrudge a bit of this triumph to Grace. She was doing an outstanding job up there, and he was silently cheering her on.

Grace took a moment to compose herself – and to let the exchange sink in to the jury – then she began again. 'Ms Shays,' she said, 'given the fact that you've never developed a close friendship with any of your colleagues, given the fact that you have now left eight law firms – four of them on *very* unfriendly terms – given the fact that nobody at McKenzie Brackman even remotely liked you at the end of your brief tenure there, despite once having liked you enough to elect you senior partner' – she paused for dramatic effect – 'do you make any room whatsoever for the possibility that you are not a nice person to be around?'

'Your Honour,' Soller protested again, 'this is total badgering of the witness!'

'Sustained,' agreed the judge. 'That will do, Ms Van Owen.'

Which was fine with Grace. The last impression she left with the jury was that of a cold ruthless bitch who not only couldn't keep a friend, but didn't care. Quite a different picture from that of the emotionally distraught woman Sollers had try to portray yesterday.

Grace kept her face cool, unreadable. 'That will be all,' she told Rosalind.

'You may step down,' Judge Travelini told Rosalind.

And as she returned to the defence table Grace glanced quickly towards the jury, and from the expressions on their faces she was almost certain the damage she had set out to do had been done. The looks on the faces of the McKenzie Brackman lawyers told her that they thought so, too.

*

Abby Perkins forced herself to remain calm as she walked down the hall of the courthouse, heading for a very unwanted conversation with Rosalind Shays and Jack Sollers. Ever since she had received the subpoena, Abby had been worried about getting up on the stand. She was certain that Sollers wanted her to be a friendly witness – at least, as friendly as possible, given the circumstances. It was the last thing she wanted to be.

She *had* been quite friendly with Rosalind when she was at McKenzie Brackman. Abby had admired the older woman's savvy and her ability to be tough; she had learned a few lessons from Rosalind which she would never forget. But Abby no longer had any illusions about Rosalind's agenda; she hadn't for some time now. And, if anything, she felt as though she had somehow been used as an emotional if not actual accomplice in Rosalind's attempt to take over the leadership of the firm.

Abby had spent some time thinking about the kind of games that Rosalind played with the people around her, and how she had been a part of that strategy. Keen and astute about people in general, Rosalind had seemed intuitively to sniff out Abby's ambivalent feelings about the firm in which she often felt like the younger sister to a group of adults: patted on the head, tolerated, but never really taken seriously. In contrast, Rosalind had treated her with the respect that she felt she should have been accorded by the rest of the group. Rosalind brought her in on cases, asked her opinions about things, and generally made her feel equal and useful. And that attitude had, for a while, earned Abby's gratitude and loyalty. Now, she wondered angrily, how much of a price was she expected to pay for having been treated in that fashion?

As she approached the door to the witness room, Abby forced herself to take three deep breaths. She reminded herself that she could dictate the way this confrontation went. Then she opened the door and walked in.

'Hello,' she said curtly, nodding to Rosalind and Sollers, who were studying some documents on the table in front of them.

'Hi, Abby,' Rosalind said, greeting her with a restrained but friendly smile. Abby did not return the smile.

'Ms Perkins,' Jack Sollers said. 'Thanks for meeting with us. Have a seat.'

'No, thank you,' Abby said politely, staring at him with cool eyes. 'I think I'll stand.'

'Listen,' Jack Sollers said in a conciliatory tone, 'this is a terrible thing for everyone, Ms Perkins. And I think you should know that we hate putting you in the middle of it all, we really do.'

Abby felt like asking him, if he hated it so much, what was she doing here? Instead she forced herself to say calmly: 'I really don't have any idea why you subpoena'd me.'

'Well,' Sollers said reassuringly, 'I won't be asking you to say anything negative about McKenzie Brackman. You have nothing to worry about on that front.'

'Uh-huh,' Abby said, not believing him for one second. Sollers was very, very smooth. She forced herself to keep her expression blank, unrevealing.

'But', he continued, 'it *is* my understanding that you didn't have any problems with Rosalind when she was at the firm. As a matter of fact, it's my strong impression that you actually considered your experiences working with her to be quite positive.' He waited for a response.

Abby realised suddenly what was happening here: Sollers was playing a legal game of divide and conquer. Split the McKenzie Brackman team into factions, keep them at odds with one another and fatally weaken their position.

'Uh-huh,' Abby repeated, giving nothing away, either in tone or expression.

'Well, then,' Sollers said with a smile, 'that wasn't so difficult, was it? All we're really doing is asking you to comment on those positive experiences in court.'

Abby looked at him, unblinking, suppressing her anger at his patronising attitude. He was expecting her to act like a good little girl, an obedient child. 'But before you put me up there', she said, 'you wanted this meeting with me to make sure that I knew what you wanted. To make sure that I would say the right thing. Right?'

Sollers shrugged expansively, obviously believing he'd gotten Abby right where he wanted her. 'Well,' he said, 'it's only natural that I would want to know — before we go on the stand with you, that is — that my understanding of your feelings towards Rosalind are . . . accurate.'

Abby looked first at Rosalind, who seemed to be study- ing her, waiting for some kind of sign. Then she looked back at Sollers. 'Believe me, Mr Sollers,' she said flatly, 'you don't want my testimony.'

A little start of surprise, quickly masked, was Rosalind's reaction. Sollers was less revealing. He seemed to absorb the hit without any effect. But when he spoke his voice had a hint of steel in it, something that hadn't been there a minute ago. 'I'd like to remind you, Ms Perkins,' he said, 'if you get into that witness chair, you will have sworn to tell the truth.'

'I'm an attorney, Mr Sollers, and I believe I know what being in the witness-box entails,' Abby replied coolly.

'Then, you will tell the truth.' It was more statement than question.

'Listen to me, Mr Sollers,' Abby said, her voice now as steely as his. 'And listen carefully. Whatever positive emotions I may or may not have felt towards Ms Shays while we were working together have long been forgotten – the last two months of her tenure at McKenzie Brackman wiped them all out.'

'Then, you're implying you have no recollection —'

Abby cut him off. 'I'm not implying anything,' she told him coldly. 'I'm *telling* you I know which side my bread is buttered. And by whom.'

Sollers's eyes narrowed angrily as he stared back at her. 'Are you telling me that you – a lawyer – are prepared to get up on the witness-stand and commit perjury?'

Abby knew that this was supposed to strike fear in her heart. But she didn't feel afraid, not at all. For every admission Sollers could get out of her that would seem favourable to Rosalind, Grace could get ten that would completely destroy the positive impact.

Abby smiled thinly at Sollers. 'I'm telling you that if you put me up there you open the door to a cross-examination,' she said, calling his bluff. 'And I'm telling you', she repeated emphatically, 'that when all the dust settles' – she glanced icily over at Rosalind, then back to Jack Sollers –

'you will get hurt.'

She didn't wait for the impact to sink in. She simply turned and walked out of the room.

Chapter Nine

'I think I speak for the entire firm, Grace, when I say that you did one hell of a job on Rosalind Shays yesterday.' Leland spoke emphatically, his tone a little more upbeat than it had been before when discussing the case. 'One *hell* of a job,' he repeated.

'Thank you,' Grace said, permitting herself a small smile of agreement. 'Not only do I appreciate the compliment, but I also have to say that I thoroughly enjoyed doing it.'

'I don't blame you,' Abby said. 'I wish I could get my hands on her.'

'Speaking of which, Abby, would you care to share with us exactly what happened at your conference afterwards?' Doug asked.

Abby, too, permitted herself a small smile of satisfaction. 'Actually I think I handled it perfectly,' she said, just a little smugly. 'I'm almost positive Jack Sollers will not be calling me to the witness-stand any time in the foreseeable future. At least, not unless he wants to risk a hostile witness.' Then she proceeded to give the staff an account of the angry exchange yesterday.

'Good for you, Abby,' Victor said with a nod.

'Thanks,' said Abby.

'Thank God we've got a break from that awful trial

today,' Doug said. 'And, by the way, Ann,' he continued, 'since we know they are going to call you, I certainly hope you can manage to get yourself out of trouble as easily as Abby did.'

Ann glared angrily at Douglas, but refrained from saying anything. They'd already got into one spat this morning, when Douglas had made it clear that a gay rights case Ann was handling wasn't what he really wanted to see the firm involved in. And Ann, already anticipating what was going to be a very touch choice for her when she was called to testify in the Shays case, didn't need any more problems coming from people within the firm.

'And now to you,' Jonathan,' Doug barrelled on, mindless of the antagonism he was leaving in his wake. 'I take it that you will be working closely with Michael on the Brian Chisolm case?'

Jonathan's expression remained cold. 'I'll be working with him,' he said without further elaboration.

Doug didn't seem to notice either Ann's silence or the omission of the word 'closely' in Jonathan's statement, and he turned to Arnie, who seemed to be lost in his own thoughts.

'Arnie,' Doug began, 'what is the status of . . . ?'

But he never finished his sentence. All eyes at the conference table were suddenly riveted on Benny Stulwicz, who came into the meeting, the way he did every morning, with the regular platter of fruit and rolls for the staff. But this morning, aside from his normal outfit of slacks, a sweater and a bowtie, Benny was wearing a pristine white turban on his head. A silent shock wave seemed to roll through the room.

'Ah . . . Benny,' Arnie said tentatively, 'what's that on your head?'

'It's my turban.' Benny smiled proudly at Arnie. 'I got it yesterday,' he added, reaching up reverently to touch the bulky headgear, which seemed to be made of yards and yards of some kind of cotton, and which couldn't have looked more out of place if it had been worn by a cow.

'You got it from . . . whom?' Arnie continued in obvious disbelief.

'From the Children of God,' Benny told him happily. 'We all get to wear them.'

Abby's eyes widened. 'The Children of God?' she echoed. 'Who are they?'

'Nice people,' Benny told her. 'Really nice people. And getting to wear this means that I'm one of them.' He seemed very pleased by this turn of events.

'Well, Benny, that's very nice of you. But really aren't we *all* the children of God?' Doug asked, only half-jokingly.

Benny's reaction was no joke. His expression changed abruptly from one of pleasure to one of indignation. 'No!' he exclaimed angrily. 'Only special people get to be the Children of God.'

'Oh, please, tell me this isn't what I think it is,' Ann said softly to Stuart.

'Is it . . . I mean, are they . . . the children of God,' Arnie picked his way carefully through his words. 'Is it a cult, Benny?'

Benny shrugged. 'I don't know,' he said. 'But I do know that it's really hard to get in. You have to do a lot of things first.'

108

'Like what?' Leland asked gently.

'Well, like pray, for one,' Benny said. 'You have to pray a lot. And, uh, they teach you this special chant that you're supposed to use when things go wrong, or when you need something real badly.'

'A chant?' Arnie echoed in dismay.

'When you need *what*?' Abby asked. 'Do you chant for things like, um, cars?'

Benny thought about it for a moment. 'Yes,' he said finally, 'I think you could do that.'

Abby's eyes met Arnie's in dismay. But Benny didn't seem to notice the distinctly unfavourable reaction that was taking place everywhere around him. He was too intent on singing the praises and spreading the word of the Children of God.

'And', Benny beamed, continuing, 'we have meetings. All the time. Just like these meetings here,' he said. 'And everybody at the meetings likes everybody else. It's neat.'

'Benny,' Abby said gently, 'is there money involved in this?' She saw that her question had puzzled Benny, and she rephrased it. 'What I meant was, do you have to pay money to them to join?'

'A thousand dollars,' Benny said calmly, nodding.

'What!' Arnie yelped.

'What?' said Stuart, aghast.

'A thousand dollars?' Leland repeated, horrified. Then, hoping against hope, he continued: 'Benny, you haven't paid them the money yet, have you?'

Benny nodded tentatively, suddenly seeming to sense that something was wrong. 'Well, yes, I have,' he said. 'Yesterday,' he added. 'I got a special cheque from the

109

bank.'

'Oh, no,' Abby groaned, resting her forehead in her hands.

'Benny, you didn't, did you?' Arnie exclaimed.

Benny nodded. 'Yeah,' he said. 'Is something wrong?'

'You bet something's wrong! Giving money to people like that is crazy!' Arnie said angrily, wondering how people like these so-called Children of God could live with themselves. Picking on the most helpless of society's members.

'It's *not* crazy!' Benny protested. 'They're my friends!'

'They are not your friends!' Arnie snapped. 'They only want to take advantage —'

'No!' Benny yelled.

'Benny, listen to me,' Arnie said.

'No!'

'Benny, please,' Abby said.

But Benny had stopped listening to anyone in the room. With his hands clapped over his ears and his eyes squeezed tightly shut, he was making a series of garbled moaning sounds. 'Nammm noo, paaa nay . . .'

'What the hell . . .?' Leland began.

'Benny, stop it!' Arnie tried to be heard over the chanting.

'Naamm noo ayy no . . .'

'Oh Jesus,' Doug said. 'Do something! Somebody do something!'

'Do something!' Ann said to Arnie.

'Benny,' Arnie tried again.

Benny opened his eyes long enough to see that everyone in the room was still upset, and then he promptly turned

110

and left, while the rest of the bewildered staff looking at one another helplessly.

'What the hell are we going to do about this?' Doug asked finally.

'I know what I'm going to do about it. I'm going to my office and I'm going to put in a call to Judge Lobel right now,' Leland said decisively. 'And I'm going to schedule a motion as quickly as possible to see what – if anything – we can do about this.'

'Good idea,' said Stuart.

'Arnie,' Leland said, 'can you cover this? You're closer to Benny than anyone else here.'

Arnie nodded grimly. 'You bet,' he said. 'I'm not going to let some bunch of half-assed phoney religious quacks take advantage of him!'

'Hey, hey! Wait a minute here,' Victor said. 'Listen, you guys, what if this is something Benny genuinely wants to do? I mean, he's retarded, but he thinks and feels and acts on things, just like the rest of us do. I don't know if we really have the right to do *anything* here. Just because we think this cult is bullshit doesn't mean Benny doesn't find something in it that he wants for himself.' He looked around the conference table.

Leland nodded slowly in agreement. 'OK,' he said, 'I suppose we do have to allow for that possibility, as remote as it may be. 'But,' he added, 'since we all do feel some responsibility for Benny here, let's at least try to stop payment on the cheque until we find out. I don't want to see him lose a thousand dollars for nothing.'

There were murmurs and nods of agreement all around the table.

'OK,' Doug said, relieved to be moving on. 'That does it for this morning. We're done.'

As the lawyers gathered their notes together and stood up, Michael glanced over at Jonathan. 'That may be the most expensive turban anyone ever bought,' he said, trying to lighten up the air between them. But Jonathan simply nodded, stone-faced, and headed for his office.

Ann looked quizzically at Michael, who shook his head. 'Moral dilemma,' he said.

'Really,' Ann said, her voice dripping with sarcasm, 'what a delightfully different problem for anyone on this staff to have.' Then she swept out of the room.

Stuart looked at Michael and shrugged apologetically.

'I know, Stuart,' Michael said. 'It's OK.'

'Good,' said Stuart. 'It's nice to know that *something's* OK around here.'

'I wouldn't bet on it,' Abby said under her breath as she walked by.

'My goodness,' Arnie remarked. 'What a happy group of campers.'

'Shut up, Arnie,' said Michael.

*

'Are you ready for this?' Abby asked Roxanne, late that afternoon in the ladies' room.

Roxanne shrugged. 'I suppose so,' she said, 'although I took a vow that I'd never, ever allow myself to get fixed up on a date again.'

Abby smiled. 'I know, but this isn't really a date. We're just meeting them for coffee, and if no one likes anyone

112

else it's no harm; no foul.' She touched up her lips with a pale pink gloss and surveyed her reflection in the mirror. 'Right?'

'Right,' Roxanne sighed. 'I suppose.'

'Come on, Rox, at least it's a cup of coffee with a single man, and for a half an hour you can stop worrying about what you're going to do about Arnie and about your dad.' Abby looked over at Roxanne.

'You're right,' Roxanne said finally. 'I *am* sick of all my problems. I could use a little diversion.'

*

'Burning the midnight oil, Counsellor?' Victor stuck his head into Grace's office. At seven-thirty they were the only ones left, and the lights were dimmed everywhere except in Grace's office.

Grace swept a strand of blonde hair off her face and nodded. 'Well, it's definitely not burning the candle at both ends,' she joked. 'It's nowhere near that much fun.' She sighed and pointed to a scribbled list in front of her. 'You wouldn't believe how many people I've talked to who are willing to tell me exactly how much they hate Rosalind Shays, and exactly why. But when it comes to getting up on the witness-stand and testifying under oath . . . well . . .' She shrugged wearily.

Victor came all the way into the office and sat down on Grace's Moroccan-print couch. 'I know, they don't want to go on the record,' he guessed. 'Right?'

Grace nodded again. 'Right. I think I've managed to line up two or three people who will actually talk, but I'm not at

113

all sure they won't back out at the last minute. And I'm certainly not going to risk my relationship with anyone who does back out by subpoenaing them as hostile witnesses. It's not worth it.'

'No,' Victor agreed, 'it's not.'

There was a moment of quiet which lengthened into a slight tension between them.

'Listen, Victor,' Grace said finally, breaking the silence, 'you've been incredibly gracious about what Leland did, and I don't know how to thank you enough. I mean, the time you've spent working on our side has been invaluable . . .' She shook her head impatiently. 'No, that came out all wrong,' she said. 'It sounded condescending, which is the furthest thing from the truth of the matter. I guess what I mean is . . .' Her words seemed to trail off as she realised she was starting to babble.

'Grace,' Victor said quietly, 'you don't have to explain. There are a couple of really good reasons for my exemplary behaviour.' He flashed that dazzling smile, and Grace could feel the thump of her heart in response to it. 'Whether I'm the lead or the second counsel on this case,' he continued, 'this is my job. And I wouldn't let anything as petty as resentment over something Leland did get in the way of that. To tell you the truth, I'm not even certain he was wrong any more. You did one hell of a job on Roz, and I admire you for it.'

'Thank you,' Grace said. She looked down at her desk, then up again at Victor. 'What's the other reason? You said a couple of good reasons.'

They stared at each other for a moment, and Grace could feel the tension rise again. She thought she knew exactly what he was thinking, and she also thought that he could probably read her mind as well.

'You,' Victor said simply. 'You're the other good reason.'

Grace felt her breath catch in her throat. She'd been right after all.

Victor seemed far less ill at ease with the situation. He smiled. 'Don't look so terrified, Gracie, he said. 'I'm not going to do anything that will embarrass you or pressure you, or make it uncomfortable for us to work together here. I just thought I should clear the air between us.' He gazed at her across the room, his dark eyes intense yet somehow relaxed.

This man, Grace thought, is perfectly comfortable with his own passions. And, as unexpectedly as she realised that, she also realised that the attraction between them – the attraction that was strong and enduring enough to carry through several years and several lovers in between – was something that she wanted to know more about.

'What are you thinking?' Victor asked. 'Half a dozen different expressions just played on your face.'

Grace laughed, a little uncomfortably. 'My secret's out,' she said. 'I've got a great poker face in court, but outside of court . . . well, no poker face at all.'

Victor seemed to study her, to assess her. Finally he nodded. 'Let's get out of here,' he said.

'To . . . where?' Grace asked hesitantly.

Victor smiled. 'How about across the street for a drink?' he suggested.

'Oh . . . that's fine,' said Grace, wondering if she would rather that he had just leaped across the desk and grabbed her. Half-relieved, half-disappointed.

Victor seemed once again to read her mind. He laughed. 'I think we need to talk about this, Grace,' he said. He stood up and came round to where she sat behind the desk. One hand caressed her cheek so softly that she wasn't even sure it had actually happened. 'This could be real complicated,' Victor said softly. 'And I don't want to make any mistakes . . .'

'Shut up, Victor,' Grace whispered. Then she stood up and cupped his chin with her hands. She titled her head and kissed him softly on the mouth.

'Oh Christ,' Victor sighed, as the kiss became a lengthy heated exploration.

Finally they broke apart. 'Are you sure about this?' Victor asked softly.

'No,' Grace shook her had. In the subdued lamplight of the office, her hair looked like gold. 'I'm not sure about anything.'

Victor stroked her hair. 'Tell you what,' he said, 'let's go get that drink and put the rest of this on hold. OK?'

Grace looked up into his hypnotic eyes and knew that he was right. That, no matter how she felt right now, this was no decision to be undertaken lightly. 'OK,' she agreed.

*

'Look, Roxanne, there's Victor and Grace.' Abby pointed towards the door of the the Bar, the after-hours watering-hole where half the legal talent in Los Angeles seemed to wind up.

Abby was grateful for the distraction. Gene Borlander, the good-looking accountant who had asked her to coffee and had so obligingly provided a date for Roxanne, had proven himself to be a real bore. Not nasty, not weird, not even really dislikeable. Simply . . . boring. After all, how much could anyone really care about the ins and outs of the Government's newest tax guidelines? Too bad, Abby thought with a mental sigh, because he really was very nice-looking and a very nice man.

'What?' Roxanne said. 'Oh, yes.' Apparently uninterested in the arrival of Victor and Grace, who, after all, were working together what seemed like round the clock on the Rosalind Shays case, she promptly turned her attention back to her date.

His name was Sandy Cole, and he was a real surprise. A pleasant surprise. Not, perhaps, strictly handsome, Roxanne thought, but definitely attractive. A lanky frame and slightly messy brown hair; intelligent eyes behind wire-rimmed glasses. A sense of humour. And a father who was suffering from Alzheimer's – far more advanced than Murray's. They had got along well enough before the topic arose, but there had been a genuine reserve on both their parts. Casual, superficial chit-chat, the kind that – afterwards – Roxanne would say to Abby was 'OK, but no real spark'.

And then Roxanne had, after glancing at her watch, mentioned that she had to get home. And Sandy had asked why. And Roxanne had surprised herself by telling him the truth: that she had a father who was ill and scared, and she simply didn't feel right about staying out too late. And that had led to the revelation on Sandy's part about his own father, and then to a further admission that his marriage had broken up eighteen months ago, due in part to the strain that having his elderly and disabled father living with them

117

had put on an already shaky relationship.

Abby sighed and looked covertly at her own watch. She wondered how soon she could get the hell out of there. She wondered exactly why Grace and Victor, generally two of the world's most reserved people, seemed to be so flushed and and animated tonight. She wondered why she even bothered to try to meet men. Then she glanced over at Roxanne and Sandy, and smiled to herself. At least, she thought, *something* had gone right tonight.

Chapter Ten

'How do I look?' Ann Kelsey asked Stuart nervously. This was the morning she was being called to the witness-stand, and the butterflies in her stomach simply would not go away. She'd managed to take two bites of toast before feeling like she'd throw up if she ate any more; and the three or four cups of coffee she'd choked down weren't helping her nerves any, either. 'Do you think I should have gone with the grey suit instead of this one?'

They were standing in the hallway of the courthouse, and Ann, pale as a ghost, was clutching Stuart's arm for reassurance.

'You look fine, honey,' Stuart said with a supportive smile. 'It's how you feel that I'm a lot more worried about.'

'Me, too,' Ann admitted. 'And I feel awful. Oh, Stuart,' she said, 'I'm really scared.'

Stuart studied his wife's angular, pretty face, which today looked drawn and unhappy. 'Listen, Ann,' he said, 'have you really thought this thing through? Have you decided what you're going to say?'

Ann shrugged unhappily. 'Of course I've thought about it,' she said. 'You know that. It seems as though ever since this suit began I haven't been able to think about anything else.'

'It is a little overwhelming,' Stuart admitted, thinking back to the way Sollers had treated him on the stand.

'If I repeat that conversation, Stuart, we're going to be out an awful lot of money.' Ann's eyes were shadowed and troubled.

'Yes,' we are,' Stuart agreed calmly.

'We can afford it better than anyone else in the firm,' Ann added, aware that their financial status was in no danger.

'That's true,' Stuart said, nodding.

Ann chewed nervously on her lower lip. 'It would be kind of hard to remember exactly what I said back then, don't you think?'

Stuart nodded encouragingly. 'It really *was* a long time ago,' he said. He knew he was walking a fine line here: Ann ethics were unassailable, and whichever way this decision went would undoubtedly cost her a great deal emotionally. He absolutely couldn't allow himself to encourage her one way or the other, although secretly he had to admit that he was hoping that for once his wife would be able to put self-protection before the strictest interpretation of the truth.

'Yes,' Ann said with a nod. Then she looked at Stuart. 'I mean, *anyone* could forget precisely what they talked about that long ago, couldn't they?'

'They absolutely could,' Stuart reassured her.

'Oh Jesus,' Ann said, slumping against the wall. 'I don't know what I'm going to do.'

Stuart put a comforting arm around her. 'You're going to do what you feel you have to do, Annie,' he said.

*

'What do you think she's going to do?' Doug whispered to Arnie, who shrugged fatalistically.

'Face it, Doug,' Arnie said, 'Ann Kelsey's not exactly known for dissembling. I have the distinctly strong feeling that the best we can hope for is a convenient and temporary lapse of memory.'

Doug looked at Ann seating herself in the witness-box after being sworn in, and tried silently to will her to say the right thing – the thing that would protect the firm. If there was ever a time that pragmatic Douglas Brackman was going to allow himself to believe in anything as metaphysical as telepathy, this was it.

Sollers, looking like the cat that caught the canary, was standing directly in front of the witness-box. 'Would you consider yourself a friend of Rosalind Shays, Ms Kelsey?' he asked pleasantly.

'Well, he certainly didn't waste any time on frivolous questions,' Doug said gloomily.

Ann remained composed, looking back coolly at Sollers. 'I don't harbour any ill will against her, if that's what you're asking,' she said.

Soller's thin smile was given in recognition of her evasive answer. 'But would you consider yourself to be a *friend*?' he repeated with emphasis on the last word.

Ann paused for a moment. 'No,' she said finally, 'I wouldn't.' She had the intuitive feeling that Sollers was going to use this opportunity to move in immediately for some kind of kill, and his next words were proof of her assumption.

121

'In fact', Sollers said seriously, 'you were completely opposed to her even joining the firm in the first place, were you not?'

'Yes,' Ann admitted, 'I was.'

'And once she was actually working at McKenzie Brackman you repeatedly clashed with Ms Shays, isn't that correct?'

'Well,' Ann said hesitantly, 'I wouldn't say we clashed *repeatedly*, but yes, there were a few instances when I felt that —'

'Thank you,' Sollers said, cutting her off in midsentence. 'And the truth is that you loathed the idea of her becoming senior partner, true or false?'

'True,' Ann said flatly. She knew she was being trapped by his questions, but she just didn't see a way out of this mess.

'You also had a pet nickname for Ms Shays, didn't you?' Sollers asked simply.

'Objection,' Grace said loudly. 'That has no relevance to this line of questioning.'

'Your Honour,' Sollers said, 'I'm attempting to show that if this witness had any bias or predisposition before Ms Shays was forced to leave the firm —'

'Object!' Grace said sharply. 'We've already established that the plaintiff was not in *any* way forced to leave the firm!'

'Strike that from the record,' Judge Travelini told the court clerk. 'Mr Sollers, please rephrase.'

'I'm attempting to prove that in Ms Kelsey's case any bias she held before Ms Shays . . . *left* the firm went *against* my client.'

'I believe the feelings of hostility towards Ms Shays have already been established,' Grace argued.

'Your Honour,' Sollers said calmly, 'I think it's important for the jury actually to see the *degree* of hostility at work here.'

Judge Travelini nodded. 'I'm going to allow it, Counsellor,' she said.

Grace sank back into her chair. 'We're in trouble here,' she whispered to Victor.

He nodded in agreement. 'Let's see if we can deflect this a little, even just by objecting often enough.'

Grace shrugged. 'I don't know if we can,' she said. 'Look at the jury – they're all ears for this. Damn Sollers anyway!'

'Now, Ms Kelsey,' Sollers began again. Ann could practically see him rubbing his hands together with glee, and she braced herself. 'What *was* your pet name for my client?'

'I . . . I'm not sure I know exactly what you mean,' she hedged.

'Oh, come now, Ms Kelsey,' Sollers said with false jocularity. 'I've subpoena'd your colleague, Ms Perkins, and several secretaries at McKenzie Brackman, all of whom heard you call Ms Shays your pet name. Not once, but several times. And, of course, I can also recall your husband to the stand to verify what was repeatedly heard in the office.'

Ann glared at him, feeling both helpless and furious. She'd be damned, she thought, if she'd let this bastard get his claws into Stuart again. Even though that particular reaction on her part was undoubtedly the one Sollers was counting on.

'What was the name, Ms Kelsey?' he repeated, his tone a little less friendly.

'The witness will answer the question,' Judge Travelini said in a no-nonsense tone of voice.

'We're screwed,' Grace murmured.

Ann took a breath, then looked from from Sollers. 'The Queen Bitch,' she said quietly, wishing she could just disappear.

'Ah, yes,' Sollers said, nodding judiciously. 'The Queen Bitch.' He paused and stroked his chin. 'Now,' he said, 'given how very unwilling you must be to help my client, having publicly dubbed her . . . well, what you dubbed her . . .' He paused again, giving the jury the maximum amount of time to absorb the terrible insult that had been done to Rosalind Shays by this nasty and overtly hostile witness. 'Well,' he began again, 'with that attitude in mind, I'm going to ask you now to recall a certain conversation you had with Ms Shays after she was forced from her position as senior partner.'

'Objection!' Before Jack Sollers had even managed to finish his sentence, Grace was up out of her chair like a bolt of lightning, her words overlapping with his. 'This calls for hearsay,' she said emphatically.

'It's not hearsay,' Jack Sollers protested. 'It's an admission as well as a declaration against interests, your Honour.'

'Sweet Jesus,' Leland muttered.

'The objection is overruled,' the judge said.

Doug groaned softly. 'We're dead,' he muttered, 'unless she does the right thing.'

Next to him, Stuart squirmed uncomfortably. He felt so sorry for Ann, having to undergo this public embarrassment; at the same time, he found himself both devoutly hoping that somehow she would manage to find a way to stonewall what he was certain was inevitably coming and resenting Douglas for giving voice to that precise feeling. And what the hell was the right thing anyway?

'Thank you, your Honour,' Sollers said humbly. Then he turned his attention back to the witness-stand, his eyes boring into Ann's like lasers. 'Do you remember the conversation I'm referring to, Ms Kelsey?'

Ann shrugged. 'I had lots of conversations with Rosalind Shays when she worked at Mckenzie Brackman. I certainly can't be expected to remember every single one of them.'

Sollers didn't so much as blink at the attempted evasion. 'No, of course not,' he agreed. 'But the one I'm talking about is a very specific and unusual conversation that took place in the ladies' room immediately after Ms Shays lost the senior partnership. Do you recall that particular conversation, Ms Kelsey?'

'No,' Douglas whispered. 'No, no, no – just say no, Ann!'

'You're right,' Victor told Grace under his breath. 'We're screwed.'

'Blue and tattooed,' Grace added gloomily.

Ann glanced at Grace and Victor, as if for support. But reading in their eyes that there was no way out of this except a blatant lie she tried once again to hedge. 'I can recall talking to her in the ladies' room quite a few times,' she said.

'But during *this* conversation', Sollers said, 'do you

recall telling Ms Shays that if a man had done the things she'd done at McKenzie Brackman he would be hailed and praised as a hero and a strong leader?'

'I'm . . . not sure,' Ann said.

Sollers was like a terrier with a bone. 'Do you recall telling Ms Shays that it was only because she's a *woman* that she was met with this kind of hostility? That it was only because she's a woman that she was being punished, chased out of the firm?'

'I . . . I don't recall that specifically,' Ann said. 'I don't think I ever used those words.' She wondered miserably if her excuses sounded as feeble to the jury as they did to her. There was absolutely no doubt in her mind that they sounded feeble to Jack Sollers: it was written all over his face.

'But did you use words to that effect?' he pushed on.

'I never used any words like *punished* or *chased out*,' Ann said firmly.

Sollers's eyes narrowed, and his tone was cold. 'Did you or did you not, Ms Kelsey, represent to Ms Shays that things might have turned out quite differently for her if she had been a man? Regardless of the specific phrasing, did you say that? Yes or no?'

'I didn't . . . I mean, she was really upset. In a gesture of sympathy I *might* have said . . .'

Sollers leaned forward, fixing her with his eyes. 'Yes or no?' he insisted. 'Did you tell her things might have been different if she were a man? *Yes* or *no*?'

Ann looked frantically towards Grace and Victor, and saw that they wanted her to say no. She also understood that, of all the lawyers at McKenzie Brackman, those two would be the most likely to understand how serious this

126

ethical dilemma was to her. After an agonising minute had passed, Ann made the only choice she felt she could make: she was an officer of the court, and she was under oath. 'Yes,' she said quietly.

She could see the disappointment on the faces of her colleagues – even Stuart's – and found herself wishing that she could just disappear, out of this courtroom and as far away as possible – preferably to another planet where they didn't have lawyers or courtrooms at all.

'Just one more question, Ms Kelsey,' Sollers said smoothly.

'What now?' Arnie muttered. 'What else is left to nail her on?'

'When you said that to my client,' Sollers said, 'when you basically said that she had been discriminated against because of her gender, were you giving her sympathy? Or did you really mean it?'

Ann struggled with herself, wanting to be able to dismiss what she had said as an attempt to comfort an upset colleague. But she was still under oath. She stared Sollers in the eye. 'I meant it,' she said, knowing that as the words emerged she was giving the jury a damned good reason to award the sun and the moon to Rosalind.

Sollers smiled grimly. 'Thank you, Ms Kelsey,' he said. 'Nothing further.'

*

Late that afternoon, the lawyers were back at McKenzie Brackman and gathered in the conference room, which Ann Kelsey was beginning to see as some sort of gateway to

Hell, the office equivalent of the River Styx or something. She knew she was in for a lambasting – this meeting had been called specifically to see if there was any way they could alter the course the trial was taking. The course she had set by being unable to lie under oath. Ann felt anger and resentment coming her way; but, she reflected, she also had a right to be angry. How could anyone really expect an officer of the court to lie?

The gathered staff was quiet, until Leland came briskly into the room and sat down. 'All right,' he said, glancing quickly around, 'we all know why we're here. I think we'd better come up with something fast or we are going to lose this trial.'

'But it's only just started,' Stuart protested, coming to Ann's defence before anyone had even mentioned her name. 'How can you say we're losing?'

'Oh, we're losing all right, Stuart,' Doug snapped. 'Thanks to Ann Kelsey here.'

Ann suddenly felt her temper rise. 'Don't start with me, Douglas,' she warned him.

'I'm not starting anything – I'm just sticking with the facts!'

Ann glared at him. '*I'm* the one who had to make the decision up there, not you. I was under oath – an oath to tell the truth! And that's what I did – I answered the questions that were asked. You think it was easy, Doug? Well, I wonder if *you'd* find it so damned easy to lie on the witness-stand!'

'You buried us, Ann!' Douglas said.

'OK,' Leland said, 'OK. Both of you, simmer down. Rehashing Ann's gaffe on the stand is of no use at this

128

point.'

'Gaffe!' Ann repeated angrily.

'She didn't make a gaffe!' Stuart chimed in.

'The point is, where do we go from here?' Leland said, ignoring both of them.

'We'd thought about getting Arnie up on the stand . . .,' Grace began.

'I don't know if that's the right move at this point,' Leland said thoughtfully. 'It makes me a little nervous, to tell you the truth.'

'Why?' Arnie asked defensively.

'Why?' Doug echoed in disbelief. 'Possibly because you have a shaky reputation for honesty, at best —'

'Give me a break, Doug,' Arnie said crossly.

'– and because', Doug continued, 'Rosalind Shays worked here! She knows that you're the sleaze factor in this firm, and she's going to make sure that Jack Sollers picks at you like an open sore!'

'Stick it, Doug!' Arnie snapped.

'What lovely imagery,' Grace said to Michael Kuzak.

'Which – the open sore or sticking it?' Michael asked as Arnie and Doug continued to carp at one another. 'Or both?'

'That's enough, Arnie. You, too, Doug,' Leland broke in. 'Come on, this isn't a schoolyard.'

'Hey!' Doug said, his voice rising, 'don't you get it? I'm not just talking because I love the sound of my own voice, folks! Our malpractice insurance does not cover sex discrimination! We are looking down a very long barrel of liability, and the last thing we need is our own people killing us with their stupid testimony!'

'My testimony was the truth, you idiot!' Ann snapped.

'Hey,' Victor said, as the accusations continued to fly. 'Hey, shut up!' He got the attention of the startled lawyers. 'Come on, everybody just calm down and try to think rationally. Grace took a big chunk out of Rosalind yesterday. Both her credibility and her sympathy are shaky in the minds of the jury now.'

'Well, they were until Ann got up there and created more sympathy for her,' Doug muttered.

'Shut up,' Doug,' Michael said. 'Just listen to Victor, OK?'

Victor looked around the table and continued in a calm voice. 'No matter what damage has been done up to this point,' he said, 'our side hasn't even begun our defence yet. We have a long way to go, and since we don't know exactly what else Jack Sollers may have up his sleeve I think we should stick with the planned programme.' He looked at Arnie. 'Are you ready, Arnie?'

'Perfectly,' Arnie said succinctly.

'OK,' Victor said, 'there we are. We start with Arnie and we get better – no offence, Arnie, but no one expects divorce lawyers to be the most above-board guys in the world anyway. And Grace and I have a few tricks and surprises of our own lined up.' He smiled briefly at Grace. 'This thing is not over,' he said.

Leland nodded in satisfaction. 'He's absolutely right,' he agreed.

Arnie smiled wolfishly. 'You just ask the questions, Grace, and I'll pull us even. Sollers won't be able to lay a glove on me.'

McKenzie eyed the blond lawyer sceptically. 'Let's not

130

get too cocky here, Arnold.'

Arnie shrugged easily. 'I'm not being cocky; I'm just telling you the truth. He can't touch me.'

Leland nodded again, then rose out of his chair. 'We're adjourned here,' he said, feeling grateful that they'd got through this meeting with relatively few damaged egos.

The lawyers filed out, Ann heading quickly down the hall towards her office, obviously wanting to be alone.

'You got a minute, Counsellor?' Victor asked Grace.

'Sure,' she said, smiling easily at him.

Inside her office, Victor closed the door and pulled her tightly against him. Then he kissed her.

'Hey,' said Grace, laughing and flushed. 'What do you think you're doing?'

Victor shrugged and smiled at her. 'All I asked you was if you had a minute,' he said, his hands on her waist. 'I didn't say it was to discuss the Rosalind Shays case, did I?'

Grace smiled back at him, then pulled his mouth down to hers. When they finally broke apart again, she shook her head, bewildered. 'Wasn't it just last night that we agreed to take this slowly?' she said.

Victor nodded. Then, in between kisses to her neck and her ear, he murmured: 'We did. And it's been eighteen whole hours. Don't you think that counts as taking it slowly?'

Grace felt herself begin to melt into him. 'Go away, Victor,' she said weakly, 'before someone walks in and invokes that rarely used morals clause in our contracts.' God, she thought, this man was sexier than anyone she had ever met; she wanted him so badly she felt shaky.

'OK,' he said, laughing. He opened the door and looked

back at her, his dark eyes filled with promise. 'I think we'd better get together later,' he said.

Grace simply nodded, then watched as he disappeared down the hallway. She turned and walked over to the window, staring out but not even seeing the LA smog-and-skyline spread before her. This might, she thought, be the most dangerous thing – professionally and personally – she had ever done. An affair, a love-affair, with a man in the firm she had just joined. Where would it go? Bemused, Grace reminded herself that her lengthy relationship with Michael Kuzak began in earnest when he showed up wearing a gorilla suit during her wedding to someone else. Grace had been unable to resist it; she had simply left her bouquet, her bewildered groom and her startled parents behind, and walked off with the ape.

She sighed and shook her head. Obviously the mature level-headed woman that was the Grace Van Owen most people knew had an entirely different side to her personality. And that side was not at all tame or level-headed; that side took risks. Big risks. And Victor Sifuentes, complex intense Victor, looked and felt like the next big risk. Grace smiled a little, thinking how peculiar life could be. Then she mentally shook herself and went back to her desk, ready once more to tackle the complicated task of getting the better of Rosalind Shays.

Chapter Eleven

Doug Brackman knocked on the door to Arnie Becker's office and stuck his head in. 'Are you busy?' he asked a little timidly.

Arnie smiled cynically at him. 'Yeah, Doug, you bet I'm busy,' he said. 'I'm busy being the "open sore" of the firm, just waiting to see who's going to pick at me next.'

'I'm sorry I said that,' Doug said humbly. 'I really am, believe me. I guess I just got a little carried away, what with all the emotions flying around this place lately.' He moved tentatively into the middle of the office, then just stood there uncertainly, looking at Arnie.

'Forget it,' Arnie told him with a dismissive wave. 'We're all under a lot of pressure right now, and everyone's popping off at the mouth. Besides, I've been called worse.' He paused to think. 'Well, I've *probably* been called worse anyway.'

Still Doug didn't move. He didn't talk. He simply remained standing, looking as if he was completely confused about something.

Arnie looked at him quizzically. 'I said the apology's accepted, Doug. Is there something else on your mind? Because, if there isn't, I'm about two weeks behind on my work, and —'

'Well, the thing is . . . uh . . . well, I really need to ask your advice on something that's kind of touchy,' Doug said finally.

'Touchy, Doug?' Arnie queried, one eyebrow raised. 'Like the name of a doctor who treats venereal disease completely confidentially?' Arnie was unable to resist the chance to snipe, accepted apology or not.

Doug didn't even rise to the bait. 'This is serious, Arnie,' he said, sinking into the chair facing Arnie's chrome and glass desk.

'How serious?'

'It's about Marilyn.'

Arnie looked surprised, then nodded thoughtfully, tilting back in his chair. 'OK,' he said, 'shoot.'

Doug proceded to tell Arnie about the death of Senator Miller in Marilyn's bedroom – gun, holsters, spurs and all – and how he had had to call in some big favours to keep the real circumstances of the flamboyant man's death hidden from the media.

At the end of Doug's recital, Arnie laughed and shook his head. 'You know what's amazing, Doug?' he asked. 'For the squarest, most uptight guy in the entire firm, you've really managed to land yourself in some strange places over the past couple of years.'

'I know,' Doug said gloomily. Sollers's opening statement had been an all too painful reminder of what Doug's life had been like in the recent past – especially the reminder of his passionate affair with the woman who had been his own father's mistress, a woman who was a good twenty years Doug's senior.

'So what's the problem?' Arnie asked. 'It sounds like you took care of it pretty neatly to me.'

134

'The problem is that I just can't take this relationship any more,' Doug confessed. 'It's too hard on me.'

'What do you mean?'

Doug frowned. 'The only reason that Marilyn agreed to date me in the first place is that I told her I could deal with what she does for a living. I swore up and down the line that it wouldn't bother me. But I was wrong. I guess I overestimated myself.' He sighed. 'It's impossible, Arnie. I just can't come home to her and ask her how her day was, and have to hear about spurs and cross-dressers and gerbils.'

Doug was absolutely serious, so Arnie forced himself not to laugh at the description, which nevertheless certainly brought up some interesting images. 'Why don't you just tell her to quit her job or find something else to do?' Arnie suggested.

Doug shook his head glumly. 'She won't do it,' he replied. 'She trained to be a sexual surrogate, and that's what she says she is. There doesn't seem to be anything else that even really interests her – professionally, that is.'

'So what do you want to do?' Arnie asked, thinking Doug was taking a long circuitous route to whatever it was he wanted advice about.

'I have to end it between us,' Doug said finally. 'That's all there is to it.'

Arnie shrugged. 'So,' he said, 'end it. What's the big deal? Why do you need advice from me? I'm hardly the therapist type.'

'I need your advice because you're the resident expert on wriggling off hooks,' Doug said. 'And I mean that as a compliment,' he added hastily. 'I need to do this . . . well, *gently*, I guess. I don't want to hurt her. The thing is,

Marilyn is very involved in our relationship. I think– no, I *know* she's in love with me.'

Arnie smirked knowingly at Doug. 'And you need to find the easiest, quickest way out, right?'

Doug nodded, relieved to have it out in the open. 'Right,' he said.

Arnie thought about it for a moment. 'Well,' he said finally, 'if you ask me, Marilyn's done wonders for you. I think the two of you really make a good couple. You seem happy with her. But if you're *certain* this is what you want to do. . . .'

'I'm sure,' Doug said firmly.

Arnie shrugged. 'OK. In that case, this is what you do. You take her to a nice expensive restaurant. Say, Brasserie or Metro. Make sure it's a quiet one. A place where she won't dare make a scene. You have a little wine, you have a little Salad Russe – then you lean across the table and take her hand. And you say – with all the humility you can fake – you say: "Marilyn, I'm overwrought with ambivalence.'"

'Oh, come on!' Doug said sceptically. 'Overwrought with ambivalence? You can't expect me to say that. You can't expect her to believe it!'

'Trust me,' Arnie assured him. 'It will work. You just drop the bomb quickly and with accurate aim, and I guarantee she won't make a peep – it's too public a place. She might even admire your honesty – I *love* it when that happens. Although', he said thoughtfully, 'Marilyn may be a little too smart for that. Anyway, you tell her it hurts you more than it hurts her, you say goodbye, you pay the bill and you head for the door. Don't even think about looking back. Oh, and tip the valet on the way in so that your car will be waiting for you the minute you step out of the door. Voilà!'

'Gee,' Doug said with a frown, 'that sounds so . . . *cold*. I mean, I was kind of hoping to come out of this and still be friends.'

Arnie waved off the idea. 'Big mistake, Doug,' he said. 'You won't be friends. What's called for her is a complete severance. A clean break. Trust your instincts on this, Doug – there's a good reason why you came to *me* for advice.'

Doug nodded, his face still unhappy. 'I guess you're right,' he said.

'Of course I'm right,' Arnie assured him with a smile. 'I'm *always* right about this stuff.'

'OK,' Doug said.

'Do it exactly the way I told you,' Arnie added.

'Don't get creative, and don't deviate from a pattern which is known to work. Got it?' He stared at Doug.

'Got it,' Doug said, looking utterly miserable.

*

The partners were holding a special meeting that afternoon, one to decide on promotions and rises for the associates in the firm. It began well, with a discussion of Victor Sifuentes. The one thing they all seemed to be able to agree upon was that Victor deserved to be made a full partner.

'His work has been consistently outstanding,' Leland McKenzie said, acknowledging the verbal support Victor received from his colleagues.

'And maybe this will help the fallout from you taking

137

him off lead counsel in the Shays case, too,' Stuart said thoughtfully.

'I had a perfectly good reason for that,' Leland defended himself. 'And everyone here knows it! Besides, Grace is doing an outstanding job.'

'We all know that, Leland,' Doug reassured him.

Grace, feeling slightly awkward because of what was – or wasn't – happening between her and Victor, simply remained silent, speaking only when the vote was taken, adding her yes to the others.

'All right, then,' Leland said, satisfied, 'it's unanimous. Victor is now a full partner. Next up, Abigail Perkins.'

'Not a chance,' Doug said promptly.

'Agreed,' said Arnie Becker.

'Why not?' demanded Ann, offended by her colleagues' outright immediate rejection of Abby. 'What's wrong with Abby?'

'She's just not good enough to make partner,' Doug said succinctly.

'That's not true!' Ann retorted. 'That's not true at all!'

'Oh, come on, Ann . . .,' Arnie began.

'All right, now,' Leland interjected before this could escalate into a full-blown battle between the partners. 'Hold on a minute.' He looked around the table. 'I want you to remember something here. We promised Abby when she returned to the firm that she'd be considered for partnership.'

'*Considered*', Doug reminded him, 'is not the same thing as *guaranteed*.'

'But she deserves it,' Ann protested. 'Abby Perkins has been doing extremely good work. She's turned into a

138

damned good lawyer; and I, for one, think she should be recognised for it.'

'Maybe so, Ann,' said Michael diplomatically. 'I don't think there's any question about the quality of Abby's work. But face it – not *everybody* can make partner. Victor makes eight full partners, and Joanthan Rollins comes up in two years.'

'And don't forget CJ and Tommy Mullaney,' Stuart reminded them.

This mention of the two newest additions to the McKenzie Brackman staff made them all pause for a moment. CJ was a spitfire all right, but she was no team player. And as for Tommy Mullaney – Leland had made it quite clear that the unconventional lawyer's style wasn't his cup of tea at all.

And it was Leland was spoke first. 'C. J. Lamb has no interest in making partner – she can barely make the morning meetings, she's a complete maverick, and I'm certain she intends to stay that way. As for Tommy Mullaney, he doesn't stand a chance of making partner – at least, not while I'm here.'

'I think Tommy's good,' Grace said, coming to his defence.

Leland shook his head. 'It has nothing to do with being good,' he aid. 'He's a loose cannon. I don't like the way he operates. Besides, his employment history speaks for itself; he's self-destructive, and I'm predicting he won't even last here. He's never managed to last anywhere else.'

'I disagree,' Grace said firmly.

Doug held up a hand. 'Wait a second, folks,' he said, 'we're digressing with CJ and Tommy – they're not even up for review right now. Can we please just stick to Abby for the moment?'

'This *is* about Abby,' Leland told him. 'C. J. Lamb and Tommy Mullaney are not future partners, so they shouldn't be used as reasons to exclude Abby Perkins!'

'Come on, Leland,' Arnie said, 'forget about Abby. Just give her a merit badge for 'most improved player', and leave it at that. The truth of the matter is that Abby has zero profile, and a partnership isn't some kind of reward to just be handed out to anyone who performs their job adequately . . .'

'She performs far more than adequately!' Ann flared.

'Look,' said Arnie pragmatically, 'the only real question is what's in it for us, right? With Victor, it's obvious: he's already made a hell of a name for himself in the legal community, and there are lots of firms who would love the chance to steal him away from us. With Abby, ask yourself the same question: what's in it for us? The answer is . . . nothing.'

'What about acknowledging someone's loyalty?' Ann challenged him.

'What about it?' Doug said with a shrug.

'Oh, please, Ann, give me a break,' Arnie said with a pained expression. 'Loyalty. Big deal.'

'Well, that's exactly what I'd expect to hear coming from you, Arnie!' Ann snapped. 'Loyalty's never been one of your more noticeable qualities!'

'Come on, Ann,' Stuart spoke up, 'I hate to join the chorus, but what they're saying is true. Abby is no miracle-worker . . .'

'And neither are you!' Ann said to her husband.

140

'Well, thank you very much!' Stuart retorted, thoroughly offended. 'I happen to bring in as much as you do to this firm . . .'

'You do not!' Ann said sharply.

'Enough!' Leland said. 'Both of you, that's quite enough.' He glared at everyone. 'Some days around here,' he said crossly, 'I feel like I'm running a cross between a pre-school and an encounter group!'

'Let's just put it to the vote and get it out of the way,' Michael suggested.

'Fine,' said Doug.

'Well, I vote yes,' Leland said firmly. 'And I seriously recommend that the rest of you think about it and do the same.'

'Yes,' said Ann, seething.

'No,' said Arnie flatly.

'No,' said Michael.

'No,' said Doug.

'No', said Stuart, glaring angrily a his wife, who glared back.

Grace hesitated. Finally, she said: 'No.'

'OK, that's it,' Doug said briskly. 'Five to two, no partnership.'

Ann got angrily up and prepared to leave the room. 'I can't believe you people,' she said with disgust.

'Hold on, Ann sit back down.' Doug looked around the table at the lawyers. 'One more thing. We do not announce or reveal the results of this meeting to *anyone* before March the fifteenth.'

'What on earth are you talking about?' Ann asked, bewildered.

141

'We've got to face some hard cold facts, Ann,' Douglas told her. 'We have three offers of employment out to third-year law students who will respond to us by that date.' He stared at Ann. 'Since two of them are women who could already be wary of our firm being tagged with the sex discrimination label, we can't have the news about Abby leaking out. It could very well tip the balance away from their deciding to go with us.'

Ann's jaw dropped. 'Are you serious?' she asked in disbelief.

'Very,' Doug assured her.

'That's absolutely disgusting,' Ann said. 'You can't do that!'

'Oh, yes, we can,' Doug said.

'Listen, Doug,' Grace said, trying to interject a note of reason into the proceedings, 'I think that Ann's absolutely right on this one. If we're not going to make Abby a partner, we at least owe her the courtesy of telling her.'

'No,' said Douglas.

'I agree,' Arnie said. 'We can't jeopardise the firm that way.'

Ann looked at Leland, hoping he would put an end to this nonsense. Leland shook his head. 'I'm sorry, Ann,' he said. 'But I agree with Doug on this one. If the news leaks out that the man is "in" and the woman is "out", it could really cost us. We tell *nobody*.'

'But, Leland . . .,' Ann began.

Leland shook his head. 'This is a partnership meeting, Ann. You have the fiduciary responsibility to all of us. You tell *nobody*.'

Ann rose and walked to the door. Then she turned and

142

looked at them, her disgust at their tactics written on her face. 'This place is really a pile of shit, you know that?' She asked. 'I hope everyone here is happy to know that, while we may have got rid of Rosalind Shays in the flesh, her spirit is certainly alive and well and flourishing among us!' And with that statement and one more intense glare for her husband she stormed out of the meeting.

*

'Mike, got a minute?' Victor said, coming into Michael Kuzak's office.

'Sure, sit down,' Michael said.

'I . . . I have to ask you something,' Victor said, his expression serious.

Oh Christ, Michael thought, he's going to ask me about the partners meeting, and how the hell am I going to not answer him without making him think that he was passed over? 'What's on your mind?' he asked, bracing himself.

'I'm really a little unsure about how to approach you on this,' Victor said tentatively. The issue of a possible romance with Grace, and the triangular emotional ripples it could produce at work, had been weighing heavily on his mind. 'I guess the best thing is just to start.' He paused for a moment to collect his thoughts, and then plunged in. 'It's about Grace,' he said.

Thank God, Michael thought. Then, just as quickly, he wondered what Victor was talking about. 'What about Grace?' he asked.

Victor, usually an unruffled and unflappable man, seemed a little nervous, Michael thought.

143

'We're getting . . .' Victor began. 'Oh, hell, Mike. There's no way to mince words. There's something happening between us.'

Michael simply stared at him, bewildered. 'Grace and you?' he repeated. Then, suddenly, be began to understand exactly what Victor was saying. 'Do you really mean something is going on between you two . . . *romantically*?' he asked.

Victor nodded, his handsome face serious. 'Yes.'

Michael just continued to stare, but Victor could see that there was a different quality to this stare – this one was more hostile than confused.

'Look,' said Victor, 'neither of us meant for this to happen. It just kind of . . . well, it sneaked up on us.'

There was still no verbal reaction from Michael Kuzak, although Victor could have sworn that the emotional temperature in the office had just dropped from normal to zero.

He tried again. 'I want this to be above board, Michael. I guess what I'm trying to say is . . . well, I suppose I thought it was fair that you knew, and that if it bothered you you had the chance to say so.' He paused, his dark eyes meeting Michael's frosty expressionless stare. '*Would* it bother you if Grace and I began seeing each other?'

Michael just continued to stare at Victor, his eyes narrowed. Finally, he spoke. 'Yes,' he said flatly. 'It would bother me.'

Chapter Twelve

If Arnie Becker hadn't become a divorce lawyer, he would have made an excellent actor. With his polished present-ation, his blond good looks and his easy smile, he sat in the witness-box as though testifying was something which he did every day. Calm, relaxed, even congenial, it was plain to see that the jury was impressed with this witness. Which, Grace thought thankfully, was a nice change for their side. She had taken him carefully through a series of questions all designed to lead up to his assessment of the way in which Rosalind had been treated at the firm and, more important, the way in which she had left it.

Arnie spoke calmly, no trace of nervousness or con-descension in his voice. Looking thoughtful and serious now, he proceeded through his testimony. 'Removing Rosalind Shays was certainly not the kind of action we normally take, and it was most definitely not done casual-ly. It was a very risky move for us.'

'Risky?' Grace repeated, making sure the jury remem-bered the description. 'How so?'

'Well,' Arnie said, 'in order to survive in these days of high-profile legal battles and more lawyers than most of society knows what to do with '– here he paused and flashed a charming self-deprecating smile towards the jury-box – 'a law firm absolutely has to project both stability

145

and unity to the outside business world.'

'Can you elaborate on that, Mr Becker?' Grace asked sweetly. 'I'd like the jury to get an in-depth look at how these decisions are made – in particular, how this very *risky* one was made.'

'Playing musical chairs with the senior partnership of a firm can severely and permanently undermine those objectives I just mentioned – unity and stability. The truth of the matter is that the consequences of that kind of seemingly impulsive shifting around at the top can be *devastating* to a firm. It is not the kind of thing that occurs frivolously.'

'What about out-of-office politics?' Grace asked him, heading off that line of questioning on Jack Sollers's part.

Arnie shook his head. 'Not really, no,' he said. 'I'm not saying that McKenzie Brackman is free of office politics – no company is; what I'm saying is that we only elected to replace Rosalind when it became apparent that there was absolutely no choice in the matter.'

'Why?' Grace queried. 'What did Ms Shays do that was so awful?'

'Well,' Arnie seemed to hesitate, 'there were many things; but, first, I want to say that personally I happen to like Roz. I think she's a genuinely unhappy person who presents herself as an ogre as a form of self-protection —'

'Objection!' Jack Sollers said loudly.

'Sustained,' Judge Travelini said with a slight frown. 'Mr Becker, please refrain from character assessments unless directly asked, and confine your answers to the question given.'

'Of course,' Arnie said humbly. 'What was the question?'

God, he's good, Grace thought. 'I asked you what Ms Shays did that was so terrible,' she reminded him.

'Yes . . . well, initially it was the alienation of the associates. She took on a client who publicly supported apartheid in South Africa, and she completely ignored the protests of Jonathan Rollins, our black associate. Then she went behind Victor Sifuentes' back and settled a case right out from under him. Victor is Hispanic,' he added, speaking to the jury. From his seat at the defence table, Victor bit back a smile as Arnie turned his attention back towards Grace. 'Now, I really don't think that Roz is overtly racist, but she did demonstrate no regard whatsoever for our minority employees.'

'This is ridiculous,' Jack Sollers protested.

'I'm only telling you what I saw,' Arnie said ingenuously.

'Mr Becker,' the judge said, a note of warning in her voice. 'Stick to the issue at hand.'

'I'm sorry, your Honour,' Arnie said.

'What else did she do, Mr Becker?'

'It was the sum total of everything she did and didn't do,' he said. 'There was this fundamental incompatibility with people that came from Roz and ultimately spread through the firm like some sort of a cancer. Her . . . well, her underlying dishonesty simply became prohibitive.' Arnie sighed. 'We felt sorry for her. And that's the reason that she chose *not* to fire her. But Rosalind Shays as senior partner?' His cocked eyebrow and expression of disbelief almost spoke for itself. '*Please!*'

Grace smiled. 'Thank you, Mr Becker. Nothing further.'

Jack Sollers approached the witness-box with an attitude

147

and posture that was palpably hostile. He glared at **Arnie**, then began in a tone dripping with sarcasm. 'Mr **Becker** claims something called "fundamental incompatibility", he said to the jury. 'Mr **Becker**,' he said, addressing **Arnie** directly, 'I'd like to explore that a little. Isn't it true that you yourself secretly defected from McKenzie Brackman in the middle of the night last year?'

'I did *temporarily* leave the firm,' Arnie acknowledged.

'The truth is that you sneaked out and you stole clients. And the truth is that the firm sued you, isn't that correct?'

'We had a disagreement,' Arnie replied, shrugging his shoulders as if the vitriolic temporary split had been nothing more than a petty squabble about the office filing system.

'And is that what you consider *unity*, Mr Becker?'

'Truth be told, one of the real reasons that I left at all was because Rosalind Shays was brought in.'

'Really?' Jack Sollers asked in a tone of surprise. 'But one minute ago, you said you liked her, didn't you?'

'*Personally*,' Arnie said firmly. 'But professionally I couldn't endorse her methods. And, to *me*, putting her into a leadership position represented a major shift of this firm's moral centre – something that didn't sit well with my conscience.'

'I wonder where Arnie ever picked up a phrase like "moral centre",' Stuart murmured to Doug.

Sollers looked gleefully. 'Your conscience!' he exclaimed. 'Let's talk about that for a moment. You have had sexual relations with several of your divorce clients, haven't you, Mr Becker?'

'Objection!' Grace said. 'Relevance!'

'Goes to explore this man's moral centre, your Honour,' Sollers said quickly.

'I'll allow it, Counsellor,' the judge said to Grace. 'He opened the door.'

'Uh-oh,' Stuart said softly. Beside him, Doug nodded grimly. This was not a topic you wanted let loose with Arnie Becker on the stand.

'So, Mr Becker, regarding your moral centre – you've slept with clients, you've slept with opposing counsel, with —'

Arnie leaped in before Jack Sollers could reel off any more professional or personal categories of the women he'd slept with. 'Yes, Mr Sollers,' Arnie said, 'I *did* have relationships with people I represented, all of them *before* I became a happily married man. I don't see any reason to apologise for that. None at all!' He turned to the jury. 'As a person who works very hard, the truth is that most of the people I meet are *through* my work, and the fact that social or even romantic relationships did result from my professional associations is an indictment of neither my integrity nor my sense of ethics.' He glared at Sollers. 'And I'm personally offended at your suggestion to the contrary!'

Sollers seemed to be at a loss for words.

'My God,' Doug breathed, 'he actually managed to turn that around to his advantage!'

'Amazing,' said Stuart.

Leland McKenzie smiled.

'Please bear with me,' Jack Sollers began again, 'but I find myself a little bewildered, Mr Becker. Now, *you* say that Rosalind Shays was ousted because of a fundamental incompatibility.' He paused, frowning in seeming confu-

149

sion. 'But Ann Kelsey testified that it was because Rosalind was a woman.' He started straight at Arnie, his eyes challenging and anything but confused. 'So the question is, which one of you is lying?'

'Objection!' Grace flared.

But Arnie held up a palm as if to motion her off. 'No, wait it's OK. Actually it's very simple. Ann Kelsey wasn't lying. She was *mistaken*.'

Stuart groaned. Beside him, Ann went rigid.

Sollers smirked. 'That's kind of a big mistake to make – under *oath*, and with a huge judgement on the line, wouldn't you say?'

Arnie shook his head firmly. 'No. The simple fact is that Ann Kelsey tends to . . . well, suffer from a kind of hypersensitivity on male – female issues.'

'Oh?' Sollers said in disbelief. 'Would you care to clarify that statement?'

'Certainly,' Arnie replied, all business. 'Her reactions stem from a basic insecurity on her part, a fear that she only became partner on her husband's coat-tails.' He paused and looked pityingly at Ann, who was practically vibrating with fury. 'I'm sorry, Ann,' he said with as much sincerity as he could muster, 'but it's the truth. This insecurity can tend to cloud her judgement, and while there's absolutely no doubt in my mind that she was completely honest when she gave her statement I have to say that her assumption was totally misplaced.'

Arnie smiled a dazzling smile at the jury, while Jack Sollers retreated in defeat, and Ann Kelsey looked daggers at him across the courtroom.

Michael Kuzak and Jonathan Rollins, attempting to shield Brian Chisolm from the endless violation by cameras and microphones lining the criminal-court building, pushed their way through the throngs of reporters and news crews. The Brian Chisolm case had just been upgraded from carnival sideshow to full-blown three-ring circus, complete with Derron Holloway posturing and proselytising and feeding the media frenzy outside Brian's trial.

'Jonathan, I need to speak to you privately,' Michael Kuzak said, displeasure written all over his face. 'Brian,' he told their client, 'will you excuse us for a minute?'

Brian Chisolm nodded and left the witness-room in the criminal-court building. When the door had shut behind him, Michael whipped angrily around and slammed his briefcase on the table.

'What the hell did you think you were doing out there?' he demanded.

Jonathan, impeccable in a navy pinstriped suit and oxblood tie, looked coolly back at Michael. 'What's your problem, Michael?' he asked.

'My *problem* is that I'm sick to death of your attitude,' Michael said furiously. 'And you know exactly what I'm talking about – that little bullshit truth-by-omission performance that you just put on for the camera crews!'

Jonathan just stared at him, his own eyes unfathomable.

Kuazk wanted to shake him. 'A reporter asks you whether you think your client is innocent, and you have the nerve to say "No comment"!'

'I thought it was fairly appropriate under the circum-

151

stances,' Jonathan said coolly.

'Oh, did you? Under what circumstances, Jonathan? Under the circumstances that Derron Holloway just provided by suggesting to the media that you are only on this case because we need a black lawyer?' Michael's voice was shaking with anger. 'Or the circumstances that you just created by letting everyone out there think that Derron Holloway is right?'

Jonathan shrugged. 'What's the big deal, Mike? I thought the object here was just to get through this trial.'

'That's complete crap, Jonathan, and you damned well know it!' Michael wasn't even trying to control himself now. 'Acquiescence to a question like that borders on malpractice. The cameras were pointed at you, for God's sake, Jonathan, and you say "No comment"?'

'I'm sorry,' Jonathan said flatly.

'*Sorry* won't do it, and you know it!' Michael glared. 'I've got a job to do here, and I happen to *need* you! In case you haven't noticed, there's a lynch-mob mentality building here that's going to hang an innocent man, and you just helped *fuel* it!'

A moment passed, during which neither man appeared to be backing down. The air between them was thick with tension.

'I said I was sorry,' Jonathan repeated finally.

Michael grabbed his briefcase. 'You listen to me,' he said in a low angry voice. 'You get your head in this trial no matter *what* your problem is. Because I don't give a rat's ass what it is; what matters is the trial. And if you can't see that, then maybe you'd better start rethinking exactly what it is that you want to do with your future, because being a lawyer sure doesn't seem to be working for you!'

With that, he slammed out of the room, leaving an angry but – to his own surprise – thoughtful Jonathan behind.

*

Michael Kuzak's state of mind was still black when he arrived back at the office and saw that Grace Van Owen's door was open. Without really thinking about what he was going to say or why, he walked abruptly in.

Grace looked up from the papers she was perusing, surprised. 'Hi, Mickey,' she said. 'What's going on?' She hadn't lived with the man for all that time for nothing: she knew Michael's dark moods very well indeed.

'For the record,' Michael said angrily, 'I think it's completely unprofessional!'

Grace's expression went from surprised to bewildered. 'I beg your pardon?' she said. 'Mickey, what are you talking about?'

'You and Victor,' Michael said. 'I think it's bad for the firm and I think it's bad for morale!'

Grace looked down to hide her shock and her anger. After a moment had passed, she looked up again. 'Look, Michael,' she said calmly, '*if* Victor and I were seeing each other, what business is it of yours?'

'Probably none,' Michael admitted. 'But . . . well, you're a partner, Grace, and he's still an associate. At least for now. You know how dangerous that can be.'

'Dangerous?' Grace repeated. 'Actually no, I *don't* know how dangerous it can be.'

'As a partner in this firm, it is —'

'Give me a break, Michael! Your objection to it really is that I'm a partner and he's an associate?' Grace's eyes widened in disbelief.

A storm of emotions passed across Michael's face as he considered an honest answer to Grace's question. 'No,' he admitted finally. 'He's a friend, and you're my ex-lover. I think that's the truth. How about it?'

'At least it's honest,' Grace said softly.

Michael's smile was tinged with bitterness. 'Yes,' he said, 'it is.'

Grace sighed. 'Listen, Michael,' she said, 'this isn't something anyone expected. And it's certainly not something I want to rub in your face. I can completely understand your reaction – I don't know how comfortable I'd be if you suddenly started dating . . . well, *Abby*. But what *you* have to understand is that truly it just isn't any of your business.'

Michael looked at Grace, his face a mixture of anger and sadness and recognition of the truth of her words. 'Fine,' he said shortly. 'I just wanted to let you know how I felt. Victor's the one who came to me. He's the one who asked me if I'd mind. And I was honest with him, too, Grace. I said yes, I would mind.' He turned to leave the office. At the door he looked back. 'I guess it didn't really make a difference, though, did it?'

And with that he whirled around and walked out, leaving Grace frustrated, uncomfortable and angry. She glanced at her watch and decided she might as well pack up and leave. It was certainly late enough, and she could take the briefs she'd been studying home with her. There, in her own

154

home, surrounded by the things she loved, maybe she'd be able to give her work the attention it needed.

Grace threw a stack of papers into her grey leather briefcase and pulled on her jacket. It was time to get away from the office, which was – as far as she could see – turning into something resembling a soap opera. As she reached the bank of elevators, Victor emerged from one of them.

'Grace . . .'

'I need to talk to you,' she said, surprising herself. 'Now.'

'Can it wait just a minute? I need to make a call on this case, and —'

'I said *now*,' Grace snapped and stalked into his office.

'Grace, what —?'

Grace whipped around to face him, her usual calmness gone. 'Who the hell do you think you are?' she demanded angrily.

'What?' Victor asked, taken aback by this unexpected attack. 'What are you talking about?'

Grace pulled herself up to her full height and glared. 'You have hell of a nerve,' she said. 'One' – she held up one finger 'you and I do not have a relationship.'

'What . . .?'

'Two!' A second finger was raised. 'We are not sleeping together. And, three,' she spat, 'I haven't even said that I would go out with you!'

Victor glanced uncomfortably towards the open door, well aware that anyone passing by could hear what Grace was saying. Besides, what had made her so angry? 'Why are we talking about this now?' Victor asked softly.

'Because', Grace said, a flush rising from her throat to

155

her face, 'you went to Michael Kuzak and made this – whatever this is – *public*! I can't believe you did that. What did you need – Michael's stamp of approval?'

Victor groaned. 'Oh Jesus,' he said, 'what did Michael say to you?'

'What the hell does that matter?' Grace flared. 'I think what really matters is what you said to Michael! How dare you?'

'Look, Grace —' Victor's attempt at apology or explanation was cut short.

'Damm it, Victor!' she said. 'If there is something happening here between us, then that's what it is: between *us*. There's no third party involved, this has nothing to so with Michael.'

'He still loves you,' Victor said softly.

Grace was stunned into silence for a moment. Then she shook her head. 'I don't know if that's true,' she said, 'and quite frankly it doesn't matter. How Michael Kuzak feels about me doesn't give him the right to decide who I see. And it doesn't give you the right, either.' She stared at him, frustrated and furious and far more upset than she wanted to be. 'You'd better get something straight, Victor. Whatever you and I may or may not become, I'm in charge of my own life. I make up my own mind, and I don't need anybody's permission – for anything.'

Victor wanted to grab her and hold her and tell her that he'd never thought anything different from that; but he knew that this wasn't the moment. And he felt ashamed of having gone to Michael. 'I'm sorry,' he said finally. 'I didn't think it through, and I did the wrong thing.'

Grace's eyes were cool and uncertain. She shook her

head. Then she walked to the door. 'I don't know,' she said to him. 'If it's this much trouble now, maybe we should just forget the whole thing.'

'Grace, wait . . .,' Victor said, but she was already gone.

Chapter Thirteen

Following Arnie Becker's advice, Doug made a lunch reservation at Nic Anthony's on Melrose, a restaurant which catered chiefly to the entertainment business, but the very uppermost reaches of it. Elegant, subdued, yet still cutting-edge chic, Nic Anthony's was the spot where pay-or-play deals were discussed, where normally reclusive stars felt comfortable eating, and where top-level studio executives lured other top executives into their own personal shark-pools. Doug figured that in such elevated surroundings Marilyn would be both too distracted and too impressed to react immediately – that is, emotionally – to the break-up.

Doug was already seated when Marilyn entered, looking extremely appealing in a pale yellow suit and high heels, a broad-brimmed straw hat framing her face prettily. It was that kind of place: a woman could actually walk in in a hat and gloves and look as if it was the norm. Marilyn allowed herself to be escorted to the table, and smiled happily at Doug as she sat down. They exchanged affectionate pleas-antries while the waiter uncorked a bottle of California Chardonnay for them. Once Doug had sipped and nodded his approval, the waiter poured and got discreetly out of their way.

'Marilyn,' Doug began, 'the reason I asked you here was

to talk about —'

Marilyn held up a hand and shook her head. 'Let's order and just enjoy being here for a while, Doug. We can save the serious talk for later – there's plenty of time for that.'

That didn't give Doug much latitude, and he chafed nervously throughout the next forty-five minutes while they made smalltalk and Marilyn enjoyed the surroundings. Finally, their salads nearly eaten, the wine-bottle almost empty, Doug plunged in again.

'Listen,' he said seriously, 'there's something we need to discuss.'

Marilyn nodded in agreement. 'It's about the Senator, isn't it?' she asked understandingly. 'I had a feeling you were a little flipped out by what happened. But, Doug,' she continued earnestly, 'you were so good about it. I mean, you handled the whole thing so beautifully discreetly.' She shook her head in admiration. 'I just don't know how I can ever repay you,' she said.

Feeling like an utter heel, Doug nodded. 'Actually', he forced himself to continue, 'this concerns a bigger picture than just what happened with the . . . Senator.' He nearly choked on the word. 'Marilyn,' he said, 'this is very difficult for me to tell you, but the truth is that I'm overwrought with ambivalence.' He tried to gaze soulfully into her eyes, but all he met was a bewildered expression in return.

'Excuse me?' Marilyn said. 'What are you talking about?'

'Marilyn, I adore you,' Doug said, deviating slightly from his Arnie-coached speech. 'It has nothing to do with that. But . . . I want to terminate our relationship.'

Marilyn simply looked puzzled. 'Because of one dead

159

client in a holster?' she asked in disbelief. 'You can't be serious!'

'But I am,' Doug insisted, mustering up all the sincerity he could. 'Look, it goes beyond what happened the other day. But the truth is it did affect me adversely – having such a shocking confrontation with . . . well, with what you do for a living.'

'The way you met me was through what I do for a living,' Marilyn reminded him a little sharply. 'Or has that little fact conveniently slipped your mind?'

'No, of course it hasn't,' Doug replied, thinking she was putting up more of a fuss than Arnie had promised. He lowered his voice, hoping she would follow suit. 'I'm sorry, but I just can't handle what you do. And I think the honest thing would be just to end this relationship and walk away.'

Marilyn's face flushed, and her voice rose. 'The *honest* thing!' she exclaimed disdainfully. 'I was *always* honest! I told you right from the beginning that you didn't want to get involved with a sexual surrogate!'

Doug saw two men at an adjacent table turn and stare quizzically at them. 'Shh!' he said. 'For heaven's sake, keep your voice down!'

'Why?' Marilyn asked, her voice still raised. 'Are you embarrassed? Because *I'm* not. I never was!'

'Shh!' Doug repeated urgently. 'No, of course I'm not embarrassed.'

'Douglas, when you began to hound me to go out with you and I was adamant about not doing it, I remember one thing quite clearly: I listed all the reasons that it wouldn't be a good idea, but you insisted that my occupation was not a barrier.'

'I didn't think it *was*,' Doug said miserably. 'But now I realise —'

Marilyn wasn't through. She interrupted him in mid-sentence to say: 'We've invested a lot of time in this relationship, Douglas. We've been together exclusively for over half a year now . . .'

'Not exactly exclusively,' Doug said. Arnie, he thought, I'm going to wring your neck.

'Oh, great!' Marilyn snapped. 'Now you're going to get insulting! Well, I'm not through!' She glared at him. 'Why is it that now you're suddenly choosing to bring out a problem which is obviously so fundamental – and must have been from the very beginning?'

Doug glanced sideways and saw that the men had lost interest. Good, he thought frantically. Now, if he could escape before the words *sex* or *surrogate* cropped up again, maybe it would all be all right. He took a deep breath. 'Marilyn,' he said softly, 'please believe me, this hurts me more than it hurts you.'

She stared at him disdainfully. 'That may or may not be true,' she said, 'but either way it's beside the point. You owe me an explanation here. I want to know why you specifically told me that my job wasn't an obstacle if it was?'

Doug shrugged unhappily. 'I guess I didn't really know myself back then,' he said.

Marilyn looked pained. 'Oh, please!' she said. 'Give me a break. You knew yourself well enough to come to me and admit that you needed help, because you were a bald impotent workaholic . . .'

'Oh God,' Doug muttered as the heads at nearby tables turned in astonishment. He wondered if he could – in this crowd – try to pass this off as some sort of audition for a soap opera.

Marilyn didn't even seem to notice the attention they were attracting. She simply kept on in the same vein. '. . . who couldn't even think about sex without breaking wind!'

Doug snagged the arm of a passing waiter. 'Could I get the bill please?' he said, trying to keep a note of desperation out of his voice. What he really wanted to do was crawl under the table until Marilyn had finished her tirade and left the restaurant.

'Marilyn,' he hissed, 'I really don't think this is the time or place.'

'Oh, yes, it is!' she retorted angrily. 'If you're going to lay something like this on me in public, I'm going to tell you exactly what's on my mind!' She stared at him for a beat, then said in a more reasonable tone: 'You were a mess, Douglas, and I changed all that.'

'Overwrought,' Doug said frantically. 'I told you I'm overwrought . . .'

'I made you happy; we made each *other* happy!' Marilyn's voice was rising again.

'Shh!' Doug said.

'No!' Marilyn looked too angry to be fighting back tears, but she was clearly distraught. 'I helped you become what you are, Douglas. For the first time in your life, you've been able to have gas-free intercourse!'

'Marilyn,' Doug moaned, as a woman at the next table gaped, wide-eyed. 'Please . . .' This was definitely not going the way Arnie had promised it would.

162

'Please *what*?' She demanded. 'This is the end? Are you kidding? You owe me a lot more than this, Doug.'

'I'm sorry . . .'

'You should be!' She glared angrily at him, not giving an inch.

Doug summoned all the courage he could find. 'Marilyn,' he said softly. 'It's over. It really is. And I really *am* sorry.'

'I'm sorry, too,' Marilyn said. She got up abruptly, her napkin floating to the floor. 'You are not an honest man, Doug Brackman . . .'

Doug cringed. Now everyone in hearing range would know exactly who he was.

'You lie to yourself,' Marilyn continued, 'and you lied to me. And that's even worse is that this doesn't even sound like you. It's like you read some article in the *Playboy* advice column on how to get rid of an unwanted lover.' Now she *did* seem to be struggling to keep back the tears. 'That, or you talked to Arnie Becker to get some pointers from him.'

Doug reddened.

'Never mind,' Marilyn said, picking up her purse. 'It doesn't even matter at this point. You're a liar, and I'm leaving.'

She turned on her heel and strode rapidly to the door, then disappeared into the sunlit afternoon. Doug rested his head in his hands. Thanks a lot, Arnie, he thought. He heard a discreet cough, and looked up to see his waiter at his side. 'Will you be having any dessert today?' he asked.

*

163

'I'm not sure if having Lobel on the bench is going to help or hurt us,' Arnie whispered to Abby as they took their places in civil court. True to his word, Leland had phoned the judge and promptly set up a hearing at which they could discuss Benny's sudden conversion and the money it entailed.

Also present were the founders and leaders of the so-called Children of God sect. Arnie's face was set in a frown of disapproval as he glared at the sweet-looking middle-aged couple who had identified themselves as Herbert and Elaine Rose. Their turbans looked about as natural to them as Benny's did to him. Their lawyer, Lawrence Bradley, had just identified himself to the judge. Only Benny wasn't present – a fact which Abby found fairly discomforting. After all, this had to do with him, not with them. And he wasn't so retarded that he couldn't make lots of decisions for himself. She whispered her doubts to Arnie.

'Listen,' he said softly, 'no one is disputing that, But you and I know that people like this can rip off other people who are . . . well, even if they're just naive. Come on, Abby, we're protecting Benny. If this all proves to be above board – something which I personally doubt – then fine. Let him go ahead and walk around looking like he's been in the neuropsychiatric ward. All I'm doing here is trying to help.'

'I know,' Abby agreed with a sigh. 'It's just that it seems somehow . . . well, *unfair*.'

Lawrence Bradley's introduction finished, Judge Lobel wasted no time. His lined dour face annoyed, he spoke.

'Mr Becker, I'm not sure I understand this complaint,' he

said.

Arnie stood up respectfully. He and Lobel had crossed swords a few times in the past, and he was taking care to appear attentive, thoughtful and as serious as the occasion warranted. 'Your Honour,' he began, 'based upon certain information and beliefs, we are convinced that the contract entered into between Benjamin Stulwicz and Herbert and Elaine Rose of the Temple of the Children of God was done so fraudulently. We further believe that the Roses clearly took advantage of Mr Stulwicz's retardation when they enticed him to join their cult —'

Bradley stood up. 'Your honour, I object,' he said forcefully. 'I happen to be a member of the Children of God myself. We are a recognised religious organisation, not a cult. And on behalf of my clients, as well as personally, I deeply resent both being called a cult and the false assertion that we prey on the retarded.'

Judge Lobel considered the lawyer's assertion seriously.

'Your Honour,' Arnie countered quickly, 'we certainly aren't in court to offend anyone. All we are doing is seeking the return of Mr Stulwicz's thousand-dollar membership fee, feeling as we do that Mr Stulwicz isn't able to grasp the importance of that kind of investment. And, further, we seek the protection of his pledge of wages for the same reasons.'

Lobel frowned again, this time the creases in his face deepening even more. 'I can read, Mr Becker,' the judge said. 'I know exactly what you're requesting. But what I don't understand is why you and Ms Perkins are plaintiffs. Are you two the conservators for Mr Stulwicz?

Abby rose. 'No, your Honour,' she said. 'But we are

165

seeking temporary conservatorship.'

Judge Lobel regarded them quizzically, anger barely hidden under the surface. 'Ms Perkins, Mr Becker, I'm sure that both of you are aware that Mr Kuzak of your law firm was before this bench two years ago, arguing that Mr Stulwicz was fully capable of exercising his right to vote. Are you now saying that he is capable of deciding what's good for this country, but not for himself?'

Dammit, Abby thought. 'Your Honour, we honestly feel that we are acting in Mr Stulwicz's best interests —'

The judge cut her off with an abrupt motion. 'Mr Bradley,' he said sternly, 'I have a question for you.'

'Yes, your Honour?'

'For a thousand dollars initial fee and forty-five dollars a week that Mr Stulwicz has pledged to you, what exactly do you give him in return?'

'Companionship,' Bradley said promptly. 'Spiritual guidance. And the conviction of his faith.'

Arnie stifled an expletive.

'Right,' said Judge Lobel, nodding.

'Your Honour,' Bradley said, 'before you decide, we'd like to put a witness on the stand. We'd like to put Benjamin Stulwicz up.'

'Objection,' Arnie said, outraged.

'Overruled,' Judge Lobel said promptly. 'I happen to think that that's an excellent idea.' His glance swung from Bradley to Arnie. 'Since I don't totally trust either one of you,' he said grimly, 'I'd like to hear what the man says for himself. Tomorrow. Ten o'clock.' Then he banged his gavel and left the court.

'Great,' muttered Arnie. 'We've got some quick coach-

166

ing to do.'

*

'How did it go with Benny's hearing?' Rozanne asked Abby a few hours later in the ladies' room.

Abby shrugged, tired out at the end of another long day. 'He's putting Benny on the witness-stand tomorrow,' she said. 'I'm not exactly sure if I think that's a good thing or a bad thing.'

Roxanne nodded in agreement with the decision. 'I think it's a good thing,' she said. 'After all, he's a person, Abby – a very decent, nice person. Just because he doesn't think as fast as the rest of us is no reason why he can't make up his mind about things that are important to him personally.'

'I know,' Abby sighed. 'I'm really torn about this. I mean, I think Benny's perfectly capable of a lot of things, too. But whenever I'm face to face with one of those weird pseudo-religious cults the hair on the back of my neck just goes up. I can't help feeling that they're just out to take advantage of people. They're like well-organized con artists.'

'In turbans,' Roxanne added, applying fresh lip-liner. 'I wonder if we'd feel so threatened if they just wore normal clothes like the rest of us.'

Abby smiled. 'Who knows?' she said. She looked appraisingly at Roxanne. 'Are you going out with Sandy tonight?' she asked.

Roxanne smiled. 'Yes,' she said. 'He actually seems like a nice guy, and at least we have something in common, even if it is only fathers with Alzheimer's.' She regarded

167

her reflection critically. 'How about you and . . . what was his name again?'

'Gene,' Abby sighed. 'He's cute, but, God, how long can you listen to someone talk about the newest tax guidelines and their applications?'

Roxanne laughed. 'Sounds like David,' she said, referring to her former husband. 'And I wouldn't wish that on anyone.'

Abby shrugged. 'Actually', she said, 'he asked me out for tonight, and I was thinking of giving him one more chance. I mean, some people just get nervous on dates.'

'So?'

'I promised Arnie I'd help him get Benny ready to go before the judge tomorrow, and that means getting up extra early so that I can drop Eric at school and get to the office before anyone else is here. I'm too beat to think about going out.'

A peculiar expression crossed Roxanne's face. 'Abby,' she said impulsively, 'I think you'd better call Gene back and accept, and just tell Arnie to take care of this himself.'

Abby looked startled. 'Why would I do that?' she asked.

'Because you work too damned hard here, you don't get out and have enough fun . . .'

'I know all that,' Abby agreed ruefully, 'believe me! But come on, Roxanne, you know I'm working my ass off to make partner this year.'

Roxanne wrestled with her conscience for a minute, then remembered how good a friend Abby had been to her in the past. It was time to repay the favour, even if it meant breaking bad news to the overworked lawyer. 'But, Abby, that's just it,' Roxanne said unhappily. 'It's not going to happen.

At least, not this year.'

'Excuse me?' Abby said, blinking in disbelief. 'Rox, what are you talking about?'

Roxanne took a deep breath and plunged in. 'I don't know how to tell you this tactfully, but I think you have the right to know before you go sacrificing any more of your life to this firm, so I'm just going to tell you. This morning, Doug's new secretary was typing up the minutes of the partners' meeting the other day. I peeped at it while she was answering the phone.' She regarded Abby's alarmed face in the mirror and wished there was a kinder way to do this. 'They voted on the new partners, Abby. Victor's in. You're out.'

The colour drained out of Abby's face, leaving it pale and stunned. 'Are you . . . absolutely certain?' she asked finally.

Roxanne nodded. 'I'm sorry,' she said, 'but it's true.'

'But . . . that can't be right,' Abby said weakly. 'It doesn't make sense. *Why?*'

Might as well be hanged for a sheep as for a lamb, Roxanne thought. Besides, she was outraged at the treatment Abby – who worked harder than anyone else in the firm – was receiving at the hands of her colleagues. 'It seems as though . . . well, the feeling is that you don't have the profile to bring in clients.'

'Profile?' Abby echoed. 'Are you kidding? What about all the *work* I do? What about the hours I put in?'

Roxanne nodded in agreement. 'I know,' she said. 'But the upshot is that you aren't being invited into the inner circle. I probably should have kept my mouth shut, but I just think it's so damned unfair!'

Abby shook her head incredulously. 'But I had lunch with Ann today,' she said. 'Why on earth didn't she tell me? We're such close friends.'

Roxanne's lip curled in disgust. 'They decided to keep it a secret until March the fifteenth,' she said. 'Apparently they don't want to spook the women law students they've got offers out to.'

It hardly seemed possible, but Abby's face got paler. Then a crimson flash of anger suffused her fair complexion. 'Those bastards,' she said softly. 'Those incredible lying bastards.'

'Yes,' said Roxanne, 'they are.' She put a hand on Abby's arm. 'Oh God, Abby, I'm so sorry. Maybe they'll . . . change their minds.'

Abby's face was suddenly filled with furious resolution. 'They want profile?' she snapped angrily. 'Oh, boy, are they going to get it!'

'What are you going to do?' Roxanne asked, a little alarmed at Abby's vehemence.

A grim smile crossed Abby's pretty face. 'Keep a close eye on your television set,' she told Roxanne, 'and you'll see.'

Chapter Fourteen

'I can't understand it,' Arnie fumed, checking his watch for the umpteenth time. 'Where the hell is Abby? She knows what we have to do this morning, and she's *never* late!'

Benny, who sat nervously slumped on the couch in Arnie's office, shrugged. 'Maybe she had to do something with Eric at school,' he said.

Arnie sighed. 'That's whole trouble with trying to have a career and juggle a family at the same time,' he said, thinking gratefully that Corrinne was one of those rare women who seemed to be perfectly fulfilled being a full-time wife and mother. Although, if she brought up the subject of talking to (read *firing*) Roxanne one more time, he might just suggest that she go out and at least do volunteer work to keep her mind off what happened at his office. Then he thought about Gwen and the potential complications there, and shuddered inwardly. He checked his watch yet again, fuming.

'Arnie?' Roxanne tapped at the door and poked her head into the office. 'Oh, hi, Benny,' she said cheerfully, 'I didn't know you were here already.'

Benny nodded unhappily. 'Yeah,' he said with a characteristic shrug. 'Arnie wanted me to get here early so we could talk about what I have to say to the judge in court.'

'Are you a little nervous?' Roxanne asked sympathetically.

'Yeah,' Benny replied, staring down at the floor. 'I don't want to go to court.' Then he looked accusingly up at Arnie. 'I really don't want to go talk to the judge,' he reiterated.

'Benny, come on, you know you have to go,' Arnie reminded him. 'We talked about this before. You got a subpoena.'

A look akin to fright crossed Benny's face. 'But I didn't do anything, honest.'

'No, of course, you didn't, Benny,' Roxanne reassured him. 'We all know that, and the judge knows it, too.' She came all the way into the office and sat beside him on the couch, patting his hand comfortingly. 'Getting a subpoena doesn't mean that at all. It just means that the judge wants to talk to you. Or he wants to hear your side of the story.'

'What story?' Benny asked, puzzled.

Arnie tried to think of an objective way of presenting Benny with the problem. 'Why you joined that . . . He wants to know why you joined the Temple of the Children of God.' He looked at his watch again. 'Jesus,' he said, 'where the hell is Abby? I need her to help me out here.'

'Oh!' Roxanne exclaimed, flushing a little guilty. 'I'm sorry. That's what I came in here to tell you. She called to say that she'd be late; something urgent came up. She'll meet you at the courthouse.'

'Oh, great,' Arnie muttered. 'That's just great. We've got to coach Benny . . .'

'Ah . . . do you want me to help?' Roxanne offered.

Arnie smiled and shook his head. 'No, Rox, but thanks. I

172

guess Benny and I can hash it all out before we have to leave for court. I just hope Abby turns up on time there; Judge Lobel is a real stickler about promptness.'

Roxanne reddened slightly and bit down on her knuckle. 'Arnie, I . . .' Roxanne started to say something. 'I . . . ah . . . oh! There goes the phone!' And suddenly she was gone. Arnie looked after her, a little puzzled. He wondered what on earth had rattled his usually efficient and precise secretary so much this morning. Roxanne had seemed really preoccupied. Oh, well, he thought, it was probably about Murray: she certainly had her hands full there. But thinking about Roxanne's problems just led back to thinking about Corrinne's problems, and the last thing Arnie wanted to do was give that unpleasant subject any more thought. Time to go to work, he told himself.

'OK, Benny,' Arnie said briskly, 'it looks like it's just us guys. So why don't we go over this again from the top?'

'OK,' Benny said, looking miserable.

'Now,' said Arnie, 'tell me exactly why you joined the Temple.'

'So that when I die I'll live with God,' Benny replied promptly.

Arnie studied Benny's face and felt a pang of genuine compassion. 'Well,' he asked gently, 'what happens to you after you die if you don't join the cult?'

A look of fear passed over Benny's face. 'I go to the devil,' he said nervously. 'And he sticks me with a great big fork.'

Arnie rolled his eyes. Maybe convincing the judge that undue influence had been used here would be easy after all. 'Did they tell you that?' he asked. 'The people from the

Temple?' Those bastards, he added silently.

'Kind of.' Benny shrugged. 'Anyway, they said that I'd go to hell.' He looked at Arnie. 'Isn't that the same thing?'

Arnie sighed. 'To some people I guess it is,' he said. 'But, Benny, listen to me; this is really important. Personally I think that it's kind of a fib, and I also think everyone has the right to make up his or her own mind about it. I mean, if there really *is* a heaven and a hell, then don't you think that the only thing that would really make a difference about you getting in is if you are a good person?' Listen to me, he thought, giving lessons in theology.

'I . . . I dunno,' Benny said. But he seemed to be considering the merits of the idea.

'Well, think about it this way,' Arnie continued. 'Your mom died, and you would say that she was a good person, right?'

Benny nodded with conviction. 'Of course she was. She was a *really* good person. She always took care of me.'

'Yes,' said Arnie gently, 'she did. Now, your mother wasn't a member of the Temple of the Children of God, was she?'

'No,' Benny said, shaking his head negatively. 'Sometimes she went to Catholic church,' he added. 'But not too often. Usually only at Easter for the Sunrise service at the Hollywood Bowl; she thought that was really beautiful.'

Arnie nodded. 'And don't you think that she's in heaven?'

Benny looked startled; then, as the implications of the question became clear to him, upset. 'Yes, she is!' He nodded vigorously. 'She has to be!' he said. 'She couldn't

174

be with the devil!'

'OK,' Arnie said soothingly, 'I agree with you. And that's exactly the point I was trying to make. I don't think you have to belong to a church or pay money to one to stay out of hell.'

'Good, 'cause my mon couldn't be there,' Benny repeated, relieved.

'Besides,' Arnie continued on a more pragmatic note, 'you pledged all this money to them. Did they talk about that?'

'What do you mean?' Benny asked. 'They told me how all that money would be used to help the Temple and its membership, and I'm a member.'

'Yes, but did they bother to tell you how you're going to live and pay your rent and eat on forty-five dollars less every week?'

A look somewhere between stubbornness and naive faith crossed Benny's face. 'God will provide,' he said sanctimoniously.

'Oh Christ!' Arnie muttered. Why wasn't Abby here? He forced himself to remain calm. 'OK, look,' he said. 'We've known you and we've been your friends a lot longer than these Temple people have, right?'

'Right,' Benny agreed, a little suspiciously.

'And you know that nobody in this office would lie to you, don't you?'

Benny nodded reluctantly.

'Benny,' Arnie said as kindly as he could, 'you're retarded. We don't say it or talk about it very often, and we don't think about it a lot, either. But it's a fact.'

'I know,' Benny said.

'The ugly truth is, Benny, that there are people out there who *look* for guys like you because you're an easy mark.' Arnie saw a look of confusion cross Benny's face, and elaborated. 'They know they can win your trust. They think they can steal your money, and you won't even know it. As a matter of fact, they *count* on the fact that you'll still think that they're your friends even *after* they rip you off.'

'But they *are* my friends!' Benny insisted. He stared at Arnie, hurt and angry at what he was being asked to believe. 'Rose and the others, they're all so nice, and they want me to come to meetings and be with them – not just during working hours, but afterwards, too! They *are* my friends, Arnie!'

'No,' Arnie insisted, even though it was difficult to continue in the face of Benny's pain. 'They really aren't. Friends don't ask other friends to pay them so they can hang around together.'

'I . . . I dunno,' Benny said, retreating into himself. 'I dunno what you're really talking about.'

'Listen to me, Benny. *Please*.' Arnie looked at his watch again. They were due in court shortly, and somehow he *had* to convince Benny that their position was the right one. 'When we go to court, you're going to tell the judge that you made a mistake.' Benny looked mutinous, but Arnie continued. 'You're going to tell him that you were confused when you signed that piece of paper pledging your money to them, do you understand me?'

Benny shrugged. 'I dunno,' he said.

'You have to trust us here. Come on, Benny, help me on this,' Arnie pleaded. Benny's expression softened, and Arnie sighed in relief. He'd got through to him after all. He

176

pointed to a piece of paper. 'OK,' he said, 'these are the questions the judge is going to ask you. And this is what you're going to say. Pay attention.'

*

Victor watched as Grace approached her fourth witness of the morning. It must have taken a miracle of sorts, but she had actually been able to produce four former colleagues of Rosalind Shays who were willing to stand up in front of God, the court and everybody else, and talk about the uniformly miserable experiences they had had working with the woman.

Grace had made short but effective work of the testimonies of the previous three, and even Jack Sollers hadn't been able to shake their statements and descriptions, or – more dangerous – to prove that any one of them had any ongoing personal motive for impugning Rosalind Shays. Grace had done a brilliant job, Victor thought. Every one of the witnesses so far had weathered working with Shays, and hadn't suffered career setbacks or lost out on promotions; so Sollers didn't really have a leg to stand on, although he kept trying to imply that personal grudges were playing a large part in their willingness to come forward today. Victor glanced at the jury: they looked as though they were buying exactly what Grace wanted them to buy.

Well, he thought ruefully, how nice for everyone. Grace was having a terrific day. McKenzie Brackman was having a good day. The jury was entranced. Only he, Victor Sifuentes, was having a truly shitty day, unless you counted Roz and Jack Sollers, and he didn't give a damn *what* kind of day they were having – the worse for them, the better for everyone else.

But talk about avoidance, Victor thought glumly; Grace had it down to a science. She had managed to arrive in court literally two minutes before Judge Travelini appeared, which gave her just enough time for a hastily whispered conference with Leland and Doug, and absolutely no time to do anything other than say a cursory hello to Victor, snap open her briefcase and approach the bench. Since then, she had acknowledged Victor as little as possible without giving anyone else in court the impression that there was anything wrong at the defence table. Grace looked pleasant, composed and utterly distant.

'Now, Mr Garland,' Grace said to the last of the four witnesses – the Gang of Four, as she had jokingly called them. 'Could you please tell the court exactly how Ms Shays managed to create the impression with your client that she could provide more effective representation than you?' This was safe territory: Grace had a written affidavit from the client in question, who had come crawling back to Ralph Garland after he learned how he'd been lied to and manipulated.

And on and on it went, while Victor sat, outwardly calm and inwardly as stormy as the North Sea. What the hell had he done? And what was he going to do? He glanced up as Grace returned to the defence table to find yet another affidavit, and tried to read something other than a certain blank coolness in her eyes. But there was nothing to be read.

When Grace finished with her witness, Victor was determined to make some sort of personal contact, some sort of apology – even if he had to do it while Jack Sollers attempted to bully the witness in cross examination.

'Thank you, that will be all,' said Grace. She headed back to the defence table.

'Mr Sollers?' said Judge Travelini.

'No questions, your Honour,' Sollers replied.

'Then, we'll adjourn,' said Judge Travelini.

Victor groaned silently as Grace busily swept up the papers on the table and hustled out of the courtroom. Dodging through the McKenzie Brackman staff to follow her into the hall, he caught up with her just as the elevator doors opened and Michael Kuzak emerged. All three of them seemed to freeze in their tracks.

Grace recovered first. 'Well, Mickey,' she said sweetly. 'And Victor.' She glanced from one to the other. 'How cosy.' She glanced down at her watch, then up at them. 'Gee,' she said, 'I'd love to stay and chat, but I'm late for an appointment.' She smiled thinly. 'But I'm sure that's OK with you two – you seem to have so much to talk about these days.' And she swept into the elevator and punched the down button, laving Victor and Michael in the hallway together.

'So', said Michael heartily, as Doug and Leland converged on them, 'how did it go this morning?'

*

Benny was as nervous as he could be. All the coaching Arnie had done just an hour before hadn't convinced him that being in front of a judge did not mean that something terrible was about to happen. He fidgeted in the witness-box while the Rose's attorney, Bradley, questioned him.

'Now, Benny,' said Bradley, 'you first met the Roses

179

when you went to their church – is that correct?'

Benny glanced at Arnie, who nodded slightly. 'Yes,' said Benny.

Abby arrived just then, a little out of breath. 'Sorry,' she whispered to Arnie, 'something came up.'

Arnie nodded silently, intent on what was happening in front of him. This was no time to question Abby about her tardiness.

'And it's true, isn't it, that *you* asked *them* how you could join the temple?'

Benny nodded. 'I was confused. I want my money back.'

Arnie sat bolt upright. This wasn't the time for Benny to be saying that; that response was intended for later in the proceedings.

'What?' Bradley asked, puzzled. 'You were confused?'

'I didn't know what I was doing,' Benny said by rote. 'I want my money back.'

'Uh-oh,' Arnie murmured.

'I want my money back,' Benny said. 'It's a cult. I was confused.'

'Oh, no . . .,' Arnie said, standing up. 'Your Honour,' he began, 'Mr Stulwicz is obviously distraught . . .'

'Sit down, Counsellor,' Judge Lobel said sternly. Then he turned to Benny. 'Did Mr Becker tell you what to say today?' he asked gently.

Benny nodded. 'Yes.'

'Objection!' Arnie said.

'I was confused.'

'Overruled!' the judge said sharply. Then he spoke to Benny again. 'All right, Mr Stulwicz,' he said, 'that's OK. But now I want you just to forget what Mr Becker said, do

180

you understand?'

'Uh-huh,' Benny said nervously.

'Good,' said the judge. 'Now, you're under oath, and that means you have to tell the truth. You understand that, don't you?'

'Yeah,' said Benny.

'Fine. Now, when you signed that piece of paper, did you know that it would mean you'd have to pay a thousand dollars to the Temple, and that they would get forty-five dollars from your salary every week? Did you understand that?'

'Yes,' Benny said.

'Dammit,' Arnie swore under his breath. Beside him, Abby looked concerned at the direction this was taking.

'Then, you *weren't* confused, were you?' Judge Lobel pressed.

Arnie stood up. 'Objection, your Honour!' he exclaimed. 'He's confused right *now*!'

'Sit down!' Judge Lobel ordered him. He turned to the witness-box again. 'Now, Mr Stulwicz, I hope you're aware how serious it is to lie under oath.'

This time it was Bradley who stood up. 'Your Honour,' he said, 'I would move for sanctions against Mr Becker for this patently unscrupulous coaching!'

'*You're* going to try to tell *me* tell about unscrupulous!' Arnie said, infuriated. 'Look at you people, for Christ's sake! Sticking a bonnet on his head like that . . .'

'It's not a bonnet!' Bradley retorted angrily.

'Mr Becker. Mr Bradley, 'the judge began.

'Ask the witness about getting stuck with a big fork by the devil if he doesn't join their phoney church and buy his

181

way into heaven, your Honour!' Arnie exclaimed, his voice loud and angry.

'What are you *talking* about?' Bradley demanded, astonished.

'What's that if not blatant coercion?' Arnie demanded.

'We did no such thing!' Bradley shouted.

'All right!' Judge Lobel interjected sharply. 'I've heard quite enough from both of you!'

Neither lawyer seemed to agree, or maybe they simply didn't hear the judge. A humming noise had started coming from the witness-box; but Abby, sitting worriedly at the plaintiff's table, couldn't make out what it was over the legal shouting going on in front of her.

'For God's sake, he's retarded!' Arnie yelled, pointing at Benny. 'How can you do this?'

'You're a flat-out liar!' Bradley shouted back. 'You don't know what the hell you're talking about!'

'Ommm paaaa maaa naay, ommm paaah naa maay . . .'

Abby finally realised that Benny was chanting, just as he had when he'd got nervous in the conference room, trying to defend his decision to join the Temple.

'Ooom paaa naa maay . . .'

Oh, no, Abby thought.

'Mr Stulwicz,' said Judge Lobel, suddenly realising that strange noises were emanating from the witness-box, 'what is it that you're trying to say?'

Benny was obviously blocking it all out. 'Oommm paah naaa maaay . . .', he droned, his eyes shut.

'Please note the rote-like chanting for the record!' Arnie said sharply.

'Objection to rote-like characterisation!' Bradley yelled

over the increasingly loud sounds.

'Mr Stulwicz,' Judge Lobel said, his voice rising, too, 'please stop *whatever* it is you're doing – we're in a courtroom!'

'It's like he's been brainwashed!' Arnie snapped.

'Objection!' Bradley yelled.

'Look at him! *Listen* to him!' Arnie stared at Benny, dismayed. 'For God's sake, if that isn't the result of brainwashing, then it must be hypnosis!'

'Objection!'

'Benny, please stop this!' Abby said, rising and approaching the witness-box. Someone had to help Benny, she thought, and with all the shouting and objecting that was going on he was probably just getting more and more scared of what was going to happen. 'Benny,' she tried again, 'please stop; it's OK. Really.'

Judge Lobel looked at Benny, whose eyes were still squeezed tightly shut. The chanting wouldn't stop. Then the judge looked sharply at Bradley, then at Arnie and Abby. 'I've seen quite enough, Counsellors,' he said shortly. 'I'll take this under advisement. Please be back here at four o'clock this afternoon. Until then, court adjourned!'

Chapter Fifteen

Jonathan approached the courtroom that afternoon with considerable trepidation, not at all diminished by his own seemingly shifting feelings about being part of the Chisolm case. He'd been angry and recalcitrant from the very beginning and, he felt rightfully so. The firm – Michael and Leland anyway – had admitted that he was being put on display in this trial simply because he was a black lawyer. It was manipulative and offensive to Jonathan. But over the past several days Jonathan had seen behaviour in the courtroom which had shocked him to the core. It was behaviour which forced him to think more than once about the kind of justice Brian Chisolm was likely to get under these circus-like conditions.

The jury selection had been so biased that it was a joke: Judge Walter Stone had set the tenor of the trial by showing such blatant favouritism to the plaintiff's side that Michael had clashed and shouted, and finally come right out and accused Stone of being unable to withstand the pressures surrounding this case. And, according to office gossip, it wasn't an unfair accusation, either.

Even Jonathan, reluctant to see anything wrong with the proceedings, had to admit that the jury selection had been ridiculous, and that Stone, obviously afraid of political fall-out from this charged case, was bowing to the pressure. In this case, the pressure was coming from Derron Holloway, which was a change. But that didn't make it any more right or any more ethical.

Last night, unable to sleep, he'd been staring at the ceiling looking for answers, but none had come. Then Diana had nudged him gently and asked what was wrong. 'Wait,' she said, 'let me take a wild guess. It's the Chisolm case, isn't it?'

'Of course,' Jonathan sighed. He rolled over to face her, and saw that she, too, was wide awake. 'Thanks for not beating me up over this,' he said.

She smiled at him understandingly. 'Know what?' she said. 'Maybe the reason I'm not beating up on you is because I don't think it's wrong for you to be on this case.'

Jonathan looked at her in astonishment. 'Are you kidding?' he asked. 'I'm sitting there at the defence table looking black, letting myself be exploited. What can be right about that?'

Diana shrugged. 'Don't you think that Derron Holloway's exploiting things just a little, too?'

Jonathan shook his head, 'No,' he said. 'Well, yes,' he amended. 'But he's doing it to make a point. What's *my* point?'

Diana sat up. 'I'm not sure that there *is* a point, for you,' she admitted. 'But I'm *also* not sure you should be feeling guilty about the side you're on.' She looked at him seriously. 'Listen to me, Jonathan,' she said, 'Derron Holloway may speak up for minorities, but he is also a rabble-rouser and a blatant rejectionist.'

'His methods are a little offensive sometimes,' Jonathan admitted. 'But I think he manages to do some good sometimes, too.'

Diana shrugged. 'Yes,' she agreed, 'he does. But mostly he gets a lot of publicity and a lot of cheers, when all he offers up is a lot of rage.'

Jonathan thought about it for a moment. 'Sometimes rage is a start.'

'But look what it started this time,' Diana pointed out. 'A public demand for a conviction, no matter what. Innocent or guilty, there'd better be a conviction to keep the peace. That's what Holloway has started. And, worse,' she said soberly, 'that's what Stone and the DA seem to be giving in to.'

Jonathan shook his head. 'Maybe,' he said. 'But I certainly don't know that Brian Chisolm is innocent.'

'The point is,' Diana told him, 'whether he is or isn't, it seems to be totally irrelevant to what's happening in that court.'

Now, in the light of day, as Jonathan walked through the doors to the courtroom and joined Michael at the defence table, he thought about what Diana had said. And he found himself agreeing, at least in principle, that the process of justice was being subverted here. And that was wrong.

'Here,' he said in a whisper, handing the deposition of Brian Chisolm's partner to Michael. 'Sorry it took so long.'

DA Marcia Fusco was in the middle of her opening speech to the jury. '. . . and Officer Chisolm *claims* he was fired on first, by two unknown drug-dealers. But, ladies and gentlemen, there is absolutely no evidence to suggest that these alleged drug-dealers ever existed. No stray bullets were found, and although Mr Chisolm never took a lie-detector test —'

'Objection!' Michael roared, leaping to his feet.

'Ms Fusco,' Judge Stone admonished her, 'you know better than that. Members of the jury will disregard that statement. Whether or not the accused took a polygraph is of no relevance.'

Michael moved closer. 'Move for a mistrial,' he said.

'Approach,' Judge Stone told the lawyers. 'You're not getting a mistrial,' he said in a hiss.

'What?' Michael said, outraged. 'You can't allow —'

'She didn't say he failed it, Mr Kuzak . . .'

'She implied he refused to take it!'

'She did no such thing,' Judge Stone retorted. 'I see no prejudice.'

'This is outrageous!' Michael said.

'You keep your voice down, Counsellor.' Judge Stone looked extremely angry.

Michael didn't. 'You let Holloway grandstand,' he said loudly, 'you let biased jurors be seated, and now this . . .'

'Your motion is denied,' the judge said loudly. 'Ms Fusco, continue.'

Michael sat down beside Jonathan, so furious that he was practically vibrating. 'What are you going to do?' Jonathan whispered as Fusco came to the end of her statement, finishing with a dramatic promise to prove that Brian Chisolm was a murderer. Jonathan had to side with Michael on this one: allowing the trial to go forward after Fusco prejudiced the jury with her seemingly innocent reference to the polygraph test was unconscionable. But, then, Judge Stone didn't seem to have a hell of a lot of conscience to begin with.

'Watch,' Michael said grimly. Then he arose and faced

the jury. He paused dramatically in front of the jury-box, then began.

'Serving justice,' he said, 'that's why we're here.' He looked at each of them. 'The problem is, it's premissed on the assumption that we have impartial jurors and a fair judge. Well,' he said with a shrug, 'I have to tell you that after the jury selection process I have my doubts about you – the jurors . . .'

'What's he doing?' Brian Chisolm whispered to Jonathan in a voice filled with panic.

Michael pointed to Stone. '. . . but none at all about that big chicken bastard up there in the robes!'

Jonathan felt his jaw drop.

'Oh my God!' Brian Chisolm said.

'Mr Kuzak!' Judge Stone roared. 'You're in contempt! Bailiff! Take him into custody!'

'This man', Michael said in a loud clear voice, his finger still pointing at Stone, 'only cares about one thing: getting his sleazy lazy ass re-elected!' As the bailiff approached and grabbed his arms, he continued, his voice even louder: 'Staying on Holloway's good side so he doesn't get reamed in the press!'

'Oh Jesus,' Brian Chisolm said. For the first time, Jonathan felt a pang of genuine pity for the man.

As Michael was dragged from court, he continued to rant. 'Got to call a mistrial now, Judge! You've got no choice!'

In the stunned silence that followed Michael's exit, the judge took stock of the situation. 'Members of the jury,' he said, clearing his throat, 'Mr Kuzak just tried – and failed – to get this trial called off for reasons that have nothing to do

188

with the issue before you.' He looked straight at Jonathan. 'Mr Rollins, you will please continue.'

'*What?*' Jonathan couldn't believe his ears.

'Your Honour,' DA Fusco protested, 'under the circumstances —'

'No!' Stone yelled, turning on her. 'Mr Kuzak isn't going to get his way on this. Mr Rollins, pick up where he left off.'

'You can't be serious,' Jonathan began.

'Quite serious.' Judge Stone glared at him, while all around, the press, the jury and the curiosity-seekers murmured their disbelief. 'Pick up where he left off *now!*'

Jonathan's head was spinning; it was a jumble of his own ambivalence, of Michael's *real* intent in getting himself dragged out of court, of the disgusting behaviour of the judge on the bench in front of him. He saw Brian Chisolm staring at him, quite obviously frightened that Jonathan, who hadn't exactly kept his feelings about the case under wraps, was going to let him hang. Last night's conversation with Diana echoing in his head, he abruptly made up his mind and stood up.

'All right,' he said amiably. He looked at the jury, then directly at Stone. 'To pick up where my learned colleague left off, your Honour,' he said, 'you are indeed a big chicken bastard who is only worried about re-election —'

'You're in contempt, too!' Stone roared in shock. 'Bailiff! Take this man away!'

'But he forgot a couple of things!' Jonathan shouted over the noisy furore that had erupted in the court. The bailiff grabbed his arm and began to lead him out. 'He forgot to call you a stupid bastard!' Jonathan declared. And he forgot' – the doors opened before him, and over his shoulder, Jonathan yelled – 'to ask you who you bribed to get the robe!'

*

'OK, Benny. Now, don't worry about this; there's absolutely no reason to panic here,' Arnie assured him with a desperate look at Abby. They were about to go before Judge Lobel for what Arnie sincerely hoped would be the last time – he couldn't handle another scene like the one in court this morning. And it didn't help matters that Abby had been strangely reticent, almost distant. Obviously, Arnie thought, she was preoccupied with her own problems, but why did she have to bring them to work with her?

'Benny,' Abby said, suddenly snapping to attention and putting a friendly hand on Benny's arm, 'Arnie's right. There's nothing to be scared of. This is going to be quick and easy, you'll see.'

'Oh . . . OK,' Benny said hesitantly. But Abby could see that he was still nervous.

'Listen,' she said, 'the only thing that's going to be decided in there this afternoon is if you get your money back from the Temple or not.'

Benny stared at her, puzzled and upset. 'But I don't care about that,' he said.

'We know you don't,' Arnie told him, 'but we think you need some protection from this kind of thing. Like we talked about in the office, remember?'

'Uh-huh,' Benny said.

Looking at Benny, Abby realised she still had some

190

doubts about what they were doing. But she kept them to herself; at this point, it was a little late to switch sides. The bailiff came to the door of the courtroom and motioned them in. Once inside, they stood behind the plaintiff's table and waited for Judge Lobel, who looked positively grim, to deliver his opinion on the case. At the defence table, the Roses and their attorney, Bradley, also stood.

'I have considered this matter very carefully,' Judge Lobel said, coming right to the point. 'And, for all the evidence put before me, I have to say that I see no real proof that Mr Stulwicz was acting under undue influence when he signed the financial agreement with the Temple of the Children of God.'

Abby felt Arnie stiffen in dismay beside her.

'In fact,' the judge continued, looking directly at Abby and Arnie, 'if there is anybody in this courtroom who is guilty of any sort of brainwashing, it was more than likely Mr Becker and Ms Perkins.'

Abby felt a little tremor of shock run through her. She might have had her doubts about what they were doing, but she certainly hadn't expected to be reprimanded in this manner.

Judge Lobel continued to stare sombrely at Arnie and Abby. 'Counsellors,' he said, 'your behaviour here was contemptible. Mr Stulwicz clearly trusts you. And you repaid that trust by bringing suit without so much as consulting him about the matter.'

'But, your Honour . . .' Arnie protested. 'We thought we were doing what was best . . .'

'I'm not through,' the judge told him sharply. 'You obviously both coached and somehow coerced him, and it's quite clear that you got him to recite rehearsed answers up here. In short,' he said, his mouth set in a grim line, 'it was the two of *you* who treated him as an object to be manipulated, instead of a person to be cared for. And it doesn't matter a tinker's damm to me if you thought you had his best interests in mind. What you did was still wrong.'

Abby felt herself sag a little under the indictment; the worst part about it was that she didn't entirely disagree with Judge Lobel – he was actually voicing some of the same doubts and worries that had plagued her about bringing this suit in the first place.

'Petition for a temporary restraining order denied,' the judge concluded. 'The costs of both parties will be paid by McKenzie Brackman. That's all.' He banged his gavel.

Abby and Arnie remained where they were, dismayed by the verdict, while beside them Benny simply seemed uncertain what to make of it. Then the Roses approached them.

Abby watched in astonishment as Mrs Rose handed a cheque to Benny. 'Benny,' she said kindly, 'here's a cheque, to give you your money back.'

'I don't understand,' Arnie said to her.

'I'm sure you don't,' said Bradley their lawyer.

But Mrs Rose ignored Arnie and Abby, speaking directly to Benny. 'From your testimony,' she said softly, 'it seems that you aren't completely sure about us, Benny. She paused and looked at him with a friendly smile. 'And, if that's the case, you probably shouldn't be with the church.'

'But I don't want the money back . . .,' Benny began.

Mrs Rose shook her head. 'Our lawyer tells us that there's nothing to stop your lawyers from bringing another action against us down the road. 'I'm sorry,' she said sadly, 'but we just can't afford it.' She paused, then smiled again. 'I really *am* sorry,' she reiterated. 'We're going to miss you.'

'I'll miss you, too,' Benny said.

He shook hands with Mrs Rose, then Mr Rose, and watched wistfully as they walked away. Arnie put his hand on Benny's shoulder.

'Come on, Benny,' he said quietly, 'let's go home.'

Benny shook Arnie's hand off. 'I'll take the bus,' he told them.

'But . . . why?' Abby asked, bewildered. 'We have a car; you don't have to . . .'

Benny shook his head stubbornly. 'I don't want to go with you,' he said.

Arnie and Abby exchanged looks of perplexed dismay.

'Hey, Benny,' Arnie said placatingly, 'it's all right; there's nothing to be upset about any more. It's all over now.'

Benny looked at them, hurt and anger in his eyes. 'You made my friends go away,' he said accusingly. 'Why did you have to do that?'

Oh God, Abby thought, her heart breaking for Benny. 'Benny,' she assured him, '*we're* your friends.'

Benny looked from Abby to Arnie, then back again. 'No,' he said, shaking his head, 'you're only my friends when we're at work. But after work you don't want to be with me.' He paused and gazed at the door through which the Roses had disappeared. 'They liked me,' he said. 'They liked me all the time.'

Then he turned and walked away, leaving Abby and Arnie feeling worse than they had before.

*

Grace tried to work, diligently studying the brief she had brought home with her. But her concentration kept drifting, and finally she simply gave up and turned on the television. That didn't hold her attention, either. At the unexpected sound of her doorbell chimes, Grace glanced at the clock and saw that it was nearly ten-thirty. She padded to the door barefoot, wondering who could be visiting unannounced at this hour. When she peered cautiously through the peephole and saw Victor standing on her doorstep, she wasn't exactly surprised. After all, there was definitely unfinished business between them. She opened the door and stared at him silently.

'Grace,' he began. 'I know it's presumptuous and rude to come by this way . . .'

'Yes,' Grace agreed coolly, trying to quell the physical impact that Victor made on her – even when she was angry, 'It is.'

'And I'm probably the last person on earth you want to see . . ..'

'Close,' Grace agreed.

'Can I come in anyway?'

Grace hesitated for a moment. But Victor's penitent expression and obvious concern won her over. After all, she told herself, they had to talk about what had happened. They had to establish their status in order to go on working together. It was the only mature thing they *could* do. And it definitely didn't have anything to do with the way Victor looked in a faded khaki T-shirt, old jeans, and a well-worn

194

bomber's jacket. Or with the way he was looking at her, clad only in a football jersey which reached halfway down her thighs.

'OK,' she said.

They stood in her front hallway, more than a little awkward with each other.

'Well,' Grace said finally, 'do you want coffee or a drink or . . . anything?'

Victor shook his head. 'I'm not going to stay long,' he said. 'I just thought we really needed to talk about what happened.'

Grace nodded, chewing on her bottom lip.

'Look,' Victor began, 'I'm not sure what else I can say except I'm sorry. *Really* sorry.'

Grace nodded again. 'So am I,' she said.

Victor sighed. 'Going to Michael was a completely knee-jerk reaction; it was something from out of the past.' Grace looked puzzled, and Victor continued. 'You don't muscle in on another guy.'

'Oh, come on!' Grace said in disbelief. 'What do you think this is – high school? And since when am I anybody's property? Even when I was going with Mickey, I wasn't "his"!'

'I know that, Grace,' Victor said softly. 'I told you it was a knee-jerk reaction, and that's exactly what I meant. Where I grew up, the machismo attitude was a prerequisite for everything you did in the rest of your life. I know it's no excuse, but I guess I just didn't think about it; I felt like I owed Michael an . . . *explanation* or something. And I didn't think about how it would make you feel.'

Grace nodded, softening. 'So . . .?'

195

Victor smiled at her. 'So I apologise, and I'll keep on apologising until I'm sure you've really forgiven me. And then I'll try like hell to get things back to where they were going.' He looked at her, his dark intense eyes full of desire.

'OK,' Grace said, feeling like things could get out of control fast, and not at all certain if she wanted them to or not.

'Am I forgiven?' Victor asked her softly.

Grace hesitated for a moment, knowing the rest of the evening and God knows how long into the future rested with her response. 'Yes,' she said in a half-whisper. 'You're forgiven.'

'Oh Christ, Grace,' Victor murmured, pulling her tightly to him. 'Jesus, I was so scared you'd just turn it off and never give me another chance.'

'I don't think I could turn it off if I wanted to,' she said softly. 'And I don't want to.'

When Victor bent down and kissed her, Grace felt again what she had felt before with him – that this was different, that this was something so passionate and so removed from all other experiences that it seemed to come from another world. The temperature in the hallway seemed to have zoomed up at least fifteen degrees.

She felt his hands moving under her jersey, and she broke contact with his mouth just long enough to pull it impatiently over her head and toss it aside. It was as if they had no time left, as if this was going to be the last chance either of them ever had to make love. Her hands were pulling his T-shirt up, his were caressing her breasts and stroking her thighs and promising that what was about to

196

happen would be a trip to another dimension.

They never made it upstairs to Grace's bedroom; they didn't even make it to the couch in the living-room. On the cool slate tiles of the entryway, Victor and Grace claimed each other. And when it was over each of them seemed to sense that something in their lives had changed, irrevocably, for the better.

Chapter Sixteen

Victor watched Grace with both admiration and a certain private sense of amusement as she took her place in front of the judge and jury the next morning. Looking at her, he thought, no one would ever guess the kind of night the two of them had spent together – or the fact that both of them had admitted they couldn't wait for the next night, either. In court Grace was her usual impeccable cool self, all business – and seemingly unemotional. But Victor knew that, beside the intimate secret she was carrying around inside, she also had one hell of a surprise in store for Rosalind up her sleeve.

'Your Honour,' Grace said, 'at this time the defence would like to call Mrs Susan Raab to the stand.'

Victor glanced covertly over at the plaintiff's table and saw that Rosalind had gone stiff with shock. That's right, Victor thought, even a calculating iceberg like you would have to be shocked by the fact that your own daughter is being asked to testify here.

'Objection,' said Jack Sollers promptly. 'This witness is not on their pre-trial list.'

Like Stuart Markowwitz wasn't on yours, Victor thought smugly.

'Your Honour,' Grace cut in, 'we just decided to call this witness last night. I tried to notify counsel this morning. I left a message with his office.'

Jack Sollers approached the bench. 'Your honour,' he said, 'side-bar.' Grace joined him, and they spoke in muted tones so that the members of the jury couldn't hear the contents of the controversy. While they were speaking, a slender pleasant-looking woman in her mid-thirties entered the courtroom.

'This witness has no relevance to this case,' Sollers told the judge.

Grace shook her head. 'That's not true. Our entire defence is mounted on the supposition that Ms Shays is a very difficult person to get along with,' she argued. 'Ms Raab has known her far longer than any other witness we could call, your Honour, and we feel she is competent to impeach.'

A quickly repressed look of anger crossed Jack Soller's face. 'I'm sorry, your Honour,' he said, 'but this has all the earmarks of a cheap attempt to —'

Judge Travelini shook her head impatiently. 'I'm going to have to go with this witness, Mr Sollers. I believe Ms van Owen is correct. Now, if you want to adjourn after direct, that's fine with me. But this trial is dragging out long enough. Let's try to keep it moving.' Then she nodded to the waiting bailiff. 'Swear the witness in,' she told him.

As Susan Raab took the stand, it was obvious to Victor that she was both uncomfortable and nervous at the part she was being asked to play in this. And, he thought, how could you blame her?

'Raise your right hand,' the bailiff told her. Susan Raab did as she was told. 'Do you swear to tell the truth, the whole truth and nothing but the truth, so help you God?'

199

'I do,' Susan Raab replied softly.

Grace approached the witness-box. 'Please state your full name for the record,' she told the witness.

'Susan Raab,' the woman replied nervously.

'Ms Raab,' Grace said, 'you are in this courtroom under subpoena today, are you not?'

'Yes,' Susan Rabb said quietly.

'Could you please state your relationship with the plaintiff, Rosalind Shays?'

Susan Raab stared down, refusing even to look at Rosalind. Then she said: 'She's my mother.'

Victor watched the members of the jury react in surprise and curiosity. He had to admit, this had been a brilliant idea of Grace's. As long as it didn't backfire; and, knowing what he did about the relationship between this mother and daughter, he had very little doubt that anything could go wrong.

'Your Honour,' Grace addressed the judge, 'we seek to treat the witness as hostile.'

'Granted,' Judge Travelini said.

Grace turned her attention back to Susan Raab. 'Where do you live, Ms Raab?' she asked.

'I live in Glendale,' the witness replied.

'And that would be Glendale . . . California?' Grace queried.

'Yes,' Susan Raab said.

'And where does your mother live?' Grace continued.

'Pacific Palisades,' Susan Raab said.

'Do you know how far apart those two cities are?' Grace asked.

Susan Raab shrugged uncomfortably. 'I'm not exactly

sure,' she said. 'Probably about an hour's ride in a car, but I'm really not certain.'

Victor could feel the interest of the jury perk up even more. How could this woman not know the distance between her mother's house and her own?

'And before this moment, in court, when was the last time you saw your mother?' Grace asked pointedly.

'Objection,' Sollers said.

'I'd like a little latitude,' Grace told the judge. 'This *is* a hostile witness.'

'Go ahead,' Judge Travelini agreed.

'Ms Raab,' Grace asked again, 'Please tell the court when the last time was that you saw your mother.'

'I'm . . . not exactly sure,' Susan Raab said, flushing a little.

Victor glanced towards the plaintiff's table and saw that Rosalind, like her daughter, was refusing to make eye-contact. Her gaze was firmly fixed on the ground.

'Was it more than a year ago?' Grace persisted.

'Yes,' Susan Raab said quietly.

'More than . . . *five* years ago?' Grace asked.

Susan Raab paused for a moment. 'Probably,' she said finally.

'Was it more than ten years ago?'

Susan Raab finally looked Grace directly in the eye. 'Look,' she said, 'I'm just not sure. I already told you I don't know.'

'All right,' Grace said. 'Are you married?' she asked.

'Yes,' Susan Raab said.

Grace nodded thoughtfully. 'Do you have any children, Ms Raab?' she asked.

'Yes,' Susan Raab replied tersely.

'And what are their ages?'

Victor smiled to himself. Grace was moving towards the dramatic end-point with finesse and style, and she had the jury hooked.

'I have a seven-year-old son,' Susan Raab told her, 'and a five-year-old daughter.'

Grace paused for a moment, building to her climax. 'Have they ever met their grandmother?' she asked pointedly. There was no reply from the witness. 'Ms Raab?' Grace said. 'I asked you if your children had ever met their grandmother, Ms Shays.'

There was still no reply from Susan Raab, who bit her lip and refused again to meet Grace's eye.

'Witness will answer the question,' Judge Travelini said.

Susan Raab looked up, an expression of anger and unhappiness on her face. 'No,' she said, 'they have never met their grandmother.'

Victor could see that the intended effect was working on the jury. This admission from Ms Raab was more startling than even her appearance in court today.

'Why is that?' Grace persisted. 'Is it too long a drive?'

'Objection!' Jack Sollers snapped.

Grace held up her hands in a placating gesture. 'Question withdrawn,' she said. Then she turned her attention back to the witness-box. 'Can you tell the court *why* your children have never met their grandmother?' Grace asked.

Again, there was only a stubborn and uncomfortable silence.

'Ms Raab,' Judge Travelini said, a note of warning in her voice, 'I don't want to have to tell you again. Answer the

202

question.'

Susan Raab glanced up at the judge, then looked at Grace, conflicting emotions on her face. 'My . . . mother and I . . . well, we just . . . we just don't get along,' she said softly. 'That's all.'

Grace milked the moment, first staring at Susan Raab in the witness-box, then looking pointedly back at Rosalind Shays.

'Do you have any more questions for the witness, Ms Van Owen?' Judge Travelini enquired.

'No,' Grace said. Then she walked back to the defence table and sat down. The silence in the court was deafening as people absorbed the emotional content of the previous exchange. OK, thought Victor, just try to top that one, Jack.

Finally Jack Sollers arose and approached the witness box. 'Ms Raab,' he said. 'I have only one question for you. Do you love your mother?'

Tears welled up in Susan Raab's eyes. 'Of course I do,' she said softly.

Jack Sollers stared from the witness to the jury, making sure the impact had hit. 'Nothing further,' he said.

'You may step down, Ms Raab,' the judge told her.

All eyes in the courtroom remained focused on Susan Raab as she made her way hurriedly to the exit. And every-one knew that not once – not even at this emotional finale – did Susan Raab meet her mother's eyes.

*

'I simply cannot believe she's doing this!' Ann exclaimed. 'What on earth ever possessed her?'

She, along with the rest of the staff at McKenzie Brackman, were gathered in the conference room watching, of all things, the Phil Donahue show. It was hardly a normal way to spend the hour between three and four o'clock in the office; but, then, Abby Perkins's appearance on the show – as an opponent of gun control – wasn't exactly business as usual, either.

Up on the small screen, Phil Donahue, with every silver hair in place, ever-present microphone in hand, prowled among his various guests on stage, searching for the next controversial place to land. Right now, the audience – and the McKenzie Brackman staff – were hearing the opinion of Professor Henry Bennett, an outspoken and well-known proponent of gun control, while Abby and the other guests looked on.

'It's a national disgrace! Do you realise that *hundreds* of children are killed every year as the result of accidental gunshots in their own homes!' Bennett was saying. 'That alone should be reason enough to enforce stricter laws on gun control.'

'But', Donahue said, playing his usual role of the devil's advocate, 'think about this. Does that really have anything to do with gun control? Or are those horrifying tragedies really the result of parental negligence in those homes?'

Bennett shook his head vehemently. 'But that isn't really the point,' he said. 'It doesn't matter which way you look at it; the answer has to be the same. The plain fact is that when you put guns into the mainstream of society, as we have done in this country, you literally *beg* for this kind of tragedy. And making permits to carry guns more accessible will only serve to exacerbate an already terrible problem.'

Donahue glanced quickly down at his notes, then up at Abby. 'I'd like you to meet Ms Abigail Perkins,' he said. 'Ms Perkins is an attorney with the Los Angeles firm of McKenzie, Brackman, Kuzak and Becker.' He paused dramatically and looked at his audience. 'Two years ago,' he told them solemnly, 'Ms Perkins was attacked by a deranged ex-client who was armed with a lead pipe. She was alone in her office, and she defended herself from a murderous attack the only way she could – with a handgun. She shot her attacker . . . and she killed him.'

There was scattered applause from the audience, while Abby nervously fidgeted with her hands.

In the McKenzie Brackman conference room Leland shook his head in bewilderment. 'This isn't precisely what we might have hoped for in the way of publicity,' he said.

Doug nodded in agreement. 'Really, couldn't she have done a show on adoption or something? Something less controversial than this?'

'I don't know,' Arnie said thoughtfully, 'this might not be such a bad thing after all. Having a tough female lawyer on our team certainly won't hurt us.'

'Don't be ridiculous!' Ann snapped. 'This is simply absurd!'

'Come on, you guys, save the analysis for later,' C. J. Lamb spoke up. 'Let's not talk over Abby here.' She pointed to the screen.

'Ms Perkins,' Donahue continued, 'you didn't have a permit to carry a gun, did you?'

'No,' Abby admitted. 'I didn't, although I tried to get one. I was turned down.'

'Turned down?' Donahue's eyebrows went up. 'But

why? A young woman working downtown, and a woman with no criminal record . . .'

Abby shook her head. 'That didn't matter. The truth is that permits are nearly impossible to get unless you carry large amounts of cash or jewellery, or you're in private security. Regular responsible citizens – people like you and me, people who may genuinely have as much fear for their lives as anyone else – are simply not allowed to carry firearms. At least, not legally.'

'Oh, wonderful,' Ann said. 'She's advocating legal disobedience!'

'Which means,' Donahue said, leading the debate in the direction that would be sure to produce the most fireworks, 'if you had followed the letter of the law and left your handgun at home . . .'

'That's right.' Abby nodded in grim agreement. 'Or even if the attack had happened on the street . . . I'd be dead,' she said.

'But come on, Ms Perkins, you're a lawyer. You must know from your practice just how dangerous this freedom of access to firearms can be. You must have been involved in cases where there was a shooting in the house, right?'

Abby nodded. 'We've had several cases like that come through the firm,' she said.

'So how does that make you feel about what Professor Bennett was saying? What *about* the safety issue?' He glanced at his notes again. 'According to the latest national crime statistics, eight thousand people a year in this country are killed by handguns. And a lot of them *are* kids who are shot by accident, just like the Professor was saying.'

'I find that appalling,' Abby replied promptly. She

seemed to have lost her initial nervousness, and was projecting herself as a clear and confident spokesperson. 'As', she continued, 'I'm sure everyone here does. But what's equally appalling is selling guns to people with criminal records or a history of mental illness. I do *strongly* favour gun registration, with mandatory waiting periods and background checks . . .'

'Well, thank God for that!' Ann said sarcastically. 'A little bit of reason emerges . . .'

'Oh, come on, Ann, I think she's doing great,' Roxanne defended Abby. You hypocrite, she thought, remembering Abby's hurt when she discovered that Ann hadn't told her about not making partner.

On the screen, Professor Bennett was outraged. 'The idea of passing out pistols as if we live in Dodge City is contemptible. And —'

'No, *I'll* tell you what's contemptible,' Abby broke in, her voice tense and filled with emotion. 'That our government can't seem to stop the flow of drugs into this country, or put a halt to the way those drugs are ravishing our young people. What's contemptible is that government can't seem to stop the rising crime rates, or stop automatic weapons from getting into the hands of every gangbanger in this country! But that same government wants to pass laws that stop guns from getting to you and me, when every dealer and pimp and psycho out there seems to have easy access to them! Who the hell is sticking up for *our* rights?'

The audience broke into a spontaneous cheer for Abby's bravado and her point of view, just as the show broke for a commercial. In the conference room, the staff seemed collectively stunned by what they had just seen on the

207

screen.

'Gee,' said Arnie, obviously surprised. 'I didn't know she had it in her. Abby always seems like such a little mouse.'

'Oh, for heaven's sake, Arnie, she shot and killed a man!' Roxanne said. 'That's not exactly what I'd call mousy!'

'I remember her mentioning that she's been invited to do this show, but I could swear she said she wasn't going to do this,' Ann mused.

'Well, then, I guess something must've changed her mind,' said C. J. Lamb, with a wink at Roxanne.

Roxanne suddenly realized that C. J., who'd only been with the firm for a month, must have somehow intuited the partnership problem also. Or else she'd got it on the secretarial grapevine. CJ was completely egalitarian, a free spirit befriending clerk and judge alike according to the way she felt. That attitude, Roxanne thought, obviously paid some hefty dividends in the way of shared confidences.

The commercial ended, and the debate on screen continued.

'I mean, we have to think about this problem realistically,' Abby was saying, 'if the police can't protect our children, then they should let us do it ourselves!'

'And what do you think about that, Professor?' Donahue asked. 'You have to admit we've got a problem here. Take a look at the crime statistics. Like it or not, we're living in an urban jungle.'

The Professor shook his head stubbornly. 'I refuse to believe that arming citizens with weapons is the only solution!'

'Well, it was certainly *my* solution!' Abby said vehemently. 'And the only reason I'm alive and on this show today is because I had that gun.'

The audience broke into applause once again, and Donahue motioned for them to hold it down. 'OK, folks,' he said genially, 'everyone gets a turn to speak their mind here.'

'I feel like I'm watching *Calamity Jane*,' Leland remarked.

Donahue he turned his attention back to the Professor. 'What do you say to something like that, Professor Bennett?' he asked.

'I say it's ridiculous!' the Professor said adamantly. 'If everyone is armed, then you might as well admit that our society has failed. If you give in to the violence, then we become a society of violence!'

'We're *already* a society of violence!' Abby insisted impatiently. 'We can't turn our back on that reality, Professor, no matter *how* much we'd like to!' She paused and looked at the audience. 'What I'm saying is, deal with that fact instead of pretending it doesn't exist. The time has come to let us – the good people – fight back!'

'Oh my God,' said Ann, obviously dismayed at the reactionary political point of view she believed Abby was putting forth.

'Time for another break while we all cool down.' Donahue gazed into the camera. 'Lawyers who kill. We'll be right back.'

'Oh my God,' Ann said again.

'I still can't believe it,' said Arnie. 'Abby, of all people ...'

'Just full of surprises, isn't she?' CJ asked cheerfully. She smiled at Roxanne again, and gave a covert thumbs-up. Roxanne nodded in satisfaction. Chalk one up for the underdogs, she thought.

*

'And she was so impressive!' Roxanne told Sandy Cole. 'It was great!' She'd just finished recounting the tale of Abby and Phil Donahue and the partnership injustice. This was their third date, and Roxanne was beginning to feel quite relaxed with Sandy, who seemed to be a genuinely caring and sensitive individual. If he was a little on the shy side, that was fine with Roxanne – she certainly wanted male companionship, and some romance in her life was welcome, but she was in no hurry to plunge into a whirl-wind affair.

'It certainly sounds like an interesting place to work,' Sandy said with a smile. 'More interesting than the accoun-tancy firm anyway.'

'But you like it, don't you?' Roxanne asked.

They were in Sandy's car, heading back to Roxanne's house after a Caribbean dinner and a stroll down the reno-vated Santa Monica promenade.

Sandy shrugged. 'I do like it,' he said. 'I mean, it's the kind of thing – figures, that is – that I've always been good at.' He glanced over at Roxanne shyly. 'But there's some-thing else I'd really like to do,' he said.

'What?' Roxanne asked curiously.

'Well . . . I already do it,' Sandy said. 'I write poetry.'

Roxanne was surprised – and impressed. 'Really?' she

210

asked. 'That's great. It must be so nice to have that kind of creative drive.'

Sandy seemed relieved. 'I'm glad you think that way,' he confessed. 'The few people I've told it to have had different reactions – you know, like I'm flaky or something.'

'There doesn't seem to be *anything* flaky about you,' Roxanne said with a smile, 'and why would writing poetry seem that way anyway? I mean, did anyone think Robert Frost was a flake?'

Sandy laughed. 'You've got a point,' he said. He pulled up in front of Roxanne's house and turned to her. 'I'd like to meet your father,' he said, 'if that's all right with you.'

Roxanne hesitated. Her first reaction was negative; exposing a possible romantic relationship to her father was dangerous ground. Murray was so likely to act like a maniac. Then, again, Sandy's own father had Alzheimer's, and he had got used to some pretty bizarre behaviour himself.

'Sure,' said Roxanne, 'come on in.'

They walked up the flagstone path that led to the red front door, while Roxanne fished around in her bag for her keys. She opened the door to the cheerful front hallway and peered into the living-room. 'Dad?' she called out. 'You here?' There was no reply, and Roxanne shrugged, 'He's probably watching TV in the study,' she told Sandy. 'Here, let me take your jacket, and we'll go find him.'

Television canned laughter emanated from the back of the house. 'This way,' Roxanne said, leading Sandy down a dimly lit hallway. 'Dad?' she said again, peering into the small cosy den. Murray was asleep in the recliner that Roxanne had bought for him on his last birthday. 'Dad?'

she said.

'Sandy . . .,' she began, as a pang of fear began to travel through her.

'It's OK, Roxanne,' Sandy said, moving swiftly up beside her.

In the dim light of the study Murray looked peaceful and relaxed. Sandy put his index and middle finger to the side of Murray's throat. Then he looked at Roxanne and shook his head. 'He's gone,' he said quietly.

'Oh God,' Roxanne said, a sob in her throat. 'Oh God, and I wasn't even here . . .'

'Don't,' said Sandy, putting an arm around her. They both stared at Murray Melman's peaceful corpse. 'Don't blame yourself; it was quick and painless for him, Roxanne, and that's the best you can hope for with something like Alzheimer's. Honestly,' he said softly, 'it's better this way.'

Chapter Seventeen

Grace's anger at both Victor and Michael had melted away after the night that she and Victor first made love. There was a new bond between them which somehow didn't seem new at all, she mused. It was as if they'd been moving unknowingly towards this very point since the day they'd met, some five or six years before. And now that it had finally happened she couldn't imagine anything feeling more right than this did. Although she and Victor agreed to postpone any talks about the future for a while, although they had agreed to keep the relationship a secret for now, Grace had a strong intuitive sense that this was no ordinary affair, that this was leading somewhere important. And she was equally certain that Victor felt the same way about her. The thought made her smile.

It was probably this new feeling of happiness and good-will which made her more than willing to lend a helping hand to Michael – and, tangentially, Jonathan – in the increasing knotty mess of the Chisolm case. Michael and Jonathan's grandstanding *had* accomplished one thing; Judge Stone had been forced to declare a mistrial, and was going to be forced to find twelve brand-new jurors. But that certainly didn't solve all the problems. Judge Stone was still presiding, and everyone at McKenzie Brackman knew he was politically corrupt and equally unable and unwilling to set the atmosphere for a fair trial.

It was that conviction which had brought Grace here, to the shadowy recesses of the underground parking-lot that served the criminal-court building. Michael Conover, the Presiding Superior Court Judge – the man who could, if he chose, unseat Stone and put someone else behind the bench – had reluctantly agreed to meet her even though it wasn't strictly correct behaviour. He and Grace went way back together, and he knew she wouldn't be asking for this if it wasn't important. Still, he had set the meeting somewhere that he knew they wouldn't be seen or overheard. Now Conover stood by his car waiting to hear what it was that Grace had to say.

'You know, I'm not exactly comfortable about meeting like this,' Conover said to Grace, glancing around unhappily.

'Neither am I. It does sort of make you feel like Watergate, doesn't it?' Grace agreed. 'But listen to me, Michael. This is an extremely serious problem, and someone has got to tackle it.'

'I understand that,' he said, nodding his head. 'But this is *ex parte*, Grace, and *you* know *that*.' He referred to the fact that she shouldn't be talking to him about the Chisolm case at all.

'It's not as if I'm not the lawyer of record,' Grace protested.

Conover lifted a cynical eyebrow. 'You know better than to try that, Counsellor. It's your *firm's* case, and that makes this meeting inappropriate. The rest is all semantics.'

'I'm sorry, Michael,' Grace said, 'but this has to be dealt with somehow, and this is the only way I can think of to do

214

it.'

'OK,' Conover said, 'we're here, and the clock is running. Shoot.'

'It's about what's going on with the Chisolm case,' Grace said.

'I'm aware of that,' Conover said drily.

'But are you aware that this entire city is on the verge of a race riot? Or that the District Attorney's office seems to think the solution is to convict an innocent cop?' Grace demanded. 'For God's sake, Michael, if this trial keeps on the way it began, we could be starting something here that would make us look as bad as Miami did when they let that cop off for killing an unarmed Cuban! Remember that? Three days of riots, and a good part of the city going up in flames?'

'But that's exactly what *you* want, isn't it?' Conover queried. 'To get this cop off, right?'

Grace shook her head. 'No,' she said firmly. 'Even though personally, I'm certain he's not guilty of murder, that's not the point I'm trying to make. In my opinion, if Chisolm is convicted with Stone as the presiding judge, it will be as unfair a verdict as the one in Miami – just in the other direction.' She paused, her mouth set in a grim line. 'And it taints this city's judicial process just as much, too.' She looked steadily at Conover. 'What I want, Michael – and it's what you should want, too – is to see that Brian Chisolm gets a fair trial. To make sure that he isn't rail-roaded to the gallows by Derron Holloway and his hand-picked jury, and a judge he just happens to have in his pocket!'

'That's a very serious accusation, Grace,' Conover said

soberly.

'At best, Judge Stone is a victim of hysteria who can't seem to keep his priorities straight,' Grace told him. 'But what's worse is that he's more afraid of losing the next election than he is of subverting the system he's sworn to uphold!'

'Judge Stone has served with distinction for seven years,' Conover countered.

'Maybe,' Grace said doubtfully. 'But he can't control Derron Holloway. Stone let the DA talk about a lie detector in front of the jury, Michael, and he wouldn't declare a mistrial – even after he had Michael Kuzak taken into custody!'

'But he *did* wind up declaring a mistrial,' Conover countered.

'Only after locking Jonathan Rollins up, too,' Grace reminded him. '*And* after DA Fusco insisted on one! Come on, Michael, you just can't ignore the stench of corruption on this one.' Her voice rang with conviction. 'Stone's a bum and a sleazebag, and you're the presiding Superior Court Judge. You *have* to take responsibility here.'

Conover took a deep breath, thinking. Then he nodded, convinced. 'OK, I'll do it,' he said. 'I'll get you a new judge.'

Grace breathed a sigh of relief. 'Make sure it's somebody who can take the heat, Michael. Somebody who can stand up to Holloway and the pressures he's bringing to bear here.'

Conover nodded again. 'You just tell your guys to be ready,' he said. 'If we stall on this now, the public outcry is just going to get louder. And that', he added, 'isn't going to

216

help you.'

'That's not a problem,' Grace said firmly. 'We're ready now.'

'OK,' Conover said, 'I promise I'll get you a good judge.'

*

Murray's funeral consisted of a brief memorial service at which people spoke of the departed in both fond and rueful terms, citing his buoyant spirits and unique peculiar approach to life. It was all done with a certain reverence and a great deal of affectionate appreciation for someone who had made people laugh all his life. Roxanne stood, sombre in a black suit, with Sandy Cole on one side and Arnie Becker on the other.

'I still can't believe it,' she whispered, her eyes filled with tears, as she looked at the coffin. 'It was so fast!'

'Rox,' Arnie said gently, 'it's really better this way. Thank God he didn't have to suffer the deterioration that goes with Alzheimer's.' He put a gentle arm around her shoulder. 'And thank God you didn't have to suffer that, too.'

Leland stepped to the podium and, in his usual dignified manner, gave a short but pithy speech about Murray and his effect on the firm. 'He never could be accused of being stodgy,' Leland said in fond reminiscence. 'And if he sometimes did the unexpected . . . well, the unexpected was what Murray Melman lived for.'

Roxanne felt a flood of memories wash over her: Murray singing to her when she was a child; Murray comforting her when her first boyfriend broke her heart by demanding his St Christopher medal back; Murray telling her that she was good enough, smart enough to do anything she wanted to do, be anything she wanted to be. Of course, there were the other memories as well, these not nearly so comforting. There was Murray disappearing for three whole years of her childhood, right after his divorce from Roxanne's mother; Murray being kicked out of the retirement home he lived in; Murray going on the air, posing as a McKenzie Brackman lawyer, telling the press that they were very upset by the outcome of this case or that. The last incident Roxanne recalled with a shudder.

But, over all, Roxanne could still feel the essence of Murray – maddening, loving, one-of-a-kind. And she did know, on some level, that this quick ending to his life was better than the alternative. A tear rolled down her cheek as Leland's speech came to an end. That was it: the funeral was over. Roxanne had no desire to see her father interred, but she waited until everyone had hugged her and given her their condolences; and then, when only Arnie and Sandy were left in the room, she asked them to leave her alone for a few minutes.

'I understand, Rox,' Arnie said, 'and please take some time off.'

'No,' Roxanne shook her head vehemently. 'I'll go nuts if I don't have something to do. I'm coming right back to the office.'

Arnie studied her face to see if she really meant it, or if she was simply putting up a brave front. But Roxanne looked as though she meant every word, so finally Arnie nodded. 'You do what you think is best,' he said. Then he gave her a hug and a kiss, and walked out, thinking that this might be the perfect time to put a scheme he'd had in mind into action.

'Sandy?' Roxanne said. 'Give me a couple of minutes, OK?'

Sandy nodded understandingly. 'Sure,' he said, 'I'll be outside.'

Left alone, Roxanne walked over to her father's coffin and stared down at the man who had been her father, at the face which seemed so peaceful and altered, so different in death. Murray – the Murray she knew – was gone. For a long time, she simply stood there, looking down. Then finally she bent down and kissed him softly on the cheek. 'Bye, Daddy,' she said softly. 'I'm going to miss you.'

*

A few hours later, Roxanne, subdued but calm, was back at work, searching for a brief which Arnie frantically claimed he had misplaced. Roxanne was glad she had decided to come back to work it had been the right thing to do after all. The idea of sitting around at home was just too depressing, even though everyone around her was trying to be so kind. What she needed was distraction, and the bustling office seemed to be the perfect place to get it. She had already turned her desk and his office upside down, but there was no trace of the elusive papers.

'Arnie,' she said without looking up, as she heard him come in, 'I swear I've looked in every single logical place, and I can't find anything on the Samuels case at *all* . . .'

'Rox, leave it alone for now,' Arnie said. There was

something about his tone which made Roxanne look up. She was startled to see that Arnie wasn't alone. Corrinne was with him, and she seemed just as surprised to come face to face with Roxanne as Roxanne was by her presence in the office.

'Hi, Roxanne,' Corrinne said, trying to mask her discomfort. 'I wanted to tell you how sorry I am about your dad.'

'Thank you,' Roxanne said stiffly. She was perfectly aware that Arnie must've talked to Corrinne about their little conflict, and she wasn't at all certain how much Corrinne was capable of meddling – or whose side Arnie would ultimately take.

The awkward silence just lay between them, until Corrinne said: 'Well, Arnie, what about the lunch you promised me?'

'We aren't going to lunch – at least, not yet. This is more important,' Arnie said calmly.

'What's more important?' Corrinne asked, puzzled. 'What's this all about?'

But Roxanne had already figured it out. 'It's a ploy', she told Corrinne, 'to get us together.' She began to walk angrily past them, but Arnie snagged her arm and forced her to stop.

'Hold it right there,' he said. 'Both of you just stay here. I have something to say.'

'This is ridiculous,' Corrinne said, obviously annoyed, as she, too, turned to leave. But Arnie put his other hand on her arm.

'No,' he said, 'it's anything *but* ridiculous.' He looked at Roxanne. 'Look, Rox,' he said, 'I know this is a rough time for you, but that's one of the reasons I wanted to do this now. I thought this might be the perfect time to make it clear that you are incredibly important to me, and that I will always be here when you need me.'

He glanced from Corrinne to Roxanne again, but could detect only a slight softening on Roxanne's face. 'OK,' he said to them, 'if you won't talk to each other, you can at least listen to me.' No response was forthcoming from either woman. 'Both of you,' Arnie said, his temper rising, 'sit yourselves goddam down so we can get this stupid mess cleared up once and for all.'

Roxanne and Corrinne both sat, surprised by the vehemence in Arnie's voice.

'That's better,' he said. He looked first at Roxanne. 'Roxanne,' he said earnestly, 'you are my best friend, and you have been for a long, long time. Nothing can change that,' he told her. 'You are . . . well, *irreplaceable* in my life on so many different levels that I couldn't list them all, even if I tried.' His intelligent grey eyes met Roxanne's and he thought he could sense her growing receptivity to his words. 'You know my deepest, darkest and most unpleasant secrets, and you love me anyway. And you will never, ever know just how much that means to me, or how I cherish our friendship.'

He paused to collect his thoughts, then turned his attention to Corrinne. 'You are my wife,' he said simply. 'Nothing in the world can change that. You are the woman I swore to love and honour as long as we both live, after I'd spent a lifetime avoiding saying those words,' He smiled softly at her. 'I want to laugh with you and fight with you and grow old with you, Corrinne. And I know that I will also never be able to tell you how much you really mean to me.'

Both women had settled down and were listening attentively now; and Arnie hoped that he had calmed the fears that each of them seemed to have about the other's importance in his life. He looked at Roxanne again. 'But the thing is, Rox, that some things do change. I'm married now, and it would be silly and untrue to deny that it makes a difference in my life. Of *course* it makes a difference, to all of us. And it also means that you have to share me.' He smiled at Roxanne. 'But it doesn't mean that I love you any less than I did before.'

He looked again at Corrinne, who seemed genuinely moved by what she was hearing. 'And you, Corrinne, my beloved wife, have to accept the fact that Roxanne is an integral important part of my life.' He paused for a beat, gazing seriously into Corrinne's eyes. 'And she always will be,' he said.

His eyes went from one woman to the other. 'The two of you are the women I care about most in the world. There's no changing that, and there's no reason to want to. Neither one of you should feel threatened by the other. But what both of you *have* to accept is that, in accepting me for what I am, you both have to accept each other, too.'

There was a long thoughtful silence in Arnie's office. Finally Corrinne stood up and walked over to Roxanne, who did the same.

'Maybe I overreacted, Roxanne,' she said in a conciliatory tone. 'I'm sorry.'

A little smile tugged at Roxanne's mouth. 'I guess I was being pretty thin-skinned,' she admitted. 'I'm sorry too.'

She reached out her hand to shake Corrinne's, but

Corrine shook her head and, instead of extending her hand, she put her arms around Roxanne and hugged her. When they broke apart, the two women had tears in their eyes, and Arnie had a smile on his face.

*

'What's up, Grace?' Michael Kuzak asked. He and Jonathan had just been asked to drop into her office by her secretary, and it was unlike Grace to stand on such formality with him.

Grace's pretty face lit up with satisfaction. 'I've just managed to get you guys a new judge for the Chisolm case,' she announced.

'What!' Michael exclaimed, astounded. 'How the hell did you . . .?'

'Are you serious?' Jonathan spoke right over Michael's words. 'This is incredible!'

'Yes . . . well, don't go getting cocky about the case,' Grace warned both of them. 'You've still got Derron Holloway and a lot of pissed-off people to contend with.'

'I know, but this will make it so much more fair . . .' Jonathan broke off as the realisation of what he was saying struck him. 'Uh . . . who is it?' he asked.

Grace shook her head. 'Don't have the faintest idea yet,' she replied.

'*Whoever* it is, he or she can't be as bad as Stone!' Michael said happily.

'I'm going to call a spy at the DA's office,' Jonathan said, already halfway out of the door. 'See what I can find out.' And he was gone, leaving Grace and Michael alone

223

together.

'Well,' Grace said, hoping to stave off any kind of personal conversation, 'you ought to be happy, Mickey; it certainly looks like Jonathan has finally come around, doesn't it?'

Michael nodded. 'He's too smart *not* to come around,' he said, 'no matter what he said at the beginning. Listen, Grace —'

'I really have a lot to do, Mickey,' Grace said hastily. 'I'm just swamped. . . .'

'Would you please stop avoiding me, Grace?' Michael asked her softly. 'All I want to do is apologise for what happened.'

'That's all right,' Grace said, acutely uncomfortable. 'Really, there's nothing to talk about.'

'Look,' Michael said, coming around to her side of the desk and taking her hand in his, 'I think we all need to be adults about this, no matter how awkward it might feel — and I know I didn't behave in a very adult manner the other day.' He tried to smile, but it came out half-heartedly. 'Grace,' he said, 'I have to know. Are you and Victor . . .?' And then he seemed to be at a loss for words.

There was no point in lying, Grace thought. She nodded briefly. 'Yes,' she said quietly, 'we're seeing each other. But we're trying to keep it quiet for now.'

A look of pain crossed Michael Kuzak's face. 'What do you mean, "for now"?' he asked. 'Are you expecting it to get . . . well, *serious*?'

Grace met his eyes with a frank glance. She and Michael had far too much history together: she owed him the full truth. 'Yes,' she said. 'Or, at least, *I* am,' she added.

'Oh.'

'Oh, what?' Grace asked gently.

'Oh . . . I feel as if someone just sucker-punched me,' Michael replied. He tried to make the words seem light-hearted, but he just couldn't.

'I'm sorry,' Grace said helplessly, looking down at her desk. She didn't want to see the pain on his face.

'Listen, Grace,' Michael said, still holding on to her hand. 'I'm truly sorry about what seemed like meddling, but that's all gone by the wayside now. And I've been doing some serious thinking since Victor talked to me . . .' He tilted her chin up to look into her eyes. 'Grace, I know my timing is lousy – it always was. But the truth is that I'm still in love with you,' he said simply. 'And I've got to know – is there a chance for me.'

Grace felt tears well up in her eyes, and she fought to keep them back. So much history, so much time, so much real affection. But romance? Love? Finally she shook her head. 'No, Mickey,' she said softly. 'There isn't.'

Chapter Eighteen

Grace tapped lightly on the door of Leland McKenzie's office.

'Come in,' she heard him call.

She entered the spacious hunt-scene-and-mahogany office and saw that Leland was standing at the large window, staring out over the skyscrapers and bustle of the city below. He seemed preoccupied, even sad, and Grace felt a slight pang of worry about his ability to perform today. After all, Leland was her last witness, and he could well prove to be the deciding factor in the case. Grace was under no illusions: as strong an impact as the reluctant Susan Raab had made for their side, Jack Sollers's one incisive question about whether or not she loved her mother could have undone much of what had gone before. Leland had to make a strong and impressive showing on the stand. After all, he was the partner who had brought Rosalind Shays into the firm, and now he was publicly going to have to admit his own mistake, and try to make her leaving seem like the only positive resolution that could have occurred.

'Leland,' Grace said tentatively, 'are you ready?'

'Ready,' Leland replied succinctly, still staring out the window.

'The main thing', Grace reminded him, 'is to show your

authority.' It felt strange talking to the senior partner, the founding member of the firm, in this manner; but it had to be done. They simply couldn't afford any last-minute foul-ups.

Leland finally turned away from the window and faced her. 'I know exactly what I have to do, Grace,' he said with a slight touch of impatience in his voice. 'We've been over it so many times I have no doubt I could do it in my sleep.'

Grace realised she had to tackle this head-on. No matter what state of mind Leland was in, this was her job. 'Leland, look,' she said, 'you know my track record. I've prepared over a thousand witnesses for trial, and I guarantee you that *nobody* testifies exactly the way it's been rehearsed.' She paused to let the impact of the number sink in. But Leland just looked at her, his face set, unrevealing.

Grace plunged in again. 'And, believe me, when you get up on that stand you'll be nervous – no one is impervious to that. And that's OK,' she assured him. 'But nerves cause some people to be . . . well, *tentative* on the stand.' She looked at him steadily, her face and voice serious. 'And that's *not* acceptable, not at all. Particularly not at this point in this case.'

Leland nodded. 'I understand,' he said.

But Grace wasn't through. 'Leland, please listen to me. They're going to try to paint you in a bad unflattering light – they're going to go for the jugular – and you may well have an emotional reaction to it. You'd hardly be human if you didn't. But I'm telling you that you have to hide that reaction. Jack Sollers is going to try to make that jury see you as the weak ageing partner, the one who needed rescuing. Your demeanour, your presentation have to contradict

227

that impression completely.

Behind their steel-rimmed glasses, Leland's eyes held a glint of steel themselves. 'I know what I have to do, Grace,' he told her. 'I know exactly how I have to be when I'm up on that stand.'

Leland's reply didn't leave any room for further discussion. Grace knew the senior partner well enough to know that his back – and his pride – were up. She'd done all she could, and how it was in the hands of the gods.

'Well, good,' said Grace seriously. 'Because this one is going to be close.'

*

The courtroom was packed, just as it had been packed every day since the Brian Chisolm trial had begun. There were even people standing, packed three or four deep at the back of the courtroom. Nobody – especially Richard Armand, the new judge on the case – wanted to incite any more explosions at the trial, and as a result he had allowed more than the usual number of viewers in. At the defence table, Michael, Jonathan and Brian Chisolm watched sombrely as DA Marcia Fusco gently led the dead youth's mother through the horrible events that occurred the night her son was killed.

Wilma Russ, slender and reserved, was obviously trying to hold her emotions in check as she answered Fusco's questions. 'I was reading in my bedroom – that's at the back of the house – when I heard it. First, I thought it might be backfire, but in our neighbourhood' – she paused to contain herself – 'it's more likely to be gunshots. And

228

when I heard the next two there was no doubt in my mind what I was hearing.'

Fusco, calm and sympathetic, nodded understandingly while Wilma Russ took a deep breath. Then she continued the questioning. 'And what did you do then?' she asked. 'After you realised that you were hearing gunshots?'

'I got up and went to the window,' Wilma Russ replied. 'I was scared it might have been one of the little kids who got in the way – that happens, you know.' She closed her eyes, reliving that terrible night. 'So I went to the window and . . . and then I saw . . . my son.' Her voice began to quiver. 'He was just . . . lying there in the middle of the alley.'

An angry murmur ran around the courtroom, and Judge Armand glanced up sharply. 'There will be no disturbance in this court,' he said tersely.

'Did you know right away that it was your son?' Fusco asked.

Mrs Russ nodded. 'Yes, I knew it was Willie right away,' she said. 'I could tell by . . . by his gold jacket.' She bit her lip.

'And what did you do then?' Marcia Fusco's voice was compassionate, and Jonathan knew this wasn't merely an act for the benefit of the jury. You'd have to have a heart of stone not to be moved by this testimony.

'I ran outside to where he was. There was . . . blood coming out of his back.' She fought to keep the teas which were welling up in her eyes from spilling over. 'And when I turned him over there was blood in his mouth, too.' She took a deep breath. 'His eyes were . . . open. And I tried to tell him that it was all right, that he would be all right.' She choked back a sob. 'But he wasn't there any more.'

'Your son was dead?' Fusco prompted her.

'Yes,' Wilma Russ said in a near-whisper. 'He was dead.'

Marcia Fusco handed Mrs Russ a Kleenex to wipe away the tears that had brimmed over and were streaming down her face. 'Are you all right to go on?' she asked.

Wilma Russ nodded. 'I'm all right,' she said softly.

At the defence table, Michael was scribbling some notes. Brian Chisolm looked at Jonathan, misery and fear clear on his face. 'This is terrible,' he said softly.

Jonathan nodded in sombre agreement. Whether Brian meant the event itself or the impact its recounting was having on the jury didn't matter: either way, he was right.

'All right now, Mrs Russ,' Fusco continued. 'When you went outside and saw your son lying there, did you see anyone else in the alley?'

Wilma Russ looked up and seemed to gain some kind of inner strength. She pointed straight at Brian Chisolm. 'I saw that man' she said, her voice hollow, too grief-stricken even to feel the anger that Jonathan knew must be bubbling up inside her.

Maria Fusco turned to the court stenographer. 'Let the record reflect the witness has indicated the defendant, Brian Chisolm,' she said clearly. Then, turning back to the witness, she continued. 'And what was Mr Chisolm doing, Mrs Russ?'

Wilma Russ looked Brian Chisolm in the eye. 'He was just standing there with his gun,' she said. 'It was still up and pointed. And then he began to move – he came up close to us, and I was scared. But then, when he saw Willie

230

lying there' – she paused, shaken, and took another deep breath – 'he ran away. He just . . . ran away.'

'Thank you, Mrs Russ,' Fusco said quietly. She turned to Judge Armand. 'I have nothing further for this witness,' she said.

Jonathan braced himself, then rose and walked to the witness-box. 'Mrs Russ,' he said calmly, trying to mask the anxiety he was feeling, 'I'm Jonathan Rollins for the Defence, and before we go any further I'd like to express my sorrow at your loss.'

'I know who you are,' Wilma Russ said flatly.

'Yes, well . . .' Even the usually unflappable Jonathan felt uncomfortable under the woman's accusatory glance. He knew that he just had to ignore his turbulent emotions and continue. 'Can you tell the court approximately how long it took you actually to get from your bedroom window to your son after you heard the shots?'

'Maybe fifteen or twenty seconds,' Wilma Russ replied evenly.

'And it would be fair to say, wouldn't it,' Jonathan continued, 'that as you ran towards him the only place you were looking, the *only* thing you saw – at the time – was your son, William?'

'Probably,' Mrs Russ admitted.

'Mrs Russ,' Jonathan said, trying to be as gentle as possible, 'don't you think that there could have been twenty seconds, maybe thirty seconds between the time you heard those shots and the time you actually looked up from your son's body?' Jonathan winced inwardly at the image he had just painted.

'I don't know how many seconds it was exactly,' Mrs

Russ said defensively.

'No, of course not,' Jonathan said soothingly. 'Your only concern then was William naturally. But the time-lapse *could* have been twenty to thirty seconds, couldn't it?'

Mrs Russ stared coldly at him. 'So what?' she retorted.

'Well, ma'am,' Jonathan replied, 'you're sitting here in this courtroom today suggesting that my client was the only other person in that alley. But clearly there was time enough for —'

Jonathan never finished the sentence, as Wilma Russ's anger and grief finally found a place to focus and burst forth. 'I'm sitting in the courtroom because my son is dead!' she lashed out. 'I'm sitting here because' – she raised her hand and pointed at Brian Chisolm – 'that man shot him in the back!'

'Objection. Move to strike!' Jonathan shouted over the eruption of applause and support that had broken out after Mrs Russ's accusation.

'Mrs Russ,' Judge Armand said, 'that will do.'

But Wilma Russ, grief-stricken and furious, wasn't ready to be silenced. 'I've told you why *I'm* here, Mr Rollins.' She said his name with contempt. 'Now, why don't you try explaining why *you're* here!'

'That's enough, Mrs Russ!' Judge Armand warned her, as the crowd's angry disapproval of Jonathan swelled to a vocal chorus.

Jonathan had to shout to make himself heard over the crowd's reaction. 'I'm here because an innocent man is accused of murder!'

There were boos and jeers from the onlookers.

'Quiet!' Judge Armand yelled.

'He shot my boy; he shot my Willie!' Mrs Russ said, still pointing at Brian Chisolm, tears running down her face.

'It was an accident!' Jonathan said, trying desperately to find some sane way out of this nightmare.

'How can it be an accident?' Wilma Russ demanded through her tears. 'The bullet-hole was in his *back!* How can that be an accident?'

Jonathan had no answer for the grieving mother. All he could feel was a wave of relief when Judge Armand ordered the trial adjourned until the following day. Then he and Michael hustled Brian out of the courtroom as quickly as they could, angry epithets following them until the elevator doors mercifully closed them off from the crowd.

*

The beginning of Leland's testimony went just the way Grace had hoped it would; and she was pleased to see that she had prepared Leland so well – and he had steeled himself so well – that he didn't seem at all nervous or unsure. He was going a very good job of projecting the image she'd wanted: forceful, dignified and thoroughly in charge of things. She breathed an inner sigh of relief as they wound down to the real meat of the testimony.

'Yes,' Leland said to her, 'I was the one who brought her into the firm. And I certainly *did* want to see her succeed.'

Grace nodded in agreement. 'But Rosalind Shays didn't, after all, succeed – at least, in your mind – did she?'

Leland McKenzie shook his head. 'Above all else, a senior partner has to be completely trusted by her partners. She wasn't.'

233

'What else?' Grace queried.

'A senior partner has to deal honestly with clients and co-workers. She didn't.' His voice was steady and emphatic.

'And so . . . she was voted out?'

Leland shook his head. 'No,' he corrected her, 'it never came to a vote.'

'Then, in your own words, would you tell the jury what did transpire?'

'When it became clear that she couldn't win her campaign to take over the firm,' Leland said, 'she resigned.' He paused and looked towards Rosalind, who sat, calm and unruffled. 'She wasn't pushed out, she wasn't shoved out, she wasn't tricked out. She wasn't even asked to leave. She simple walked out.'

'But you've heard Rosalind Shays claim in this very courtroom that she was forced out of McKenzie Brackman because she is a woman.'

'That is patently ridiculous,' Leland said firmly. 'If we were against women, why would she have been elected senior partner in the first place?' He looked at the jury. 'If this firm is against women, why have three of the last four partners we've made there been women?' He was gathering steam and force. 'This dispute has nothing to do with gender,' he said emphatically. '*Nothing!* And Rosalind Shays knows that.'

Grace nodded in satisfaction. 'Thank you, Mr McKenzie,' she said. 'I have nothing further.' She crossed the court back to the defence table and sat down.

'Mr Sollers, you may cross-examine.'

Jack Sollers nodded, but waited a few moments before

he rose and approached Leland, drawing the suspense out. When he was standing directly in front of Leland, he began.

'You were old,' Sollers said, 'and you couldn't hack it.'

At the defence table, Grace stirred uneasily: Jack Sollers hadn't even bothered to start with a formal pleasantry. This was going to be as bad as she had predicted.

'So', Sollers continued, his voice dripping with derision, 'you brought someone in, you gave her the title she demanded, and you let her do what she was brought in to do – to build a weak firm back up.' He smiled unpleasantly. 'And then, after she'd accomplished it for your firm, for *you*' – he paused to let the emphasis sink in – 'you just took her job back, didn't you?'

Leland refused to be ruffled. 'That's not how it happened,' he said calmly.

Sollers lifted on eyebrow in disbelief. 'That's *exactly* show it happened,' he retorted. 'Oh, you were smart, Leland, I'll give you that.'

Grace looked up. 'Objection to the informality!' she said sharply. He was doing it, she thought, he was doing exactly what she had predicted. Thank heavens Leland was well prepared.

'I'm sorry. I meant to say *Mr* McKenzie,' he said mockingly. He turned to the jury. 'Of course, I forgot – it's perfectly all right for Mr Becker to sit up here and call the plaintiff "Roz". But if we dare use a *man's* first name someone's going to jump up and object as if it were a crime ...'

'Objection!' Grace snapped, trying to hold her temper in check. After all, she knew what he was trying to do. Beneath the table, she felt Victor's knee nudge her as a warning.

'Stick to the case, Mr Sollers,' Judge Travelini told him.

Jack Sollers's face was all injured innocence. 'But that's exactly what I'm doing, your Honour,' he said. 'This man', he said, indicating Leland, '*specifically* wanted a woman taking his place because he knew from the very beginning that it was only a temporary position! He knew, with the make-up of his firm, that he would far more easily be able to get rid of a woman!'

'Objection!' Grace said.

'That's crazy!' Leland snapped.

'Oh, no,' Grace said softly.

But Leland was doing exactly what he had promised not to do – he was letting Jack Sollers play him like a violin. 'She lost her job', Leland said, 'because she manipulated people as though they were chess pieces! She lost her job', he said, glaring at Jack Sollers, 'because she couldn't be trusted!'

Jack Sollers smiled and shrugged. 'Well, Mr McKenzie,' he said smoothly, 'if you are so able to breed the kind of trust that Ms Shays can't, perhaps you can explain why it was that Arnold Becker defected from *you*, not from *her*.'

'He came back,' Leland said shortly. Arnie's defection was still a sore point for him.

'Only after you sued him,' Sollers reminded him.

Leland's temper was rising, and Grace felt a sense of foreboding.

'Your client', Leland said to Jack Sollers, 'could not run the firm!'

'Oh? Then, tell us why revenues went *down* under your administration, and not under Ms Shays'. Tell us why, when Rosalind Shays left, eleven of your long-standing clients decided to go with her, and not to stay with *you* and with the firm they'd been with for so many years!'

'Objection. Relevance!' Grace said, springing to her feet. If for no other reason, she knew she had to interrupt this effectively dramatic roll that Sollers was on.

But Leland shouted over her. 'I'll tell you this! Everything I ever did was in the best interests of my fellow-partners!'

Sollers went for it, just the way Grace had known he would. 'Then, tell us why you exalted your own vanity at the expense of your partners! Was *that* in the interest of your partners?'

'What are you talking about?' Leland demanded, confused.

'Isn't it true, sir, that even though you are diagnosed as hard of hearing you refused to wear your hearing aid because it embarrassed you?'

'Oh, no,' Grace whispered. Beside her she felt more than saw Victor having the same dismayed reaction.

'And isn't it true', Sollers pressed, 'that Rosalind Shays, because she was worried about the firm being sued for *malpractice*, had to *ask* you to wear it?'

'This is totally irrelevant!' Grace protested.

'It is not irrelevant at all!' Sollers snapped. 'It goes to this man's ego, which is completely at issue. It's that ego which compromised the firm!'

The courtroom seemed to erupt in a volley of shouts and objections, as Grace struggled to make herself heard. 'Objection!' she shouted.

'An ego', Sollers continued, ignoring Grace, 'that

victimised this woman!'

'Mr Sollers!' Judge Travelini snapped.

'She victimised herself!' Leland said loudly.

'No, it was *you*, Leland!' Sollers exclaimed. 'You were the executioner! You were the one!'

'Objection!' Grace shouted as loudly as she could.

'Mr Sollers, that is quite enough!' the judge said.

'I founded that firm!' Leland yelled. 'I wasn't going to let her ruin it!'

Despite Grace's objections, despite Judge Travelini's warnings, Sollers wasn't about to let the moment pass. He turned on Leland in an accusatory stance. 'You were a scared old man,' he said vehemently. 'Scared of being obsolete!'

Leland flinched as though a nerve had been hit. 'I'm *not* obsolete!' he said sharply. 'I founded that firm!'

'Mr McKenzie,' the judge said, 'settle down.'

Leland stared first at Rosalind, then at Jack Sollers. 'I'm not obsolete,' he repeated. 'I founded that firm.'

There was a moment of silence in the court. Then Jack Sollers said quietly: 'No further questions.'

Chapter Nineteen

'Well?' Victor said. 'What do you think?' He and Grace had been discussing the possible effect on the jury of Leland's testimony before they had been so thoroughly and happily distracted.

Grace's mind still hadn't quite refocused. She looked at him crossing her bedroom, naked in the moonlight. 'God, you are gorgeous,' she said.

Victor slipped back into bed beside her. 'Thanks,' he said, nuzzling her neck. Grace felt a tingle run down her spine. 'That wasn't exactly what I was asking, but it's nice to be appreciated for beauty.'

Grace kissed him gently on the lips. 'You are beautiful,' she said.

Victor smiled. 'Is that the only reason you love me?'

Grace leaned back against the pillows with a laugh. 'Who said I loved you?' she asked.

Victor stroked the side of her face gently, then kissed her, a long lingering kiss. 'Well, don't you?' he asked quietly.

Grace was caught by something in his voice. She looked into his liquid eyes and realised that the question – although posed flippantly – was an absolutely serious one. She caught her breath. 'Oh, Victor,' she said softly, 'I don't know. No,' she amended, 'that's not true.' She gazed nervously into his eyes. 'I suppose I *do* know, but I'm scared to trust the way I feel. This has all happened so fast . . .'

Victor put one finger up to her lips to stop her from saying anything else. He shook his head. 'No, Gracie,' he said, 'it hasn't been fast at all. The only thing that's really new here is the fact that we're lovers. All the rest was in place a long time ago.'

Grace stared at him, a little puzzled and a little troubled. 'But how can that be true?' she asked him. 'First, there was Michael in my life. And then there was Allison in yours. And if Allison hadn't been raped, then you two wouldn't have broken up, would you?'

'I don't know,' Victor replied honestly. 'I'm not saying I didn't love Allison, and I'm not saying that you didn't love Michael; but the truth is that – for their own reasons – those two relationships didn't work out. And when both of us were really free to explore what we felt about each other this is what happened. Given the circumstances, it seems inevitable to me.'

'Do you really believe that?' Grace asked curiously.

He smiled. 'Come on, Grace, you know that it's possible to love more than one person in your life. It seems to be a matter of fate – or maybe it's just logistics – which of those people you wind up with.'

'Wind up with? You make it sound so . . . *final*,' Grace said.

Victor took her face in his hands and kissed her again. 'I'm just quicker to admit when something's right than you are.' He smiled at her. 'You've got to learn to stop using your legal mind to dissect romance; it doesn't work that way.'

'Romance,' Grace repeated with wonder. 'That's what this is, isn't it?'

'It's romance,' Victor agreed with a smile. 'And it's love.'

Grace ran her hand through his dark hair and studied his sculpted handsome face. She'd been right, she thought: Victor was at ease with his passions. And he was at ease with his emotions as well. It was a combination which was rare in a man, such a sense of security and so little fear of intimacy.

'Well?' he repeated softly. 'Do you love me, Grace?' His eyes shone like a cat's in the dark. 'Because I sure as hell love you.'

Grace felt as if she had been holding her breath. 'Yes,' she whispered, 'I do.'

They lay contentedly in the moonlight, Grace curled against Victor's chest. It all felt so perfect, Grace thought. Maybe Victor was right; maybe this was inevitable. Whatever it was, she knew she wanted things to stay this way. 'I do,' she said again.

'Good,' Victor whispered.

They never managed to get back to the conversation about the trial.

In the morning Grace and Victor took two cars to work, still trying to keep their relationship from becoming office gossip. So far, Grace thought, no one seemed to suspect anything. Well, that is, except for Mickey, who had retreated into a somewhat sullen silence after his last plea to her. Grace had steeled herself for that reaction, but she was still terribly uncomfortable with it. It wasn't fair, she thought –

not that she had a right to expect Mickey to be happy abou
it. No, dammit, she thought, she *did* have a right to expec
that. Their break-up had been long ago, and they had main
tained a friendship through subsequent relationships wit
other people. It was a little late for Michael to decide h
still loved her, and she suspected that half the reason h
thought he was, was because the man in the middle wa
Victor. If it had been anyone else – anyone outside th
firm, anyone who wasn't Mickey's friend – he would hav
been gracious about it. Too much testosterone, Grac
thought ruefully, as she pulled into the underground park
ing-lot.

She saw that Victor's car was already there, and he wa
nowhere to be seen. They'd made a game of seeing wh
could get to work first, and somehow Victor alway
managed to win. Talk about too much testosterone, sh
thought with a grin. She locked her car and hurried to th
elevator, making it to the office just as the morning meetin
was beginning.

'Sorry,' said Grace, flushing slightly, 'I overslept.'

From the corner of her eye, she saw Victor bite back
smile, and she carefully avoided making any eye-contac
with him. She turned her attention to Doug Brackman, wh
was going through the status of the current cases.

Jonathan grimaced when Doug got to him. 'Fusco i
springing a new witness on us,' he said. 'And this on
could be a killer.'

'Who is it?' Doug asked.

'Someone who claims he was an eye-witness to th
shooting,' Jonathan said.

'Oh, really?' Doug replied. 'At this late date? Hov

242

convenient.'

'Yes,' Michael agreed, 'a little too convenient, wouldn't you say?'

'I would,' Stuart agreed, with nods all around the table.

'Yes, and isn't it interesting that this new witness's lawyer just happens to be Derron Holloway?' Michael continued.

'Oh Christ,' Arnie sighed. 'Good luck.'

'We're going to need it,' Jonathan said grimly.

'Moving on,' Doug said, glancing down at his notes, 'we seem to have a new client.' He peered up at the lawyers. 'Thanks to Abby Perkins,' he nodded in her direction, 'and her appearance on a controversial talk show, the California Chapter of the National Rifle Association has decided to retain us.'

'Hey,' Arnie said to Abby with a smile, 'good going – they've got the bucks in a big way.'

C. J. Lamb let out a low whistle. 'That's terrific, Abby,' she said heartily.

'They're a powerful lobby, too,' Doug agreed. 'Congratulations, Abby.'

Abby smiled thinly. 'Thanks,' she said.

Jonathan glanced at her sharply. Preoccupied as he was with the Chisolm case, he still couldn't help wondering what on earth had got into Abby. She'd seemed so remote lately, so uncommunicative. He made a mental note later to stop by her office and see if everything was all right.

'And, last but most definitely not least, the Rosalind Shays trial wraps today with closing arguments.' Doug looked at Grace. 'Take no prisoners, Grace.'

Grace nodded soberly. She was still worried what the

243

outcome of Leland's testimony the day before had been. 'I know,' she said.

'Well,' Doug concluded briskly, 'unless there's anything else, that's it.

As the lawyers rose, talking and stretching, Jonathan watched as Abby slipped out of the conference room without a word to anyone. Curiouser and curiouser, he thought. Then he turned his full attention to the coming legal battle in the Chisolm case; he couldn't afford to think about anything else.

*

'Hey, Abby,' Roxanne said, 'congratulations. I just heard about the NRA.'

Abby nodded in response, her smile still tight. 'Thanks, Rox,' she said. She leaned over Roxanne's desk and spoke softly. 'And I *do* mean thanks. If it weren't for you, I'd still have been putting in my ten hours a day and weekends on the normal stuff, and still thinking it would actually pay off.'

Roxanne looked at her with concern. 'Are you OK?' she asked pointedly.

Abby nodded. 'Fine,' she assured her. 'Well,' she said with a little smile, 'a little bitter and pretty pissed off, but essentially fine.'

'Rox,' Arnie said, hurrying up with a stack of papers, 'I need –'

Abby didn't wait for him to finish interrupting; she walked away with a little wave, and headed for the small communal kitchen where pots of coffee were kept fresh all

244

day. As she was pouring some coffee into her mug, Ann Kelsey walked into the room. She looked at Abby in a peculiar way.

'Well, Abby, that's some new client you just picked up,' she said in a tone of voice which left no doubt about how she felt about the NRA.

Abby purposely ignored the implied criticism. 'Yeah,' she said, stirring a packet of sugar into her coffee, 'it's really quite a coup. I mean, this isn't small change, this is a *huge* local chapter.'

'And I take it you're proud of yourself for that?' Ann enquired sarcastically.

Abby stared coldly at Ann. 'Yes,' she said flatly, 'as a matter of fact, I am.'

'Well, I, for one, certainly can't imagine why!' Ann snapped.

Abby kept her demeanour cool. 'Do you have a problem with this, Ann?' she asked.

'I happen to have a child in my house, and I can't say I'm particularly happy sitting and watching you on national television, telling people it's perfectly OK to arm themselves and leave loaded weapons around!' Ann flushed angrily.

'I happen to have a child in *my* house, too,' Abby reminded her, letting her annoyance show. 'And if I hadn't had that gun, then my child would now be living with his father. Remember him, Ann? Eric's wonderful father? The one who got drunk and regularly beat the hell out of me? The one who kidnapped Eric?' She felt herself losing control, but she wasn't about to take this criticism lying down. Where there was no reply from Ann, Abby pressed further. 'So why don't you tell me what the *real* problem is,' she said again. 'Why don't you just tell me the truth?'

'All right!' Ann said, responding to Abby's hostile challenge. 'If you *really* want to know, I thought that your appearance on that ludicrous show was both self-serving and irresponsible!'

Abby looked her straight in the eye. 'Thanks a lot for all your support,' she said icily.

'Hey,' Ann said, backing off a little as the extent of Abby's anger seemed to hit her. 'Come on, Abby. This is me you're talking to. Friends are *supposed* to be honest with one another, aren't they? And, even if it was a little harsh, I didn't mean to attack you – I was just giving you my honest opinion.'

'Really? Your *honest* opinion?' Abby felt her temper rising completely beyond control, and suddenly she could not remain silent for one more minute, not in the face of this blatant hypocrisy. 'Well, I happen to agree with you there, Ann,' she said, freezing Ann's gaze with hers. 'I always thought friends were supposed to be honest, too. Like, for instance, if you knew a *friend* was getting royally screwed, screwed out of a *partnership*, that would be the kind of thing you'd level with your friend about.' She was pleased to see the colour drain from Ann's face as the impact of her words hit home.

'Abby . . .,' Ann began.

'You are incredible,' Abby said venomously, not willing to let Ann get a word in. 'I don't make partner because my profile is too low' – she saw the look of surprise on Ann's face, but wouldn't let her talk – 'and then I go on television and get a little publicity, *and* I manage to rake in a very

246

high profile, highly funded client, and you have the nerve to stand there and accuse me of being self-serving and irresponsible?'

'Abby, let me explain . . .'

'Explain what?' Abby retorted. 'Explain exactly how you came to be such a hypocrite? Explain how the rules of friendship can bend and change at your whim? Explain *what*, Ann?'

Ann seemed to whither under Abby's accusations. 'I wanted to tell you,' she said. 'But . . .' And there she trailed off.

Abby stared at her with disbelief. 'But what, Ann? But your obligation to the partners takes precedence over our friendship?' She shook her head in disgust. 'Believe me, Ann, I get the picture. I get it all too clearly. That part doesn't even deserve an explanation. But one thing I would like to know is how *dare* you judge me?'

When Ann didn't reply, Abby turned on her heel and left the room.

*

Jonathan and Michael watched, stone-faced, as Marcia Fusco led the surprise witness, Jerome Bailey, through his paces. Neither of them believed for an instant that this kid was for real: he had to be someone Holloway, in his zealousness to make this case stick, had conjured up, bribed or somehow aided. But how to prove that was another matter.

'And what exactly did you see when you ran around the corner in the direction of the shot?' Fusco asked the teenager.

'I saw the kid running straight at me,' Jerome said. 'And this cop was right behind him, maybe twenty-five, thirty feet away.'

'And do you see that policeman in this courtroom?'

Jerome Bailey pointed at Brian Chisolm. 'That's him,' he said, 'the defendant.'

'And what happened next?' Fusco asked.

'The cop was screaming for the kid to stop, or something like that. And when he didn't the cop just blew him away.'

'And what did *you* do?'

'I . . . well, I just stood there, kinda like I froze. I couldn't believe what was happening. Then I split – ran away as fast as I could.'

'You didn't go to the boy's aid?' Fusco asked.

Jonathan listened closely as, one by one, Fusco cut every question he might use to impugn Jerome Bailey's statement by asking it first, and sympathetically.

'No,' Jerome said, 'I was too scared that I might get shot, too.'

'Mr Bailey,' Fusco said seriously, 'you didn't come forward with this evidence for nearly two months after the shooting occurred. Why not?'

Jerome Bailey shrugged uncomfortably. 'I didn't think it would do any good,' he said, 'telling on the cops. And I was afraid that if I did they'd come after me next.'

An angry murmur of agreement rippled around the court-room.

'Then, why have you come forward now?'

Bailey glanced at Derron Holloway for support. 'Mr Holloway convinced me. He told me that I had a respon-sibility to the community, and if I saw something, if I saw

248

anything, I should tell what I saw. And that's what I'm doing now.'

Fusco nodded in satisfaction. 'Thank you, sir,' she said. 'I have nothing else.'

Rollins was up on his feet and standing challengingly in front of Jerome Bailey before Marcia Fusco had time to return to her table.

Rollins pretended to study the youth's face. Finally he began. 'So Mr Holloway convinced you that it was your civic and community duty to come forward, did he?'

'Uh . . . yeah, he did,' Jerome replied.

'Did Mr Holloway also happen to tell you what it was that you saw?'

'Objection!' Fusco said sharply.

'Overruled,' said Judge Armand, earning some grumbling in the back of the courtroom. 'Quiet,' he said severely.

Jonathan felt a bit of relief: at least this judge wasn't going to be intimidated by histrionics or politics. And since Armand was black there would be no hint of racial partisanship, either. 'Answer the question,' he told Jerome. 'Did he tell you what to say up here?' When Jerome didn't answer, he continued: 'Would you like to confer with Mr Holloway before answering?'

'He didn't tell me what to say,' Jerome said defensively. 'I saw what I saw.'

'It's true that Mr Holloway is your lawyer – now, isn't it?'

'Objection!' Fusco said. 'This has no relevance!'

'Sit down, Ms Fusco,' Judge Armand ordered her. He turned to Jerome. 'Is Mr Holloway your lawyer?'

249

'Yes,' Bailey admitted.

'Yes,' Jonathan repeated. 'Now, Mr Bailey, you said you just stood there as Officer Chisolm was shooting at William Russ – correct?'

'That's right,' Bailey said with the confidence back in his voice.

'Now, let me get this straight,' Jonathan mused. 'You testified that William Russ was running right at you, and Officer Chisolm was shooting at him – right?'

'Right.'

'And you just stood there, *right in the line of fire*?' Jonathan positioned his body between Jerome and Holloway. 'Don't look at Mr Holloway, Mr Bailey!' he said sharply. 'Look at me! And answer me. You just stood there while he was shooting *right at you*?'

'He wasn't running right at me – it was more to the side,' Jerome said.

'Well, you said less than a minute ago under oath that he was coming right at you,' Jonathan said, his voice hard. 'Did you lie?'

Bailey began to look nervous. 'I . . . make a mistake,' he said.

'A mistake,' Jonathan repeated contemptuously. 'And, the night of the shooting, you told the police you saw nothing. Was that a mistake, too?'

'I told you, I was scared to tell them the truth!'

'And are you also scared of your own mother?' Jonathan demanded.

Bailey looked confused. 'What?'

It was time for Jonathan to play his ace in the hole. 'According to your mother's statement, you never told *her* anything.' He paused to let the impact hit the courtroom. 'Two months go by and you don't tell even a single friend. You don't tell *anybody*. Why? Are you afraid of your own friends and relatives as well as of the police?' He was up in Bailey's face and not about to give an inch. When he saw Bailey's eyes look frantically into the courtroom, Jonathan shouted: 'Why are you looking at Derron Holloway?'

'Objection,' Fusco said sharply.

'Overruled!' Judge Armand said just as sharply.

Jonathan's face was inches from Bailey's. '*Why didn't you tell anyone what you saw?*'

'I don't know,' Bailey said, crumbling under the pressure.

'Well, I do!' Jonathan said, his voice loud and clear. 'It's because you saw nothing, Mr Bailey. *Nothing!*'

The courtroom erupted.

'Objection!' DA Fusco shouted. 'Objection!'

'Quiet in the court!' Judge Armand shouted over Fusco at the unruly crowd.

'Holloway got you here!' Jonathan shouted at Jerome Bailey. 'He got to you, and you're lying!'

Derron Holloway sprang to his feet. 'You're the one telling lies!' he shouted, pointing an accusatory finger at Jonathan.

'Mr Holloway,' Judge Armand said, banging his gavel. 'Get yourself back down right *now*! Mr Rollins, don't badger the witness. If you have anything else, move on!'

Jonathan paused to take a deep breath. He looked at the youth in front of him and felt a pang of pity mixed in with his anger. 'Jerome,' he said more calmly, 'do you know what perjury is?'

251

Jerome looked at him blankly.

'I didn't think so,' said Jonathan. He turned and started back to the defence table, then swivelled in his tracks. He didn't really want to tear into this kid any more than he already had, but he still had one final nail to pound into the coffin of Jerome's credibility. 'Oh, Mr Bailey,' he said, seemingly as an afterthought, 'if you happen to think up any more *facts* tonight, you'll be sure and let us know, won't you?'

'Objection,' Marcia Fusco said dispiritedly.

'Withdrawn,' Jonathan conceded. As he sat down, he caught the look of congratulations and admiration Michael was giving him, and inwardly he knew he had done the right thing.

Chapter Twenty

Michael felt a profound sense of relief at the way Jonathan had handled his defence of **Brian Chisolm**, relief and admiration. And he was happy to see that Jonathan's attitude had changed so radically during the tenure of this tough case. Somewhere inside, **Michael** was certain, Jonathan still felt as though he was betraying the black community; and the suspicion of some degree of carelessness, if not of racism, on Brian Chisolm's part was probably still alive as well. But Michael could see that Jonathan had also awakened to the very real crisis that was occurring in the court – to the fact that Chisolm was being used as a scapegoat for all the very real wrongs that had happened before – and Jonathan had been able to rise to the challenge of that, rather than going along on a purely emotional reaction.

But today, Michael knew, as he watched Jonathan going through the preliminary questions with Brian, who was in the witness-box, was going to be a telling day. Could Jonathan paint Brian as much a victim of circumstance as the dead Willie Russ? It was a stiff challenge for any lawyer, and with whatever ambivalence remained for Jonathan even stiffer.

'And what happened after you saw the boy get out of the care?' Jonathan asked Brian Chisolm.

'He started to run away,' Chisolm replied. 'I got out of

my unit and went after him. Then, when I came around this corner, there were two black males . . . engaged in what looked to me to be a drug transaction.'

'And what did you do?'

'I didn't really have time to do anything,' Chisolm said. 'One of the males pulled a gun and shot at me as soon as I came around the corner, so I dropped to my knees and returned fire.'

'And this is all standard police procedure?' Jonathan wanted to make sure that this was on record as the accepted manner in which to deal with a life-threatening situation.

'Yes,' Chisolm said, 'it is.'

'All right. Then what happened?'

'They – the two males – ran away, heading down the alley. I got up and started to chase after them, and then' – he paused, clearly having trouble with the vivid memory – 'I saw the boy.'

'The boy being William Russ?' Jonathan prompted him.

'Yes.'

'And what was he doing?'

Brian Chisolm hesitated for a moment. 'He was . . . lying face down,' he said quietly.

'And did you realise what had happened?' Jonathan asked him.

'Yes, I knew immediately that it must have been one of my bullets that had hit him.' Chisolm's voice was a little shaky, but he continued. 'The other guy had been shooting right at me. It couldn't have been his bullet, so it must have been . . . mine.'

Jonathan nodded. He wanted to give the jury a moment to absorb what Brian had just said, to understand fully that he had never tried to place the blame on anyone but himself, that he was here admitting that it had been a terrible error. But an *error*, and not murder. 'What did you do when you saw him lying there like that?'

'I think I . . . froze – at least, for a second. Then a woman came out – Mrs Russ, although I didn't know who she was. And then I . . . I ran back to my unit and radioed for an ambulance.'

'Mr Chisolm,' Jonathan said quietly, 'why did you return fire when William Russ was standing directly *in* that line of fire?'

Brian Chisolm was having a difficult time. 'I don't know – I don't have an explanation. I made a mistake.' He looked at Mrs Russ, tears in his eyes. 'I'm so sorry,' he told her. 'I screwed up. But you have to believe me – I didn't shoot your son on purpose!' His voice was shaky, but he continued. 'I know you can never forgive me for what happened, but please believe me that it was a terrible accident. *Please* know that.'

This was the place to wrap up, Jonathan thought in the profound silence that marked the end of Brian's plea. He caught Michael's eye and nodded. 'I have nothing further, your Honour,' Jonathan said, and returned to the defence table.

'Good work,' Michael whispered.

'Yeah, thanks – but let's wait and see what Fusco has up her sleeve before we start congratulating ourselves,' Jonathan whispered back.

Marcia Fusco approached Brian Chisolm and stared at him for a beat. 'Mr Chisolm,' she began, 'do you have any explanation as to why nobody else ever saw these two

255

black drug-dealers who you claim were in the alley when you shot Willie Russ?'

'Well,' Michael whispered, 'she's not wasting a minute here.'

Jonathan nodded, watching the proceedings in front of him like a hawk.

'No,' Brian Chisolm replied without any further elaboration.

'And do you have any explanation as to why we could never find the bullets from the gun that one of these men allegedly shot at you?'

Brian Chisolm shook his head. 'No,' he said simply. 'I don't.'

'And,' Fusco said, checking the transcript she held, 'when you radioed for help, you said "Suspect down" – is that correct?'

'I'm not exactly sure what I said,' Brian replied.

Marcia Fusco handed the top page of the transcript to him to look at. 'Oh, that is what you said, Mr Chisolm. Here, it's right here in the transcript. You didn't say "Bystander down", you said "Suspect down", suggesting that your bullet hit one of the men you claim you were aiming at.'

'Objection,' Jonathan said. 'Argumentative.'

Judge Armand looked at him. 'Sustained,' he replied.

'All right,' said Fusco. 'But it is true, isn't it, that you never mentioned the words "drug-dealers"? And that you never said anything about a tragic mistake?' She was throwing his own description right back at him. 'You just said, "Suspect down" correct?'

'Yes,' Brian admitted, studying the transcript. 'But then I

said, "Send help — send an ambulance," over and over. I was panicked, and as soon as I realised what had happened the only thing I could think about was getting an ambulance to that kid.'

'But surely *you* must know that ambulances respond more quickly when it's a "citizen down" or an "officer down" call, right? But still you said, "Suspect down". She stared at him, here eyes hard.

'Objection!' Jonathan exclaimed.

Judge Armand nodded. 'Move on, Ms Fusco,' he said. 'You've made your point.'

'All right. Last year, Mr Chisolm, you asked to be reassigned to a different partner, didn't you?'

Jonathan and Michael exchanged nervous looks. This was going to get nasty.

'Yes,' Brian Chisolm said.

'What was the problem with your partner — Officer Kenneth Sims, that's correct isn't it?'

'Yes,' Brian agreed. 'We just had personality differences.'

'Hm, personality differences?' Marcia Fusco repeated doubtfully. 'I see. And what was Officer Sims's race?'

'Objection!' Jonathan said, getting to his feet.

'Overruled,' Judge Armand said firmly.

'Oh shit,' Michael said softly.

'What was his race, Mr Chisolm?' Fusco reiterated.

'He was black. But that had nothing to do with —'

'Thank you,' she said, neatly cutting off his explanation. 'Have you ever been investigated for police brutality, Mr Chisolm?'

You could have heard a pin drop in the courtroom. Brian

looked at the lawyer angrily. 'I was totally cleared!' he exclaimed. 'That was just a defence lawyer with a trumped-up case . . .'

'You were investigated for committing an unprovoked assault on a teenage suspect, weren't you?' Fusco pressed.

'Investigated and cleared.' Chisolm's response was clipped and terse.

'Cleared by other *police* investigators,' Fusco added. 'What was the race of that suspect, sir?'

'Objection!'

'Overruled.'

'What was the boy's race?'

'He was black, but —'

'Thank you, Mr Chisolm,' Marcia Fusco said firmly, leaving him no room for explanation. 'I have nothing further.'

'Does the Defence have anything more?' Judge Armand asked.

'A minute, your Honour,' Jonathan said. Then he turned to Michael for a quiet consultation. 'What do you think, Michael?' Jonathan asked softly.

'She did some real damage,' Michael replied.

'I don't think we have a choice,' Jonathan whispered.

'Do you think you can handle him?'

'I think we've got to take the risk,' Jonathan said unhappily.

'Then, go for it,' Michael told him.

Jonathan rose to his feet. 'Your Honour,' he said, 'the Defence calls Derron Holloway.'

*

258

Doug steeled himself to walk into his office. His secretary, Toni, had just informed him that Marilyn was waiting inside to see him. And since he hadn't informed Toni that he and Marilyn were no longer seeing each other he could hardly fault her for letting her in. He took a deep breath and prayed that she wasn't going to make a scene, then he opened the door.

'Hi,' said Marilyn softly. She was standing by his window, dressed in a simple green dress. The strain she'd been under showed in her fatigued expression.

'Hello,' he responded.

'I'm sorry about the scene in the restaurant, Doug,' Marilyn said quietly. She didn't seem to be on the verge of any kind of hysterics, Doug thought with relief.

'It's OK,' Doug said. 'You don't have to apologise.'

'It only happened because you hurt me,' she told him directly.

Doug looked at the ground. 'I know.'

Marilyn moved over to stand beside him and put a gentle hand on his arm. 'Listen to me, Doug,' she said. 'I've been doing a lot of thinking about this, and I think that you're just being overly reactive to a . . . situation which . . . well *shocked* you. And understandably so.'

Doug felt a jumble of emotions; he had hoped he wouldn't have to confront any of this again. He looked at Marilyn, speechless.

'Douglas, I really do understand,' she said. 'But . . . I love you. And I couldn't just walk away like that.'

'Marilyn, I don't think —'

'No, Doug, I have to say this,' she told him firmly. She

259

smiled a shaky little smile. 'I don't know how it happened, but somehow I fell in love with your shiny bald head and your little pessimistic idiosyncrasies and' – she shrugged – 'I'm absolutely crazy about you.'

'Marilyn,' he pleaded, 'please don't do this.'

But she shook her head and went on. 'I can't just give up on us this way. I can't just say goodbye to six months of a wonderful relationship with you. I don't know exactly what made you so rigid about what happened, but I do know that people who love each other can work things out. And I love you, Douglas.' She stared at him. 'And I came here to talk to you because I know you love me, too.'

Doug wanted to shrivel up and die, right on the spot. How could you explain to someone that what you felt wasn't enough to overcome certain problems?

Marilyn looked steadily at him, seemingly unwilling to give up, even if he couldn't talk about it.

'How can you do it, Doug?' she asked him. 'How can you just . . . abandon it? Abandon *us*?'

Doug pulled up all the resolve he could. Marilyn was, as usual, on the emotional target. And he realised that the only thing that would make her understand, make her accept the split-up, was the truth.

'Listen,' he said quietly. 'All my life, I've viewed myself through my father's eyes.' He glanced over at the oil portrait that hung on his wall. 'I know that's psychologically unhealthy. And I know that on top of that it's probably stupid, and it probably causes me to do things which aren't in my own best emotional interests. But' – he looked at Marilyn sadly – 'the bottom line is that he'd never approve of you and me.'

260

Marilyn didn't even look surprised. She just looked as sad as he felt. 'Douglas,' she said softly, 'for God's sake, your father has been dead for years.'

There was no way to explain it further. Besides, Doug knew, Marilyn was well trained in psychology, and he was certain that this was one truth that she would unhappily accept. 'It doesn't matter,' he said. 'It . . . Oh God, Marilyn, I'm sorry . . . but it just doesn't make any difference.'

Marilyn looked at him carefully, as though she was memorising his face. Finally she sighed. 'You know, I came in here feeling incredibly sorry for myself. But right at this minute I think I feel sorrier for *you*.'

She walked towards the door, then paused with her hand on the knob. She turned and looked at him wistfully. 'Love you,' she said in a quiet voice. Then she walked out and shut the door behind her.

Doug stared at his father's dour portrait, and then at the door. 'Love you, too,' he whispered, with a lump in his throat.

*

Marcia Fusco was not happy with Jonathan's choice of witness. She had objected strenuously, claiming that there was no foundation or relevance to the call.

But Jonathan wasn't about to back down. With the damaging testimony that had come before, he had to get Derron Holloway up there. 'Your Honour,' he said firmly, 'the Defence submits this man is not only relevant, but *crucial* to this proceeding.'

Fusco began to argue. 'He has no information that bears

261

upon —'

But Judge Armand cut her off. 'Overruled, Ms Fusco. The Defence wants to call this witness, then the Defence can.'

Jonathan breathed a sigh of relief. The first hurdle was over. Now he only had to tackle the most vocal, most articulate and most rabble-rousing opponent he had ever faced. He took a deep breath and glanced at Michael, while Derron Holloway came forth and was sworn in, his voice sonorous and booming in the courtroom.

Jonathan started right in. 'Mr Holloway,' he said, 'I'm curious about something. The day after Willie Russ was killed, you went on record, publicly, calling it a murder. Now, were you, as an attorney, privy to some information that the rest of us weren't?'

'Objection,' Fusco said, jumping to her feet. 'There's nothing relevant about that question, your Honour.'

'A little latitude, your Honour?' Jonathan said.

Judge Armand nodded. 'I'll allow it, Mr Rollins, but don't dwell.'

Jonathan faced the formidable Holloway again. 'What information could you have possibly obtained that quickly that allowed you to conclude that a murder had occurred?' he asked again.

Holloway looked at him impassively. 'A white cop has a gun. A black kid who's running away winds up face down, dead, with a bullet in his back. To me, that spells murder.'

There was a smattering of supportive applause until Judge Armand told everybody to settle down.

'So', Jonathan said, 'the fact that Brian Chisolm is white influenced your thinking?'

262

'Yes.'

'And what is that, Mr Holloway, if not racism?'

Holloway looked at Jonathan curiously. 'If I'm a racist, Mr Rollins, then I can assure you it's by necessity. The necessity to combat a much larger, much more powerful *white* racism with which this society seems terminally effected. And that includes the judicial system, which – to put it mildly – often fails to render fair and equal treatment to black citizens.'

'So this entire system is unfair?' Jonathan asked over another round of applause.

Holloway regarded him with disbelief. 'The only reason this criminal was even brought to trial, Mr Rollins, is because *I* generated enough public pressure to stop the District Attorney's office from turning a blind eye – which would have been their way of conducting business as usual.'

Jonathan saw a glimmer of light. 'So you say we're here today because of your influence?'

'That's right!' Holloway said.

'And since you admit by your own testimony that your influence is racially biased, then it stands to reason that this trial is necessarily infected by racism, isn't it?'

Holloway's face was a study in contempt. 'We're here because I had the guts to ask *questions*, Mr Rollins! And to demand answers!'

'No, Mr Holloway,' Jonathan said emphatically. 'We're here today because you are a racist!'

'Objection!' Fusco shouted over the furore in the court.

'Overruled!' Judge Armand said sharply. 'Quiet in the court!' he warned. 'Or I will have every last one of you cleared out of here!'

'You admitted that your own presumption of my client's guilt was based on the colour of his skin!' Jonathan accused Holloway.

'Objection!' Fusco shouted. 'This is a speech!'

'My question is coming,' Jonathan assured her. 'Mr Holloway, if William Russ had been white, would you have come forward publicly in this manner? Would you have staged the same kind of rally that so conveniently produced Jerome Bailey as a witness?' He glared at Holloway, willing the man to give him an honest answer. 'Well,' he demanded, '*would* you?'

'If the victim had been white, it's doubtful it would have been necessary for me to do any of that,' Holloway replied evenly.

That wasn't good enough. 'Answer my question,' Jonathan said sharply. 'You're under oath! If William Russ had been white, Derron Holloway would not be here. Didn't you tell me that, sir? Answer the question! *Yes or no*?'

There was a moment of dead silence. 'I told you that,' Holloway said.

Jonathan could sense the confusion in the crowd, and he knew that he had got what he wanted. 'Then, how can this trial be anything but a product of your own bigotry?' he asked.

Holloway shook his head. Then he raised his arm and pointed at Brian Chisolm. 'If this trial is a product of anyone's bigotry,' he said, 'it's that man's.'

'Because he's *white*,' Jonathan said, hammering his point home. 'Right?' he had to get Derron Holloway to admit it: prejudice, bigotry, this kind of inflammation of the public was all the same. It didn't matter if it came from the right or the left, from black or white. It was all the same.

Derron Holloway, however, was remaining silent, stone-faced. Jonathan tried one last tack: shaming him into an admission. 'Better say something quick, Mr Holloway,' he said with a sneer. 'The crowd is waiting to cheer for their favourite rabble-rouser here, and you'd better get your act together quick . . . before you lose them!'

'Objection,' Fusco said.

'Mr Rollins,' Judge Armand said warningly.

Derron Holloway still didn't reply. Jonathan put up his hands in mock defeat. 'I have no further questions for this hero,' he said. Then, leaving Holloway to contend emotion-ally with the shocked silence of the courtroom, he returned to his seat.

Chapter Twenty-One

It was on the following afternoon – after an uneasy and anxious night – that Jonathan rose and faced the jury for his closing argument. He was still unable to decipher their expressions or reactions, still uncertain exactly what reaction – what verdict – was going to be forthcoming. Some juries were easy to read; this one wasn't. But this was the final page. This was his closing statement. And he knew it had better be as highly charged and convincing – both logically and emotionally – as he could possibly make it.

'Ladies and gentlemen,' Jonathan said, glancing from one face to the next. 'This is a case which should never have been. This is a case about trying to wrap up a couple of hundred years of prejudice and wrong-doing in the mistake – the horrible tragic mistake – that cost a young man his life.' He paused. 'There is absolutely no evidence that this man' – he pointed to Brian Chisolm – 'committed anything other than a terrible error. The prosecution has failed to produce any such evidence, because *there is none.*'

He paused again. 'Think about it,' he told them. 'William Russ's own mother told you that it could have taken thirty seconds for her to look around the alley after she heard the shots and came running out to find her son there. Plenty of time for the drug-dealers who shot at my client to have fled the scene.'

He stared forcefully at them. 'Now we come to Jerome Bailey,' he told them. 'And what kind of evidence did that witness give? If Jerome Bailey had seen what he said he saw, don't you think he would have told his own mother? Come on. Jerome Bailey, the *only* witness the prosecution could dredge up who would testify to what the prosecution would have you believe – this witness came forth two months after the shooting. And make no mistake; he came forward only after being approached by Derron Holloway.' Jonathan glanced steadily over at Holloway, who sat calmly, no appreciable expression on his face.

Jonathan turned back to the jury. 'Derron Holloway is a self-proclaimed racist, ladies and gentlemen. By his own testimony, which all of you heard, he admitted that the *only* reason Brian Chisolm is on trial here today is because he's white. And the victim was black.' He paused.

'All right, this is what we are left with; this is the prosecution's case. One witness, only *one* witness, Jerome Bailey, who as much as admitted that he was lying on the stand, to controvert Brian Chisolm's testimony that he was shot at that night. No evidence other than a liar influenced by a racist. And', he said, his voice raised emphatically, 'no motive.' He paused for a moment to let them think about that. '*No motive*, ladies and gentlemen,' he repeated sharply. 'The prosecution is here before the court, not only lacking any physical evidence, but lacking any real *testimonial* evidence. They have failed to offer you any kind of motive at all! They are asking you to believe that Officer Chisolm just suddenly and inexplicably turned into a psychotic killer that night in that dark alley. It makes no sense.'

Jonathan paced before the jury-box, staring at each of the jurors one by one. 'This is the truth, ladies and gentlemen. The prosecution has no case. Yes,' he said emphatically, 'we have a terrible incomprehensible tragedy here – no one is denying that. And yes, it was exactly what Brian Chisolm told you it was: a horrible, *horrible* mistake. But that is *all* it was, ladies and gentlemen. A mistake. For all the media circus that has surrounded this case from the beginning, for all the histrionics in and out of the courtroom, for all the feelings of prejudice and outrage and the avalanche of anger which has poured out, it is still just a mistake.'

He kept his eyes focused on the jury, trying somehow to force them to understand his point, to understand it . . . and to agree with it. Because now, finally, as the end approached, Jonathan found he very much believed what he was saying. 'These are the facts,' he told them grimly. 'A death that shouldn't have occurred happened, and for everyone connected to that night there will never by any real peace. Not for Wilma Russ, and not for Brian Chisolm. There are no other facts. Brian Chisolm is innocent.' He nodded decisively. 'Innocent.' He looked back at Brian, whose gaze was fixed on Jonathan, then looked slowly at Derron Holloway. Finally he turned back to the jury. 'It's as sad and as simple as that,' he said. Then, quietly: 'Thank you.'

Wound up and exhausted at the same time, Jonathan returned to his seat, where Michael nodded at him in satisfaction. 'Good work,' he said.

'Thanks, Jonathan,' Brian Chisolm said quietly.

Marcia Fusco rose and walked over to the jury-box. 'The

facts,' she said, echoing what Jonathan had said. 'All right, these are the facts. 'Two witnesses swore, under oath, that they saw no other man – or men – in the alley. Can the Defence offer one bit of evidence that there *were* men, that there *was* a drug transaction taking place?' She looked intently at the jury. 'No,' she said, shaking her head. 'Not only can't they offer evidence to prove the existence of these phantom criminals, but they can't even produce a bullet from the gun that Brian Chisolm *alleges* was fired at him. So, ladies and gentlemen, since no one can prove that these two black drug-dealers even *exist*, they are certainly not a factual part of this case, are they?' Fusco shook her head. 'No,' she answered her own question, 'they most certainly are *not*. Officer Chisolm is the only other person placed in that alley. And ballistics prove that the gun that killed William Russ was Officer Chisolm's gun. That the bullets from Officer Chisolm's gun were the bullets which were fired into William Russ's *back*. Those are the facts,' she said with a dismissive glance towards Jonathan. 'The *question* is whether you, ladies and gentlemen, are going to let a killer go simply because he is white. The *question* is whether hate crimes are going to continue to go unpunished in our courts. It's up to you. A white police officer shot and killed an unarmed boy. Now' – she looked at each jury member, just as Jonathan had done – 'you can choose to do something about that.' She shrugged. 'Or', she said, 'I suppose you can choose not to.' She waited for a moment, then quietly said thank you and returned to her seat.

So this was it, Jonathan thought, with a mixture of emotions. There was no more that could be done. It was all in the hands of the jury now. As he and Michael rose and accompanied Brian Chisolm out of the courtroom, there seemed to be a difference in the atmosphere. Both the virulent hatred for Brian – or Brian's skin colour – and the readiness to applaud Holloway seemed to have diminished. The histrionics were through, and what was left was a tough decision. Everyone seemed to be aware now of the gravity of the situation, and Jonathan found himself hoping that this air of gravity and thoughtfulness would pervade in the juryroom, too.

Michael glanced down at his watch. 'Who knows how long this is going to take?' he said. 'Why don't you and Brian go grab something to eat?'

'OK,' Jonathan agreed. 'OK with you?' he asked Brian, who nodded. 'Where are you going, Mike?'

'To civil court,' Michael replied. 'Don't forget – there's another trial whose outcome has me worried.'

Jonathan nodded. 'Rosalind Shays,' he said. 'Good luck.'

*

The atmosphere in the hallway outside the civil courtroom where the Shays case had been conducted was noticeably tense. Leland McKenzie, Doug Brackman and Stuart Markowitz sat together on a bench, occasionally conferring, but spending more time simply gazing into space, thinking individually about the possible outcome of the case. Arnie Becker paced the hallway, just as tense as they were, accompanied by Victor. Ann Kelsey came out of the ladies' room and walked over to Grace, who was sitting some distance from the other attorneys. She sat down next to her and put a reassuring hand on Grace's arm.

'You're a little scared, aren't you?' Ann asked sympathetically.

Grace nodded. 'You know,' she said thoughtfully, 'when I was a DA, and even more so when I was a judge, my most primary fear was letting society down. But I've got to tell you, from this case I realise that the fear of letting my friends down is a lot worse.' She laughed a little ruefully. 'I'm not sure what that says about me,' she added.

'Listen, no matter what happens – and we both know how capricious juries can be,' Ann reminded her, 'the fact is that you did a fantastic job on this. And it wasn't an easy one.'

Grace shook her head doubtfully. 'I don't know,' she said. 'If things go for Rosalind, they could easily come back with a damages judgement of four, five . . . maybe six hundred thousand.' She stared gloomily at Ann. '*That's* scary,' she added.

'That's not going to happen,' Ann told her firmly. 'No way.'

But Grace wasn't so sanguine. 'It could,' she said. 'And that would mean eighty to ninety thousand out of each of your pockets. God, no one in the firm would ever forgive me!'

'Grace,' Ann said, 'if they do find against us, it won't be because of your defence. No one in the firm could have handled it better than you did.'

Grace sighed. 'Thank you,' she said. 'But maybe we should have gone with outside counsel . . .'

'Stop second-guessing,' Ann told her. 'And stop thinking someone could have pulled some rabbit out of the hat that

271

you didn't. OK?'

Grace shrugged. 'OK.'

At that moment, Michael Kuzak came out of the elevator and walked over to where Grace and Ann sat. 'Jesus,' he said, 'it looks like an undertakers' convention in this hallway.'

Grace nodded. 'That's pretty much what it feels like, too,' she agreed.

'How'd the summation go?' Ann asked Michael.

Michael shook his head. 'Jonathan was brilliant,' he said. 'But, to tell you the truth, I don't have the slightest idea which way that jury is going to go.'

'God, could anything else be up in the air?' Grace asked gloomily.

Just then the bailiff appeared and nodded to Grace. 'The jury's in, Ms Van Owen.'

Grace nodded, feeling her chest tighten in nervous anticipation. She glanced at the other attorneys, who seemed to take a collective deep breath before they filed into the courtroom. At the plaintiff's table Rosalind – all in black again – and Jack Sollers waited, seemingly calm and collected, no sign of nerves or worries on their faces. Victor sat down beside Grace and, under the table, gave her hand a reassuring squeeze.

'Stop worrying,' he told her.

Grace watched as the jury filed in, and could read nothing on their faces, either.

'Has the jury reached a verdict?' Judge Travelini asked.

'Yes, your Honour,' said the pudgy foreman.

'Bailiff,' Judge Travelini nodded.

The bailiff took the slip of paper from the jury foreman

and handed it to the judge, who studied it for a moment, then nodded and handed it back.

Grace thought that this was quite possibly the most nerve-wracking minute of her entire career.

'Mr Foreman,' Judge Travelini said formally, 'has the jury reached a verdict?'

'We have, your Honour,' he replied.

Grace could feel the shifting tensions in the air.

'What say you?' the judge asked.

The foreman looked down and read from the paper he was holding. 'In the claim of bad faith termination, we find for the plaintiff . . .

Grace felt herself sag with defeat.

'. . . and we order the defendant to pay compensatory damages in the amount of . . . one dollar.'

Grace sat up straight and stifled a small whoop of triumph. This was the kind of award a jury made when they realised that *some* wrong had been done to the plaintiff, but also realised that either the wrong wasn't a very grievous one, or – as Grace suspected they had thought in this case – the plaintiff had contributed a great deal to her own plight.

She glanced briefly back towards the bench of McKenzie Brackman lawyers, and saw stifled smiles all the way down the line. Beneath the table, Victor squeezed her hand again.

The foreman cleared his throat. 'And we further order the defendant to pay punitive damages in the amount of . . . two point one million dollars.'

There was a moment of stunned silence in the courtroom.

'Oh my God,' Grace whispered.

'Oh, no,' Victor said softly.

Behind them, the McKenzie Brackman lawyers seemed

to be frozen in their places, looks of horror and disbelief on their faces.

Grace looked over to the plaintiff's table, where Rosalind Shays was smiling triumphantly, and Jack Sollers was positively beaming.

'Two point one million,' Grace said in utter disbelief. 'Oh Jesus, why did we ever let this thing go to trial?'

*

The afternoon passed into evening, and still the jury was out on the Brian Chisolm case. They could bring their verdict at any time within reason, since they had been sequestered for the duration of the verdict debate. It was nearly eight o'clock when the bailiff came to find Michael, Jonathan and Brian, who were sitting in relative silence in a witness-room. At this point, there wasn't much left to say. And Michael, who had delivered the bad news about the Rosalind Shays verdict to Jonathan, seemed to be in a state of gloomy shock.

'OK,' he said, standing up, 'let's go.'

'You all right, Brian?' Jonathan asked.

Brian nodded. 'Nervous,' he admitted. 'But I'm glad it's finally going to be over.'

Michael felt as though this was some kind of miserable déjà vu – coming into the courtroom, watching the jury file back in. Jonathan had withdrawn into some private place, after glancing at Derron Holloway and his entourage making their way into the courtroom.

Judge Armand took his seat. 'Has the jury reached a verdict?' he asked.

274

The forewoman stood up. 'Yes, your Honour, we have,' she replied.

'Bailiff. . . .'

Judge Armand looked at the paper with the verdict and returned it, his expression unreadable. 'What say you?'

'In the matter of the People versus Chisolm, criminal complaint number 8212, the jury finds the defendant . . .'

Jonathan held his breath.

'Guilty of murder in the second degree.'

Jonathan felt Brian Chisolm sag with shock and disappointment beside him; and, in the periphery of his vision, he saw Chisolm's wife and mother burst into tears. Holloway's supporters were cheering. But Holloway himself, Jonathan was surprised to see, was sitting quietly, his expression almost sad.

'Quiet!' Judge Armand ordered the courtroom. 'This trial is not over, and I want every person in this courtroom quiet right now!' He looked sternly around the courtroom. 'I have something to say. And I think it's extremely important that you all listen to this.'

There were a few murmurs as the crowd settled down. What now? Jonathan wondered. How could this get any worse?

'Last year', Judge Armand said forcefully, 'I saw one of my courtrooms erupt into an all-out riot.' He glanced at Jonathan. 'Mr Rollins, you were here, too.' Jonathan nodded in grim recollection of the violent mêlée that had all but destroyed a courtroom.

'That was also a controversial case – a case of white America trampling black America. And the hatred rose up and took that room.' Judge Armand glared at them all.

'Well, I've seen that hatred in this room, too, and it saddens me and it sickens me. But, as a black man, I *understand* that hatred.'

'Right on, brother!' called someone in the back of the room.

'Bailiff, get that man out of my court *right now!*' the judge thundered.

Then he looked at the courtroom again. 'That's *exactly* the kind of hatred and bigotry I'm talking about,' he said. 'I grew up in a poor ghetto neighbourhood. And I have seen every sort of abuse and bigotry there is. I have seen innocent black people shot dead by white policemen. *I have seen it!*' He paused for a moment. 'And every day I sit up here on this bench I carry that baggage with me. There is no escape from that. But, first and foremost, I sit up here as a judge. And, as a judge, my job is *not* to effect race relations, but to effect justice in the courtroom. I wish the two went hand-in-hand more than they do.'

He paused again, his face set in a scowl. 'The only evidence that incriminated the defendant in this trial was the testimony of Jerome Bailey. A witness whom I find, as a *matter of the law*, is not credible. Not at all. I know I failed to instruct the jury to disregard Jerome Bailey's testimony. The reason I failed to do so was that I wanted to avoid a repeat of what happened last year. I wanted to avoid that kind of violent disruption of the legal process. But' – and here he turned his eyes on the jury and directed his anger at them – 'if my only choice – the only choice *you twelve people* have left me – is between another riot and an unjust verdict – I'm going to have to opt for the riot.'

276

The crowd in the courtroom began to stir and murmur, wondering what Judge Armand was up to. From his seat, Jonathan felt a slight glimmer of hope.

'As a matter of law,' Armand told them, 'I find that no reasonable jury could have reached this verdict on the basis of the evidence presented.' He stared out into the courtroom again, his face a set mask of disapproval. 'I hereby set aside the jury's verdict, and enter a verdict of Not Guilty.' He looked at Brian Chisolm. 'The defendant is free to go. This court is adjourned.' He banged his gavel forcibly, then rose and strode out of the room, leaving a stunned and silent courtroom behind him.

'Oh Jesus,' Brian Chisolm whispered, 'is it really over?'

'You bet,' Michael Kuzak told him vehemently. At least one of the big cases had come out the right way, he thought grimly.

Brian looked at Jonathan, who nodded and smiled at him. 'You're a free man, Brian,' he said as Brian's wife reached them in a flurry of tears and embraces.

Then, just as quickly, Jonathan's smile faded. It felt like a hollow triumph; it wasn't anything he had done or said which had freed his client. It wasn't the brilliant defence or the essential truths that he had presented. It wasn't the way he had exposed a false witness. *Nothing* he had done had managed to rip through the fabric of prejudice and anger that had so obviously guided the jury in their decision. If it wasn't for the iron will of a judge who refused to knuckle under to the pressure surrounding the case, Brian Chisolm would be on his way to prison right now, and there would have been nothing Jonathan could do, not until the lengthy appeals process could be started.

Jonathan quietly gathered up his papers and put them in his briefcase. He stood up and turned around to find Derron Holloway staring solemnly at him. Holloway got up, turned around and left the court without a word.

Epilogue

Leland McKenzie faced Rosalind Shays across a table in Pietro's, an up-market restaurant favoured by lawyers, the kind of place to which you took a prospective client after a meeting downtown. Leland had decided that it would be better to make his pitch on neutral ground, away from the office – the place where so much of the ugliness and bitterness between them had occurred.

'Come on, Roz,' he was saying, 'you know damned well we can't make two point one million without bankrupting the firm. Without going out of business. You *won*, for God's sake!'

'And I suppose you think I should be content merely with the victory?' Roz asked caustically.

Leland shook his head ruefully. 'I know you better than that,' he told her. 'But I'm telling you I can get you one point three by the end of this week, and then we'll all be done with it. You can walk away and I can walk away, and there will still be a McKenzie Brackman.'

Roz looked steadily at him for a moment, then seemed to soften a bit. 'I don't want to put you out of business, Leland,' she told him. 'That was never my intention. But you *owe* me for what happened.'

'Rosalind,' Leland said firmly, determined to make his point, 'everything that happened you brought on yourself

279

by attacking within the firm exactly the way you attacked the opposition.'

'I was *good* for the place,' Rosalind countered emphatically.

Leland nodded. 'You *saved* the place,' he agreed. 'And I will always be grateful for that. You know as well as anybody what that firms means to me. But, Rosalind, *I* saved it, too, when I stepped back in and took over that demoralised mess. Don't break my back now. One million three. Then you get to walk away leaving me defeated, but not mortally wounded.' He smiled at her. 'It's a start.'

Rosalind hesitated for a moment. 'One million five,' she said. Then, with a small smile, she added: 'I want you to carry the bruises for a while.'

Leland did a rapid calculation his his head. It wouldn't make Doug Brackman or the rest of the partners happy, but they could at least live through it. 'One point four,' he said.

'OK,' Rosalind agreed promptly with a business-like nod. 'That will do. I'll have Jack draw up the settlement papers, and we can file the dismissal as soon as I get the cheque.'

Leland sighed with relief. 'Deal?' he said, putting out his hand.

'Deal,' Rosalind agreed, shaking it.

Their hands still clasped, they looked at each other for a long moment – old acquaintances, old adversaries – and a surprising spark flickered between them for one tiny bit of time.

It was Roz who pulled away first. 'I feel like having some champagne,' she said with a smile. 'Would that offend you?'

Leland smiles. 'Not at all,' he said. 'You can celebrate being a rich woman, and I can celebrate still being able to breath.'

Rosalind laughed in response.

'But you can pay for the champagne,' Leland added, motioning for their waiter.

'I think I can afford that,' Rosalind agreed.

*

Jonathan was surprised to find Derron Holloway waiting for him in his office one afternoon a few days after the Chisolm trial had ended in such an unexpected victory.

'Hi,' said Jonathan cautiously.

'Hello.' Holloway's expression was sombre. He had maintained a surprisingly low profile since the case had ended, and Jonathan wondered what he wanted now, here, with him. He waited.

'I guess that verdict makes you a winner,' Holloway told him.

Jonathan shrugged. 'I was expecting some rabble-rousing from you,' he said directly. 'A noisy press conference – something like that.'

Holloway studied him. 'That's why I'm here,' he said. 'I wanted to straighten things out.' He paused for a moment. 'I guess I'm too tired for a demonstration. Or maybe', he said steadily, 'there's nothing to shout about.'

Jonathan looked at him, surprised at Holloway's unexpectedly quiet rationality. Then, all of a sudden, he understood what had really happened in that courtroom. 'You handed it to me, didn't you?' he said wonderingly. 'On the

281

stand, when you admitted that you're a racist, you gave me exactly what I needed to get Chisolm off.' He shook his head in shock.

Derron Holloway didn't deny it. 'Why don't we just say . . . I think justice was served?'

Jonathan looked at Holloway quizzically. 'If you didn't believe Chisolm was guilty in the first place, why did you go after him the way you did?'

Derron Holloway shook his head. 'I thought you understood that. I didn't know if he was guilty or not – but I knew if we didn't make that trial newsworthy we'd never find out.'

'Did you tell Jerome Bailey to lie?' Jonathan asked him.

'No,' Derron Holloway said firmly. 'But I suppose I took advantage of his . . . convenient story.' He shrugged. 'After your cross-examination, though, I knew it was a lie. And I knew the DA had no case.'

Rollins was amazed. 'So . . . what now?' he asked.

Holloway looked at him. 'A couple of weeks from now,' he said, 'it will all happen again, Another black man will be dead, shot by another white cop. I'll be there, making the same noise all over again. Making sure the questions get asked.'

Jonathan was suddenly struck by the man's uncompromising attitude, no matter what he thought of his methods. And he thought about his own future – the one he had talked to Leland about. A future with the black community.

Jonathan nodded. 'Maybe one of these days I'll be working with you for the same reasons,' he said.

Holloway smiled a smile of satisfaction. 'That would be my pleasure,' he said.

Roxanne hung up the phone after agreeing to have dinner with Sandy Cole that evening. Sandy had remained a real friend in the aftermath of Murray's death and Roxanne's subsequent emotional upheaval. And he had listened and talked and listened some more. And Roxanne found that she was really beginning to take comfort from the fact that it had been quick, and not slow and painful, like that Sandy was going through with his own father.

'Rox,' Abby said, stopping to talk to her, 'Arnie, Corrinne and I are going to go bowling with Benny tomorrow night; I'm going to bring Eric, too. Can I interest you in coming along?'

'Sure,' Roxanne said. 'It sounds like fun.' Maybe, she thought, just maybe, life was going to return to some semblance of normality. Now that the Chisolm case was over, now that Leland had agreed on a settlement with Rosalind Shays.

'Good,' said Abby briskly. Both she and Arnie had taken it to heart when Benny had walked out of that courtroom, obviously wounded by their lack of friendship outside the office. They had made a vow that – no matter what – they would start including him in their personal lives more.

Abby turned and walked briskly into her office, where she was surprised to find Ann Kelsey waiting. 'Hello,' she said coolly. 'What can I do for you?'

Ann looked miserable. 'Abby,' she said, coming right to the point, 'how long is this freeze going to go on? I *told* you I was sorry.'

'And I accepted the apology,' Abby replied. 'So let's forget it, all right?'

'But you haven't forgotten it,' Ann said, frustrated. 'You've been carrying it around, looking miserable, and —'

Abby cut her off. 'I'm sorry if my looking miserable makes you uncomfortable, Ann. I'll try to look happy, OK?' She made an effort to restrain her anger. 'Look,' she told Ann, 'I would quit this place in a millisecond if I could, but I can't. I have a son to support, and I'm a sixth-year associate in a depressed market. I have nowhere to go.'

'And the only reason you didn't make partner', Ann said, 'is *because* of that depressed market. It was economics.'

'Not my low profile?' Abby snapped.

Ann shrugged. 'Listen, Abby, I shouldn't be telling you this, but I talked to Leland yesterday, right after he made the settlement with Roz. He agreed that at the next review, six months from now, we're going to push your partnership so hard no one will be able to say no.'

Abby smiled thinly. 'Especially now that I've got a high profile and the NRA retainer?'

Ann nodded. 'Yes,' she admitted. 'At least partially because of that, too.'

Abby thought about what Ann was saying for a moment, then decided to ask the one other question that had been bothering her. 'Did Leland push for me at that last meeting?' she asked. Because he had promised her when she returned to the firm that he would.

'I can't —' Ann stared to say it was confidential, then cut herself off. 'Yes,' she said. 'He did.'

For the first time in weeks, Abby's smile was genuine. The realisation that Ann was truly sorry for what had happened, and the knowledge that a partnership was within her grasp, did wonders for her mood. 'Thanks for telling me,' she said simply.

Ann smiled, too, relieved. 'That's what friends are for,' she said. 'Um, by the way, have you heard any . . . unusual gossip on the grapevine?' she asked casually.

'Like what?' Abby asked, her curiosity about office gossip suddenly renewed.

'Well,' Ann said, 'haven't you noticed that Victor and Grace seem to be spending an awful lot of time together lately?'

Abby's eyes widened. 'Now that you mention it . . .,' she said slowly.

*

'Gracie, I think it's time we went public,' Victor told her.

'Really?' Grace said nervously. 'Why?'

'Hell, *Michael* already knows,' Victor said with a shrug. 'And, really, why not?'

'Oh, I don't know; it just seems kind of scary,' Grace replied. She got up restlessly and turned to stare out of her office window. Victor walked over behind her and put his arms around her, and together they quietly surveyed the city below them.

'Why?' Victor asked softly. 'Because it makes it . . . *official?*'

Grace laughed in acknowledgement. Not for the first time, she realised how good Victor was at cutting through

285

unnecessary defences and pinpointing the emotional truths that lay behind them. 'I suppose so,' she said.

'Listen to me, Grace,' Victor said. 'I fully intend to spend the rest of my life with you. We're going to win and lose cases together; we're going to raise our kids to be lawyers or astronauts or artists –'

'Kids?' Grace echoed, startled.

'Yes,' Victor told her, 'kids and a house and anniversaries and pets and in-laws – the whole thing. What do you say?'

Then, somehow, it all felt right, and Grace didn't hesitate. 'I say yes,' she told him. Then she turned in his arms and drew his face to hers. 'I love you,' she whispered.

In the middle of their kiss, Grace's office door opened quietly.

'Oh my God!' Doug Brackman exclaimed, startled. 'Oh, I'm so sorry! I . . . I guess I'll come back later!' And he disappeared.

Grace and Victor looked at each other and burst out laughing, still in each other's arms.

'Victor,' Grace said, unable to restrain her smile, 'I have a feeling that, ready or not, we just went public.' And as she said it Grace realised that she was, indeed, ready – ready for whatever life was going to bring to them, together.

286